BEFORE YOU WERE MINE

TEACHER CHRONICLES BOOK 1

IDA BRADY

Cover design by Mila Book Covers
Formatting by Ebony McKenna
Editing by Angela James

www.idabrady.com

To Team Brida,
For all the love, support and chocolate.

To ALL the teachers out there,
Take the night off.

CHAPTER ONE

*A*lly McVeigh knew one thing. Her reputation was worth more than all the diamonds in Africa. Or in this case, all the blue-eyed dads in Woodbury. Especially this one.

She ushered father and daughter into the conference room and motioned for them to sit down at the small, circular table. All she could think about was that this blue-eyed dad was drop-dead gorgeous. In a rugged, outdoorsy kind of way.

Bad move, Ally. Big no, no.

Clearing her throat, she ignored the way his direct gaze sent an arrow of warmth to her chest. Yoda, Master Jedi's voice rang through her brain; *awareness leads to lust. Lust leads to action. Action leads to...poll position in the unemployment line.*

This was clearly what happened when she only managed four hours of sleep.

Shutting down her curiosity, she focused on the little girl beside him.

"Charlotte, I'd like to officially welcome you to Woodbury High. I know that starting a new school, especially halfway through a semester can be tricky, but I want you to know that we're all here to support you." Ally noted how the blonde-haired child kept her head lowered. Her shoulders were stiff. Her body still. She pressed on. "This orientation folder has everything you'll need in it. You have the school planner, map, timetable—the works. We'll get your email set up by Monday and you can meet a few students from class before first period as well. We assign every new student a buddy, and you can chat to them if you have any questions during the day too."

"Charlie, you should look up when someone is talking to you." Owen's tone was a mixture of gentle encouragement and weariness. While his voice was soft, his eyes were steely. Both father and daughter screamed "defensive."

"I'm sure you're nervous. That's completely natural. To tell you the truth," she dropped her voice to a whisper, "I get nervous too. In fact, it's my first week as head of junior school and I'm terrified. I get that it can be a bit scary starting something new."

The little girl's blonde head slowly inched up. Ally caught a glimpse of big brown eyes. A wary, tentative expression. It was a start.

She covered the logistics of lockers, bell times and morning home group, so Charlotte had it fresh in her mind. It also gave the child a chance to settle those rabbit-like nerves that had her stealing glances every few minutes.

"We appreciate your help. Don't we, Charlie?"

Her meek assent was barely audible in the quiet room.

"I'll show you to Mr. Taylor's office as well, he's the Student Care Counsellor—or SCC as we call him—he's someone who I think you should see on a regular basis, to help you settle in."

Owen's eyes narrowed on her face; his arms crossed. It wasn't the first time she'd seen disapproval from parents this week. It was one of the things she still combated as a relatively young teacher. Parents assumed that teaching for seven years didn't qualify her for a leadership role. They questioned her capability. Apparently, she had to be seventy, with one foot in a pension, before she was deemed worthy.

"Charlie, could you give me and Mrs. McVeigh a second?"

She slid off the chair, closing the office door behind her.

Ally lowered her shoulders. It seemed she may have another "Difficult Dad" on her hands. Lord knew she had a gutful of them already. Just this morning she had been yelled at by a very self-entitled parent who believed she should create a new accelerated program just for his "gifted" son. He had used the term a little too liberally according to the child's teachers.

The past week, the junior school office had been filled with pushy, belligerent parents who made it clear—in no uncertain terms—that they had preferred Davina Lynch as head of junior school, and she had no place in taking over the role halfway through the semester.

She must have been mad to accept the position.

Owen looked over his shoulder through the blinds, seemingly content when Charlotte wandered across the corridor to the student artwork hanging on the walls. She braced herself for the tirade.

"Mrs. McVeigh. I get that schools are jammed with kids who have greater needs than Charlie. She isn't very forthcoming; not anymore at least. I'm hoping that will change over time."

Ally allowed a small smile. "I understand."

"But I won't tolerate bullying of any kind, just because she's different. I'm sure you've seen plenty of kids like her, but the thing is, I haven't. She's my daughter and she's hurting a lot since her mother passed. It's been a couple of years now, and since then she hasn't been the same. She doesn't communicate much. Not freely anyway. She'll barely look at people.

"I know high school can be rough, but I don't want kids picking on her or thinking she's weird. We had a gutful of that at our last school, and her coordinator was as useless as tits on a bull." He ran a hand through his hair in one stiff, jerky move.

3

"Mr. Davies—"

"Owen."

"Mr. Davies, your daughter may struggle at first here, but we pride ourselves on giving all our students the support they need. I can't guarantee it'll be easy for her, but we will do our best. We are especially tough on bullying—"

"So was the last school."

"Be that as it may—"

"I don't want her to see a shrink."

Wounds. Open wounds. He all but bled them on the conference room table. Ally had met many parents. Some down-to-earth, others delusional. She could tell that his concern came from a genuine fear for his child.

Her intuition pinged. There was more to it than what he was telling her. She'd wait and see what would come of it.

"Mr. Davies, I'm being frank with you here when I say it won't help one bit to coddle her. We want Charlotte to adjust, but to also have a variety of experiences. You might need to think about whether you're enabling her to grow or causing her greater anxiety by limiting access to professional help."

He winced.

"I don't mean to offend you but seeing a "shrink" as you so delicately word it, is pretty commonplace. Not that we use that term here. It's natural to need some support, especially after the loss Charlotte has experienced. And it's clear she's uncomfortable and withdrawn."

She knew what that was like. How easy it could be to want to hide from the world.

"She's seen every quack under the sun. They don't work."

"Those quacks aren't our SCC. Mr. Taylor is trained at supporting even the most damaged child."

Owen's blue eyes turned icy. "Excuse me?"

"I'm not suggesting Charlotte is damaged, Mr. Davies, but

that Mr. Taylor is a professional who can really ease the transition for your daughter."

"Isn't that *your* job?"

Ally bit her tongue and counted back from five before responding. "Mr. Taylor has years of experience and will be able to give us an indication of what your daughter needs—specifically—in order to be supported. It might also provide her with a platform to speak about issues she can't or won't with anyone else. *My* job is to make sure Charlotte has access to all the support networks available; her teachers and peers and yes, that includes myself."

Owen looked over his shoulder, his jaw set. The war between resistance and acceptance raged over his face. She ignored the slight stubble on his cheek and wondered what the man did for a living. Lumberjack? Army officer? Not with that untidy mass of dark blond hair.

Not her business. Not her place.

Here was a man torn up about the welfare of his child—rightly so—and she was checking him out. Had she lost her mind? Maybe her friends were right. Maybe Tinder was the answer to her dating drought.

His serious expression sucker-punched her back to the present. "Fine. She can see the councillor, but if she doesn't like it, or starts getting teased, I'm taking her out. I also want her in your class so you can keep an eye on her."

"But we've already—"

"That's how I want it to be for now. I'm her dad. My priority is keeping her happy. Got it?"

She fought against the urge to rub her throbbing temples. So much for all the care she had taken to arrange Charlotte's timetable. Normally she'd argue, but there was something about this child, a haunted look about her twelve-year-old face that hit a little too close to home.

"Her timetable has been allocated, Mr. Davies, but I'll see

what can be arranged. I can't promise anything, so just keep that in mind." Ally stood, opening the door. "Now, if you'll follow me, I'll take you both to see the shrink."

Owen's lips twitched. He stood back to let her pass before following her out and down the corridor.

Ally kept her head held high. She'd hold off on adding Owen Davies to her list of "Difficult Dads" for now.

She told herself it wasn't just because he had a pretty face.

CHAPTER TWO

Owen attempted to annihilate the burning after-taste from his mouth with a take-away long black from Toast and Roast. It was a familiar bitterness that often accompanied him when he dropped Charlie to her grandparents' place. It was no less uncomfortable than when he had been an eager teenager, meeting them for the first time.

When the coffee failed to cleanse his palate, he focused on the chance encounter he had with the green-eyed goddess the day before. Ally McVeigh was…

Hell, the woman was nothing short of a dream. *His* dream. Tall and elegant, with curves that made a man's palms itch and hair as dark as midnight. A sledgehammer of awareness still lingered.

He hadn't felt *that* in a long time.

Tapping the steering wheel, he wound down the window, grateful for the blast of cold air. He needed to calm the hell down.

He wondered how any of the boys hadn't burned down the Food Tech classroom with her as their teacher. *He* was a grown man. Those twelve-year-olds didn't stand a chance.

Owen pulled into the driveway, to the house he had bought the year after Rebecca's death. It had proved too difficult to stay in their family home. He and Charlie had needed a fresh start. But looking up at the modest, two-storey house, Owen admitted it was probably too big for just the two of them. At the time, he'd been charmed by its potential. He wanted to make happy memories in their new place. But still, the guilt at leaving their old unit shook at the foundations he was trying to build.

Then he remembered how Charlie's face had lit up at the sight of the large kitchen, and he knew he'd made the right decision. He could only hope that this school would be a new start. A chance to see his daughter happy and settled.

He picked up the mail and let himself in. Sitting at the kitchen table, he sifted through the litany of bills, and sipped at his coffee.

His hand hovered over the third envelope in the pile. The logo on the top right-hand corner made his heart race. Owen's eyes flew over the contents of the letter.

The bitter after-taste scorched the back of his throat once more.

The neatly printed letter from Scum, Cheat 'Em & Co, otherwise known as Daley, Levenson and Sons made him want to tear the fancy paper to shreds. Then set it on fire.

He didn't know what pained him more. The fact that Henry and Anita had the gumption to send such a letter, or the fact that they didn't even mention it when he had dropped off Charlie just an hour before. They were some piece of work, throwing their fancy lawyers at him.

Willing the red haze away, he read through the legal jargon once more. Rebecca's parents, as a final fuck-you, were appealing for custody of Charlie.

Over his dead body.

Keys in hand, Owen was ready to race over there and give them a piece of his mind. His hand gripped the metal so tight the edges bit into his palm, pinning his feet down, grounding him in place.

In sheer frustration, he threw the keys back on the counter. Venting his anger might do him good, but Charlie didn't need to see that. He wasn't sure how he would handle this curve ball. But whatever they thought of him, his daughter's welfare came first.

He would be their punching bag for as long as he needed to be.

It's not like they ever approved of him and Rebecca.

Probably because they had been teenagers when he had knocked up their daughter. And then had the effrontery to marry her when they had turned eighteen.

They made it clear he wasn't good enough for Rebecca. That he was an unwelcome guest in their lives. An intrusion. But they were young, in love and just finishing high school. They thought they could manage any obstacle. Even Henry and Anita Langdon.

Was this their way of getting back at him? Of showing how much they loved Charlie? They saw her every fortnight. Wasn't that enough?

Owen paced the kitchen. Then picked up his phone and dialled the one person he knew would understand.

The rumble of noise on the other line made him immediately regret the decision.

"Hey, Dickhead!"

His lips twitched. "You getting that pretty boy face hammered again, brother? Might be an improvement."

"Sure better than your ugly mug. It's happy hour over here so, duh."

"Jesus, you sound like Charlie. Thought you'd be on set."

"Early scene wrap, director had the runs. Gimme a sec."

He waited, listening to the shouts and laughter in the background. His brother Jack had always courted attention. Now that he was a big shot Hollywood star, he all but swam in the limelight. And rightly so. The pretty boy had talent and was currently filming some big blockbuster halfway across the globe in Los Angeles.

"What's eating you?"

"What? No arse-kissing first?"

"Hey old man, good to hear from you. What's eating you?"

"Fucking Langdons."

"What did your charming in-laws do now?"

He was about to spew out the truth, but knew it wasn't the right time to be talking legal problems with his half-cut sibling. No matter how much he wanted to offload.

He'd normally bug his best mate, but seeing as though Phillip was trekking in some South American jungle with no technology, he'd have better luck getting in touch with the Dalai Lama.

"Just making my life extra special. Being difficult about access with Charlie, that I'm not doing a great job parenting..."

"The usual then. You surprised? They pull this bullshit every few months, don't they?"

"Yeah, but it's getting to me."

"Don't let them fuck with you. You're the best thing for that kid. Jesus, you nearly killed yourself to work and study to put food on the table. I was there, remember? If the idiots still can't see what you've sacrificed, it's not your problem."

"That was then."

"You're right. You're not the eighteen-year-old boy anymore, juggling rent, a new baby, school and a job to put food on the table. You built this business of yours from nothing, so cut yourself some slack."

Owen rubbed his face, forcing his jaw to relax.

He knew he worked a lot, but that wouldn't be forever. He never wanted to struggle like that again. Charlie would never go without. If that meant setting up the next stage of his business and travelling a bit more to give them freedom, he'd do it.

The guilt still hovered at his conscience.

"I never wanted to do this alone, Jack. It's hard not having a partner to talk to about all this. You remember what it was like when Rebecca died. Most of our friends drifted away. All my mates are now busy with their own families. Charlie is getting older. Hormones and girl things are kicking in. Who am I to give advice to an adolescent girl?"

Jack whistled. "Oh yeah, you're doomed. Wait until she starts dating...then you have no hope. Lucky for you, she has a cool uncle to help her out."

"Really? I'd like to meet him."

He drummed his fingers along the counter and wondered, briefly what their lives would be like had Rebecca not fallen ill. If Charlie still had a mother. Whether the Langdons liked it or not, he was her father. He had to be enough.

"Whatever it is you're thinking, stop."

Owen's shoulders slumped. "Do you ever wish you could just start over? Pick up everything and run?"

Jack's voice was so low against the background noise and static, that he almost missed his reply. "More than you know."

"Jack?"

"Look, your promise to Rebecca was a long time ago. She wouldn't hold it against you if you did move."

He glanced at the letter, patient as a time-bomb and knew he would stay.

Snatching it off the table he walked across the hallway to the study. The less his daughter knew about this, the better. She was starting a new school, which meant she'd be able to make some friends and hopefully come out of her shell. He wouldn't worry her with legal issues. He wanted Charlie to enjoy being a kid.

"A promise is still a promise. And she's just starting this

new school on Monday, so we'll be in Woodbury for a while yet."

Owen shoved the letter in his desk drawer.

"You know you can't protect her from them forever."

The man, for all his superficial lifestyle, was shrewd. As always, Jack managed to surprise him with his insight when he least expected it. It was probably what made him a good actor.

"The less she knows about how they feel about me, the better. I want her to have a good relationship with her grandparents. It's not like she remembers our parents and Henry and Anita are all she has left."

"She's a smart kid. Smarter than your dumb ass, that's for sure."

"Charlie says she's still happy going over there, so that's all that matters." He had shielded her from their venom over the years and would continue to do so for as long as he could.

He sat on the edge of his study desk and looked at the wooden writing table they had found at an antique shop last summer. She had been so excited that they would share the study that she insisted on going on a stationary spending spree. Which naturally meant that her corner of the room was an explosion of colour.

Like her mother, she had an eye for putting things together. She'd even begun to create a recipe book of all her food creations, as she called it. She was brimming with creativity; a trait he hoped she wouldn't lose.

Jack cut through his reverie. "She's nearly a teenager, old man. Things change and fast at that age. One week they're playing with barbies and the next it's boys."

"Christ! How the hell would you know?"

"I know she's a good kid, but she isn't your little girl anymore."

How many times had he told himself that? He knew high

school brought with it all sorts of changes. He just wished it wouldn't be too fast.

"I know. Thanks for the chat."

"No worries!" He had to shout over the growing noise. "You're breaking up!"

"Charlie will call you on the weekend."

The connection was lost even before Owen hung up. He sat down in his leather chair and knew that his brother had a point. Talking to him had eased the cold, numbing fear.

Christ, he knew the past five years had been hellish for them all. And now he had another fight on his hands.

He gritted his teeth. Nothing would get in the way of Charlie's happiness. He'd make sure of it.

Owen scrolled through the contacts on his phone. It was time he made the call to his lawyer.

CHAPTER THREE

*A*lly stood with her back to the wall and shivered slightly, sleep still clinging to her tired limbs. After a movie marathon with her besties last night—complete with pizza, chocolate and cocktails—she had assumed that her health conscious, sports-fanatic friend, Sera, would let them sleep in before demanding they go for a run.

She should have known better.

Ally refused to acknowledge the oppressive weight that sat in the pit of her stomach. The uneasy sensation had been there the moment she had opened her eyes. She focused on the drama playing out before her instead.

Sera threw back the covers that had cocooned around Maddie's sleeping form. She had just been subjected to the same brutal awakening...except in her case she had leapt out of bed as soon as Sera placed her icy hands on her back. For a woman who was strict about her fitness, she had the poorest circulation.

She might be small, but her friend had a mean streak as long as the Yarra river. A clear head shorter than Ally's 5'11" frame, what the bronzed goddess lacked in height, she made up for in boundless energy.

Sera shoved the duvet completely off the bed.

"Numpf." Maddie blindly searched for her blankets, then curled into a ball.

Ally was certain that this treatment classified as torture in some parts of the world and Maddie would agree, if she were actually awake.

She slid down to the cold floorboards and studied her two best friends. Despite the difference in personalities, they had bonded over a dry lecture on teaching methodologies in their first year of University. When they all landed a job at Woodbury High as part of the school's graduate recruitment program, it was like it was kismet.

Oddly enough, it was their contrasting views and beliefs that had forged a deeper connection than she ever antici-pated, one stronger than any she had experienced before. Her adolescence was littered with broken friendships; girls eager to share her secrets while pretending to care. She would have given her right hand to have had them in her life when things had gotten ugly at home. Ally rubbed the goose bumps at her legs, chasing away the unpleasant memories. Not now. Not here.

"Get your pretty little butt out of bed." Sera used her P.E. teacher voice. "You know the deal."

"Don't wanna!"

In one deft move, Sera reached under Maddie's tangled locks and yanked the pillow from the bed.

Ally giggled.

Maddie squinted at the offending light. "Laugh now. I'll make you pay later. Both of you."

"Oh, c'mon!" Sera's enthusiasm radiated in waves, despite the unholy hour.

"Don't you understand?" Maddie half sat up, shoving aside her fiery auburn hair. "This face needs all the beauty sleep it can get."

"Yeah, yeah princess, let's go." Sera held her wrists and pulled, only to be dragged back down.

"Don't you see what I'm wearing? I *need* my blankies."

"You mean next to nothing?" Sera replied archly, her hazel eyes disapproving of her friend's silk singlet and tiny shorts. "That's your own fault. You should wear more layers in this weather."

"Well, for your information, *mummy*, that's what I had the blankets for!"

Ally stood, the cold numbing her toes. "Alright, children, break it up!" She marched over to them. "If Sleeping Beauty here won't get up, can we just leave her in bed and go? I'm cold."

"Excellent idea!"

"No way!"

"Then shove over so I can at least get warm," she muttered, her own Lorna Jane workout gear doing nothing to stop the chills that ran down her back.

"Yes!" Maddie crowed, making room for Ally to lie down next to her. "Jesus Mary and Joseph, your feet are like icicles!"

"It's 'coz you took ages to get out of bed and I couldn't find my socks."

"Isn't it enough we have one child in this group?"

"Shut up, De Lotto and spoon me." Maddie reached behind her to throw Sera's arm around her waist. "That's better," she said when they snuggled in. "Oooh, I feel like a warm burrito."

"You're gonna pay for this you know," Sera warned, adjusting her ponytail. "We'll do core training after the run, just as payback."

"Seraphina De Lotto, does anyone ever tell you that you talk shite?"

She barked out a laugh. "Just you, Goldilocks."

Maddie, eyes closed, reached out to pat her friend's head. "Well I'm glad someone did."

Twenty minutes later, Sera had finally managed to get them both out of bed. A light fog enveloped the trees and the pre-winter chill saturated the air. They were forty minutes into their run and already Ally's legs were like jelly.

"Doesn't this feel great?" Sera jogged backwards, her bouncy, chestnut curls up in a ponytail, golden Mediterranean skin radiating good health.

"I hate you more than I do marking English essays." Maddie huffed, colour high on her ivory cheeks.

"That's ma girl!" Sera fell back in line, her shorter, slender body in stark contrast to Maddie's taller, curvier physique.

"You can say that with ease as you don't have these heavy-weights to deal with." Maddie grabbed her own breasts, currently straining beneath her top. "I envy your perky boobs that don't need reinforced sports bras."

"Trust me, I've seen girls with bigger puppies running harder and faster than you. And don't bullshit me, you love that rack of yours."

"Yes." She gulped in air at the peak of the hill. "I do. When it's in a La Perla bra. Or," she panted, "hugging French lace." She puffed hard, her slim legs pumping like pistons. "Why. Have. To. Run."

"Because you always bitch about your butt and tummy." She poked her friend's stomach, then slapped her butt. "You want to get toned and lean, this is how you start."

"Don't. Wanna. Got. Killer. Legs. All. Good." She wiped her brow.

"You may have a gorgeous body that we all envy, but you're as fit as a ninety-year-old emphysemic. The least you can do is some exercise for your health."

Maddie waved her hands around. "Blah, blah. I'm dreaming of bagels and cream cheese."

"Later. If you stop complaining."

Ignoring her friend's melodrama, she turned to Ally. "You're awfully quiet over there. All okay?"

"Yup. Just conserving energy," she panted. "Talking and running equals hard work."

"Ah huh. What's up?" Sera nudged her.

"What's on ya mind, Al?"

She gulped in air when the monster hill that never seemed to end finally flattened out.

She didn't want to talk about the voicemail she had received from her mother late last night, or the one from her father minutes later. She didn't want to hear their disapproval. Their negativity. Just another attempt to convince her she was doing everything wrong. After the week she had, she wondered if they were right.

Head of junior school was her dream job. When the temporary position had popped up—an acting role for the rest of the year with the possibility of being made permanent—Ally let her heart decide.

That was the problem. She used emotion instead of reason. So here she was—a week in the role—eager to implement so many improvements to the system, excited about connecting with these families, yet all she could focus on were her mistakes.

Where was her resilience?

She glanced at her friends. "I'm just feeling the pressure. I've no idea what I'm doing, yet I'm in charge of leading a team. Plus, a whole bloody cohort of students! Parents already question how I run things. I'm nothing like Davina Lynch. I bet she never forgot hair ties when she had Food Tech." She winced at her petulant tone.

"Ally, the woman was practically bald." Maddie cut in.

A bubble of laughter rose from her belly. "I feel like I'm chasing my tail."

"Thats 'coz The Dragon never gave you a handover. The fact that she wouldn't help you out only goes to show that she was a mad cow who wanted to see you fail. That woman held grudges. Nobody liked her and she certainly hated the world. Bitter, mad cow."

Sera's brown eyes flashed in sympathy. "You know I'm not one to agree with Madds, but she's right. The mad cow set you up to fail. She gave you no heads up on the troublesome parents, no run through of protocol. You've had to rely on your junior school team to show you the ropes on the job. It's unfair, and you know it."

"Hell, all of junior school does too!" Maddie cried, her famous, fiery temper on display. "Everyone can see she bailed before term two started because it's a longer term, with more responsibility. Camps, reports, parent-teacher interviews…"

"But I'm supposed to be leading the team, not following them."

"Look." Maddie nudged her. "Cut yourself some slack. This was the first week back of term. Things will be tits up for a while and that's okay."

The need for everything to run smoothly, to not make so many mistakes had crippled her confidence this week. "I know."

"Do you?" Sera prodded. "'Coz it's a big job you've taken on. You've heard me blather on about it." She offered a rueful smile. "Just cut yourself some slack, yeah?"

Ally nodded.

"Aaaand?" Maddie nudged her again. "What else is eating you?"

Even running, the woman was perceptive.

"It's just a new student." She tried to control her ragged breathing, ashamed at her lack of cardiovascular fitness. "Charlotte Davies is starting tomorrow. I'll be briefing all her new teachers—that includes you two. Your student lists should be updated online by the time she has class so let me know if there are any glitches. Anyway, there's a lot going on there, and to top it off she's a really withdrawn kid. I didn't just want to place her in any class."

She swung her arms and straightened her back. She didn't know why Charlotte's plight had stayed with her throughout the weekend. But it had. "She's been through a lot. Meeting her has weighed on my mind. I've lots of kids with issues and I've got the responsibility to make sure they're all okay."

"Some children will affect you more than others. Even more so now that you're head of junior school." Sera bumped her arm.

"It's going to be tough at first, Al. Even kids in my Drama and English classes come in with heavy issues, it's the nature of those subjects, just like it is your role. What's her story?"

"Charlotte's mother passed away a few years ago. Cancer. She withdrew. Became highly anxious. She barely speaks. And the dad is super protective. I got a feeling...I can't explain it. There's something more that he's not telling me."

"Dodgy dad?"

"Nothing like that. He seems above board, but she's too withdrawn for my liking. Something else is going on. I've no doubt it's tough being a single parent. But Owen is—"

"Oooh, Owen." Maddie wiggled her eyebrows. Her eyes— one blue, the other a golden brown—gleamed.

Sera signalled for them to head back.

"Well? Is he hot?" Maddie prodded.

"He's a parent!"

"Means he's hot," Sera added.

"Details! What does he look like? Is he a silver fox?"

"Not all of us are attracted to older guys, Madds."

"He's our age?"

Ally rolled her eyes. "I guess so...early thirties I suppose? If you must know, he's tall, blue eyes, dark blond hair..."

"Sounds delicious."

"And off limits. He's a parent. You know, father of a child. Can we stop having this conversation? I have an early morning meeting with him tomorrow and I don't want thoughts like that distracting me."

Their look said it all. She whacked them both. "No! No way!"

"Just a peek?" Maddie implored. "A teeny, tiny, itty bitty glimpse?"

"No." She tried to run ahead and cursed when Sera appeared beside her a split-second later.

Maddie caught up, breathing heavily. "We'll only follow you around—"

"And make kissing noises." Sera smacked her lips together.

"I hate you."

Her friends cheered.

"Running thing…successful." Maddie swallowed. "Worth… early wake-up call…De Lotto."

"We still have core when we get home, Fitzgerald."

Maddie's curses would have made a sailor blush; not even the temptation of bagels and cream cheese could wipe the scowl off her face.

The sinking sensation Ally had woken up with earlier had begun to dissipate. A very successful run, indeed.

CHAPTER FOUR

*A*lly stared in horror at the mounting pile of paperwork before her. She had intended to get in early this morning, but found herself changing her outfit three times, only to then apply make-up she usually reserved for special occasions. Stupid really. She had allowed her friends to get in her head, which meant she was overthinking every little detail.

Her stubborn streak had her spending another fifteen minutes wiping off the mascara and eyeliner she had so painstakingly put on in the first place. Which meant she needed to touch up her foundation. It was plain unprofessional to walk around with a serious case of panda eye in her position.

She ran her hand through her ponytail, resisting the urge to give it a good, hard yank. She wouldn't succumb to the frustrations of her job that seemed to keep her company more often of late. She certainly wouldn't focus on the little bubbles of anticipation that tickled the back of her throat.

She inhaled deeply and started with the stack of papers on her right. She really needed a better filing system than this. Not to mention more emergency hair ties. She was afraid that the thick elastic band she had found under her chair would snap at any given moment.

She shuddered to think what her desk, and her state of dress would be like at the end of the term. Keeping everything in organised compartments made life easier. She liked having everything in its set place.

"Morning, Ally!" The booming voice of her colleague arrived with just as much gusto as the slamming office door. Murphey Mantel waved, good cheer radiating from his large frame.

"Hey, Murph." She offered a quick smile before frowning over a worksheet, one she was certain she had saved on her computer. Ally knew she tended to hold on to unwanted baggage. With a determined nod, she threw it in the bin.

"Tackling the beast, I see."

"Attempting to."

"Aww, don't look so glum. Do it quick. Like a band-aid. Not that I can talk," he muttered, sheepishly gesturing to his cluttered desk. "I think I have a corner here, somewhere, of free space."

Her lips curved. She could always count on Murphey to make her feel better. He had been in junior school coordination for as long as Ally had been teaching at the school, plus another decade. He had a relaxed, jolly manner with the kids, who loved and respected him.

If Murphey Mantel was the Santa Claus of Woodbury High, then Paul Anderson was the Grinch, she mused when the wiry, silver haired man set his bicycle behind his desk.

Paul Anderson was what she considered "old school." He lived by the motto, "never crack a smile 'til term two." God help a child who came in crying about some petty issue, that was usually Barbara's area of expertise. Despite Paul's bark, he had the kids' best interest always in his approach. And the kids knew never to mess around with "A-dog." It was a nickname coined generations ago and had stuck with every new cohort that arrived at the school. The older kids liked to scare the newbies with tales of A-dog's bite. He was approaching seventy and had no intentions of slowing down, let alone retiring. He could have run the office with his eyes closed.

She had learned fast that junior school was a revolving door of activity. She had thought straight up teaching was tough, but this was another playing field. Life in coordination was rarely ever quiet and always colourful.

"Brisk today isn't it?" Paul's wiry frame and small, quick steps radiated energy. "Anyone want a cup?" he called from the doorway of the kitchenette.

"No, I'm fine with my tea, thanks, Paul."

"Not for me. I don't know how you manage to do it, especially in this weather," Barbara Volero chipped in, a kind science teacher in her mid-fifties. "You'd never catch me on a bike. First, lycra." She shuddered, her short brown hair framing her oval face. "And second, I'm uncoordinated."

"Ahh, that's because you've never experienced the joy of cycling out in the country," Paul countered, leaning back against his meticulous desk, wiry hands curved around the steaming mug.

Ally enjoyed the open plan office for this very reason. There was always a conversation to be had—which was probably why she never managed to get her desk tidy. Situated at the end of Red Block, the junior school office boasted of a small porch where kids in trouble could loiter, and two offset rooms; one, a small kitchenette, the other an interview room frequently used for detentions. More often than not, someone was in there, which meant the communal round table in the middle of the office became a secondary meeting space for parents or staff. Not ideal, but not a disaster either.

She focused on sorting through her paperwork. If she

shoved aside a few more folders, she'd just be able to see the aged blond wood of her desk.

The chatter of her colleagues and the hum of student voices outside began to wash over her. Fifteen minutes later, half her desk was visible. Frowning over a note she had made in her indiscernible handwriting, she didn't notice the man waiting at her desk.

"Mrs. McVeigh?"

She clutched her chest, stifling a squeal. Owen and Charlotte stood before her, a polite smile affixed to his face, a neutral expression on hers.

"Hello. Sorry. I'm trying to read my hieroglyphics." She gripped the note in her hands, fighting off the urge to fiddle with her appearance.

"Not a problem. I can see, you're—uhh, inundated." Owen's gaze skimmed over her desk.

"Guilty! Just give me a sec." Ally grabbed her phone and planner and motioned to the interview room. "Please, follow me. Charlotte, how are you feeling?"

"Good," came the mumbled reply. She quickly assessed the little girl as they sat down. The fidgeting gave away her nerves. She still avoided eye contact.

"I've no doubt you'll have a great day today. We've got so many things happening this term that you'll find something interesting to do nearly every week. But here, I've printed off an updated timetable—" she noticed Owen's sheepish grin and was glad of it. It had taken a great deal of effort to juggle the classes. She needed the right kind of teachers, not to mention peers, to coax her out of her shell. "Your buddies will be coming in this morning to take you around. Don't worry about your locker. You can leave your bag with me, and we'll get Adrian, our grounds keeper to sort it out by the end of the week. Make sure you come back to junior school for recess and lunch and I'll be here, okay?"

Charlotte nodded, focusing on her hands in her lap.

"We appreciate you being so accommodating. Charlie's been looking forward to today. As have I." His warm expression wasn't one she was used to seeing from parents. "I have to say, I think I'm more nervous than she is, to be honest."

"Trust me, that's totally normal. I've been doing this job for a while and I still can't sleep the day before a new term. Charlotte, it looks like you have Science first. I'll come along and introduce you to everyone."

Ally caught the flicker of movement at the window. When Owen bent his head, she waved away the two busybodies. Her death stare should have said it all, but her friends could be willfully obtuse sometimes.

"Everything alright?" He glanced over his shoulder. Sera and Maddie retreated. "Do you need to go?"

"It's fine. They can wait. If I could get you to update your details on this form for us before we leave, that would be great."

It took them another ten minutes of paperwork and administration before they could finish the meeting. Every minute of it increased the queasy sensation in her stomach. She didn't want to see Owen as anything other than a parent. A very attractive, ruggedly handsome parent, sure. But one who was off limits. Like Jupiter.

Boys come from Jupiter, makes them stupider.

Girls come from Mars, makes them pop stars.

Great, she was losing her mind. School yard rhymes. Schoolgirl crush.

No. One little whiff of scandal would send tongues wagging faster than she could say "class dismissed." If she wanted a substantive position, which included the full salary and all the "perks" of career progression, she still had to apply for the ongoing role at the end of the year. Which meant she would be up against outsiders for her job; those who no doubt had more experience.

In the meantime, she'd steer well clear of any complications. Dating a dad? A definite no, no.

Ally stood, resolve firmly in place. "All finished?"

Owen handed her the forms. She led them out of the office, barely stifling a sigh. Sera and Maddie were skulking by her desk.

"So glad we could catch you." Maddie said.

"I'm sure you are." Taking the opportunity to be professional, she introduced them. "Charlotte Davies is starting with us today. Charlotte, Ms. Fitzgerald will be your English and Drama teacher and Ms. De Lotto will take you for P.E."

"Welcome to Woodbury." Sera smiled at her, then lifted an eyebrow, subtly to Ally.

Maddie offered her hand to Owen. "Maddie Fitzgerald. What do you think of the school, Mr. Davies?"

"It's great. Charlie and I are excited."

"I'm so glad."

She knew that look. Approval was marked in permanent ink all over her friend's face.

"Mrs. McVeigh mentioned social clubs the school offered. Sounds like a busy place, hey, buddy?" He squeezed his daughter's shoulder, even though her eyes remained glued to the carpet.

"I left the information booklet about city camp in your orientation folder, Charlotte. It's the biggest event in the junior school calendar. You get to stay in the city for a few nights in a hotel and you'll do a whole bunch of activities around Melbourne's Central Business District."

"That's sounds fun, doesn't it?" Owen encouraged.

"The kids love it. Especially as you get to try different foods and learn about the history of Melbourne."

"We all come back five kilos heavier, despite all the walking." Maddie's exaggerated manner had Charlotte's head inching up.

"Charlie's the baker in our family so I'm sure she'll be eager to try out all the patisseries. She's really looking forward to being in Mrs. McVeigh's Food class."

"It's *Ms. Miss.* Not *Mrs.* We haven't married her off yet." Maddie winked.

Ally had to bite her lip to stop her mouth from dropping to the floor.

"Sorry. Bad habit. Sadly, all of my schoolteachers were pushing sixty and looked like crows."

She absorbed the wave of heat in Owen's expression. Was he outright flirting? In front of everyone?

Charlotte cast a quick glance in her direction. A curious expression flittered across her face.

"It's more than fine. Kids do it all the time." She channelled her mother's distant tone, immediately wanting to vomit. "Well, we'd love to stay and chat, but it looks like our buddies are here."

Bless their punctual little hearts.

"It was nice to meet you both."

"Likewise." Maddie waved.

She shot her friends a death stare over her shoulder before heading out. Their smug faces were no better than a thirteen-year-old being released from detention.

"He. Is. Delicious." Maddie caught up with her across the court-yard at the end of the day. She was already late for her faculty meeting. Not that it would stop her friend from giving her opinion.

Ally reminded her that she should be heading to her own meeting instead of hounding her about men. As usual, Maddie ignored her suggestion.

"I totally approve."

She rolled her eyes. "You're mental, you know that?"

"You never told us that he had broad shoulders. And that slightly crooked nose makes him even yummier. Like that hero from that cartoon…but hotter."

"You need to stop watching Disney films."

"What? And waste time marking boring text response essays? No, thank you. That smile of his could melt steel, *Ms.* McVeigh."

"Yes, thank you, so much, for being painfully obvious this morning."

"Obvious?" She raised her eyebrows. "Oh, Ally. Young Padawan, much to learn you have."

Her lips curved. Her friend's Yoda impression would make George Lucas proud.

"How is the delectable Mr. Davies ever going to know that you're single and extremely date-able?"

"He isn't."

"*Au contraire*, my little petal."

She stopped. "Did it ever occur to you that he has a girlfriend?"

It wasn't often that her friend was stumped. She flicked her fiery bronze hair back, and the bracelets on her wrist jangled. Ally momentarily admired her effortless style, still intact after a long day of teaching. Everything about her screamed sensual goddess. Not that she would ever tell Maddie that. The woman did not need an ego boost.

"How did you find that out, you sly fox?"

"I didn't. But it's a very real possibility. In fact, it's highly probable."

Maddie shrugged, recovering. "Well, you'll just have to find out, won't you?"

She pursed her lips.

"Oh now, don't give me that disapproving, school-marmy

look." Maddie frowned. "I'm only trying to get you dating again. A scene you appear to be avoiding of late."

"I'm not avoiding. I simply don't have the time. And—" she added, as her friend opened her mouth, "—he's a father. A new father to the school. That's off limits and I'm sure against school policy. It's not going to be a good look if I'm hitting on a dad in the first few weeks of my new role. A position that's really important to me." She shot her a pointed look.

"Wait a month and then do it."

"Maddie!"

"Okay, okay." Her dusky maroon nails flashed in defence. "I won't push...much. But you wait and see, a hot, single dad like that, with a sob story, won't stay available for long."

"That's not my concern."

"Alright. But I will add one more thing; if a man was looking at me in that way, I'd be clearing out my calendar for the next year."

Ally couldn't help the tingle of pure, female pleasure. She would not be affected by this piece of information. Not one bit. "You've lost your pretty little mind. You're just saying that to be a pain in the butt."

"Hey!" Sera flagged them down. "Uh-oh. What's Maddie done now?"

"She thinks Charlotte's dad was giving me the eye."

Sera motioned for them to keep walking. "Have to agree with her on that one. There's totally a spark of attraction from his end. He looked like all his Christmases had come at once when you left your office today."

"More like a deer in the proverbial headlights. Utterly taken with you," Maddie added. "But our Ally doesn't want a bar of it. So unrequited love it must be." She sighed with all the gusto of a drama teacher.

Sera jerked her thumb. "Good luck with this one. Gotta go. We'll chat about this later!"

"There's nothing to chat about!" She called out after her.

Maddie stopped at the oval. "I'm this way." She gestured to Blue Block. "Take our word for it. Owen 'Daddy-licious' Davies is interested. And when a man looks at me like he's seen Santa, the Easter Bunny and the Victoria's Secret Angels all rolled into one, I tend to pay attention. Think about it!" She winked over her shoulder before sauntering away.

Her friends were nuts. There was no way in the world she was going to contemplate anything more than a professional relationship with Owen Davies. He was a father. And off limits. If she wanted to even remotely have a chance of being appointed as head of junior school in an ongoing capacity, she needed to keep distractions to a minimum.

Her only priority was getting his daughter settled in and accustomed to life at Woodbury High. Anything more would be tantamount to career suicide.

CHAPTER FIVE

"*C*arried enough there?" Murphey chuckled, opening the door to the junior school office. Ally dumped the precariously high stack of exercise books from her junior Food Tech class on her desk, then flexed her biceps.

"You know me, Murph."

She considered it a win that her desk was in some semblance of order. She liked having things set out efficiently. To have processes. It was what had attracted her to baking in the first place. All those tidy measurements, the shiny, colourful bowls. Everything was ordered. Purposeful. You knew exactly what you'd get when you added a pinch of cinnamon or a splash of vanilla. Everything had its place.

The sheer creativity of playing with those ingredients had been a wonderful indulgence growing up. A piece of the world that she could control. A much-needed balm as a lonely adolescent.

The chemical reactions that occurred in the process made sense. And had nothing whatsoever to do with hormones. Or single dads.

She turned to Charlotte, who was sitting at the round table in the middle of the office.

"Come to collect your bag?"

She nodded, fidgeting with her braid.

"Adrian's going to get your locker sorted, so by tomorrow morning it should be all set. How did you find it today? You've nearly survived your first week."

Ally caught a glimpse of large, brown eyes before her head lowered.

"It was good."

The frightened expression wasn't as prominent as it had been on Monday. That was a start. She hoped given enough time with their SCC, that Charlotte would relax into school life. She had already made a few friends that she seemed to be spending time with at recess and lunch. Always a good sign.

She would need to send out the evaluation survey to Charlotte's teachers next week. She wanted to keep an eye on her progress and flag down any concerns they might have. Success in school—and how one adjusted—was largely based on how comfortable students felt not only in class but in their social circles. With Charlotte's past, she'd need to be hyper vigilant about bullying.

"Any trouble so far?"

"No."

"You're hanging out with Holly and Fee. How's that going?"

She glanced outside. "And Jeremy."

"Is that who was hovering by the door?"

Charlotte nodded. Her face would have given a flamingo a run for their money.

"Our friends do volleyball at lunch some days. We talk. He likes baking same as me. But with science stuff too—like Heston."

Ally schooled her features. "You know of Heston, do you?"

"Uh-huh. Dad used to burn stuff that he baked. Mamma

taught me, but then got sick." Charlotte rocked from one foot to the other.

It never failed to disconcert her to see children so young act so wary.

"It's such a gift to be able to feed people, to give them joy and comfort from what you bake. You'll have to show me your skills in class. Do you have a signature dish?"

"Mamma's chocolate chip cookies with apricots and nuts."

"They sound delish. I'll have to bring in my chocolate brownies and we can swap. I bet your dad loves your cookies."

Charlotte tugged at her braid.

"Here's your bag then. We'll see you tomorrow morning."

"Yes, miss."

Ally watched her walk out. Jeremy was close by her side. She was getting glimpses of a social, engaged child, but there were triggers that had her shutting down. Ally hoped the sessions with their SCC would be enough.

She didn't notice the folded note on her desk until she sat down. The scrawl was distinctly masculine. The rush of pleasure was immediate.

Dear Ms. McVeigh. Her mouth curved. The '*Ms.*' was underlined.

I want to thank you for making Charlie's transition this week a comfortable one. She's enjoying her teachers and has already made new friends. Trust me when I say that is a huge win. I have you to thank for that. Here's hoping this doesn't get lost in a pile of paperwork. Looking forward to getting to know you. - Owen

Ally read the note a few more times before tucking it away.

She wouldn't analyse the gooey sensation that settled in her stomach. Or what her friends would say.

Her fingers hovered over her handbag.

She'd read it one more time, then she'd tackle the sky-high pile of marking that she promised she'd return to her seniors tomorrow. She might even make a start on the junior ones too. She needed an incentive to keep working after all.

Two hours later Ally opened the whitewashed door of her apartment complex. She was grateful that she didn't have to lug all those exercise books up the three flights of stairs. She had enough admin work for the junior school city camp to do later this evening that would keep her up until the wee hours.

Camp was fast approaching on the school calendar and she still didn't have enough teachers willing to miss out on three days of classes to attend. If she didn't get numbers up, it would mean cancelling the whole thing. Not an option.

City camp had been running for nearly a decade at Woodbury High. It gave the Year 7 students a chance to learn about the historical and cultural development of Melbourne since its foundation—not to mention challenging their orienteering skills as they navigated through the city with a map, adhering to a strict time limit. All of it would culminate in a massive cross-curricular project they would complete when they returned to school.

It was the first real test of her abilities to organise a large-scale school event and she needed it to go off without a hitch. She couldn't afford to stuff it up.

The first thing Ally did when she unlocked her apartment door was toss her bag against the base of the couch. She ran her hand along the back of the turquoise blue chenille fabric. It was one of the first purchases she had made with her own money—one she had picked at a bargain price from a garage sale a few suburbs over. Even though she'd had it for seven years, it never failed to make her smile at how far she had come.

Whilst small, her apartment afforded her everything she could possibly need. Turning on the lights, she crossed to the open plan kitchen. It was just big enough to fit a square table that served as a study desk and meal area, usually both at the same time. The rectangular horse-shoe shaped counter had just enough surface area for her to bake.

Ally dreamed of having a proper kitchen one day: granite counters, an island bench and lots of gleaming wooden cabinets. Nothing ostentatious. She recoiled at anything that was opulent. A gut instinct reaction, one that was born of her fervent desire to disassociate herself from her parents.

Whilst she loved her apartment, she wanted a home; a decent, modest house that afforded enough space and light to bake in without all the bells and whistles. Okay, so the kitchen might be a little blingy; every girl was entitled to dream. Since she was determined not to get any handouts from her parents—not that they ever would—she knew it was something that would take a little longer to achieve.

Ally stared out the windows to the fast-fading sunlight. She would have it one day. She had been saving her pennies for years now. Soon. Soon she'd start looking at houses and see what she could afford. She straightened and filled the kettle for tea. Everything she had bought from the time she was fourteen had been from her own money; earned by waiting tables, babysitting, tutoring—anything she could do, she did, much to her parents' mortification. She could hear her mother now. Whatever would society say?

But she had done it all without asking them for a dime. Sure, she still had her university loan to pay off, but she would pay it off herself. It was a point of pride seeing the money deducted every month. A reminder of priorities. Ally didn't want anything from her parents, especially when it dawned on her that they weren't beyond guilt-tripping her to get their way.

She wouldn't be the piggy in the middle anymore. She had been pinged back and forth like a tennis ball, eager to be given the affection that only a child of ten could want, to find herself disappointed when they couldn't or wouldn't give that to her.

It was no wonder school became her refuge. No wonder, really, that she became a teacher. The whistling kettle broke the twin lines of worry between her eyes. Ally drank in the view outside her window. The city skyline in the distance—a myriad of lights and colours—called to those eager for a night of action. After her conversation with Charlotte that afternoon, she was eager for brownies.

She glanced at the note peeking out of her handbag. Having read it twice on the way home, she could recite the short message from memory. Not that she would make a big deal of it. She often received emails from grateful parents over the years for supporting their children. This was no different.

When the phone rang, Ally was busy checking her cupboards to see if she had enough grains of gold—Sera's pet name for sugar. She picked up the wall-mounted phone in the kitchen and nearly dropped the jar of walnuts she had scooped up from the press.

She clutched at the items, back stiffening before she dumped them on the counter. Her mother's waspish voice pierced her ear.

"What is the point of having a mobile device if you don't even answer the phone, Allyna? I could have been gravely ill in the hospital."

Ally smacked at her head with her free hand. She sucked in her resentment and hoped her voice was neutral. She didn't need a lecture from her mother about "tone" this evening.

"Sorry, Mother. I didn't realise. I must have switched it to silent mode when I was marking."

"Marking?" Disgust sliced through her relaxed mood. "Oh, Allyna, why don't you get a real job?"

Ally dumped sugar in the bowl. "I do have a real job, Mother. One that I enjoy very much."

"You know you should be working in finance with your father. Business makes money. If we would have known that's what you were going to do with your life, we'd have never wasted all that money on your education. We could have sent you to the public school with the other riff raff of that area."

"I thought you said you'd be dead before you ever stepped foot in the 'hood.'"

"You're missing my point! You're not some missionary teaching the poor. For heaven's sake, they don't even wear a uniform at that school."

Ally frowned at her measurements and took a step back from the kitchen counter. No point spoiling her brownies as well as her evening. She poured herself another cup of tea and carried it over to the table. Her mother thought all "proper" schools had uniforms and believed that boarding or private schools were the only respectable places in which to be educated.

"Scandalous, I know. How will they ever show their faces in public?" She sipped her tea and silently cursed when she scalded her tongue. She was heading into bad-mood-ville and wished she could end up in some witness protection program.

Knowing her parents, they'd track her down within a week.

"You're young and naive, child. Always dreaming that things are different than what they actually are."

"Right. Is that why you called? To insult me?"

"Don't be so sensitive. I'm telling you the truth. If you can't take it from your mother how do you manage a whole class-room of kids?"

Maybe because they weren't arseholes. Ally gripped her mug.

"You've distracted me. I called to tell you about your father's surgery."

"What surgery?"

"His hip replacement. I'm sure I told you. Didn't he?"

"No, actually. Is he okay?"

"You know your father. Always looks after himself. He's more than okay, though you wouldn't know it from the way he spoke. His hip has been getting worse over the years. The doctors recommend he has the operation done now whilst he's still relatively young. It won't be for at least a few months, as he's got that bloody merger to see through and won't contemplate the operation before then. But that's beside the point. What am I going to do if he becomes an invalid after his surgery?"

"Mother, you're divorced—"

"Separated."

God forbid they got a divorce. They were too miserly to split assets. Plus, what would their friends say?

"Semantics. He has more than enough people around him to help. What about his new partner?"

"You mean that *child*? She's only eight years older than his own daughter. Disgusting if you ask me."

Her mother sniffed and Ally could picture the disdain on her face.

She found it telling that all her father's ex-girlfriends were the complete opposite to her mother—young, bubbly, and often able to discuss politics, business or art at length. A far cry from the brainless, stereotypical airheads her mother insisted they were. Also telling that many of his relationships didn't last longer than a school semester. Her father's charms wore off quicker than usual these days.

"Well, what of her—" She tried to think of the woman's name. "Kerry?"

"Casey. Common as dirt if you ask me."

"I take it she's not in the picture?"

"That's irrelevant! Your father will need someone to help him from the hospital and I'm dreadful with illness. Blood and smells and such. Plus, my doctor said I'm not to be disturbed in my condition."

Ally knew all too well of her mother's "condition." As much a diagnosis of emotional blackmail as it was hypochondria.

"From what you've said, the surgery isn't for a while. Surely you can both sort out the details between yourselves?" And leave me the hell out of it. Even as she made the suggestion, Ally knew it was ridiculous. Her parents had never been able to communicate properly. The idea of them doing so now was as far-fetched as peace between warring nations.

"And what do we have a child for then? After everything we've sacrificed for you, this is the least you could do. Especially as your father is talking about updating his will again. For all you know, you might be left without a dime."

And there it was. The *actual* reason for her call. Leaving her mother with nothing in his will was a threat her father seemed to indulge in more often of late. It never failed to cause her mother to go off the rails.

"So what if he does?"

"You can't let him leave all his wealth to some floozy who wants nothing more than his money. I've put up with his indiscretions for *decades*, Allyna. It would do well for you to remind him of this. To remind him of his family obligations."

"Not a chance. He can do whatever he wants with his money. You know where I stand regarding that."

"What did I ever do to deserve such a heartless child?"

Ally scoffed not willing to rise to the bait. "If you think he needs support after his surgery you don't have to worry. He pays private health insurance, and they'll keep him in the hospital to make sure he's recovering well before sending him home."

"I meant when he returns!" Vera snapped. "He needs *help*. Someone to make him meals, do his shopping, keep him company."

"Doesn't he have a cleaner and a housekeeper?" Not to mention a million other slaves at his beck and call.

"He will need 24-hour care."

Or an institution.

"Will he schedule it in the school break?"

"What? No. Not everything revolves around you."

"I have a job, remember? I'll only have a limited number of days of carer's leave. Surely he'll be hiring a nurse if he needs 24-hour care."

"He needs family."

Clearly the angle her mother was taking in the hope she wasn't left penniless. No doubt her father was enjoying making her uncomfortable.

Their relationship was so dysfunctional that they still acted like a united couple to all their friends, sharing the same house and hosting parties, despite living separate lives. The fact that her mother was beginning to spend more time in her newly furnished townhouse than at their family home should have culminated in a clear-cut divorce. If anything, it made the bickering and mind-games even worse. Her parents were locked in an unhealthy relationship and logic held no power over their spiteful actions.

Ally shivered. Her parents were sage reminders of why all her past relationships failed. She had the worst possible role models growing up that she found it safer to protect herself from love, than risk letting history repeat itself. Her stomach pitched and rolled. She couldn't bear to think she was like them in any way.

Experience with her parents taught her to pick her battles. Her mother's waspish attacks just weren't worth the headache.

"I can't take heaps of time off. I'm head of junior school now, so I need to work."

"After everything we have done for you! Honestly, I don't know what else you think we expect."

She stopped her mother before the guilt-trip continued. Her jaw was beginning to ache. "Tell me what the dates are, and I'll see what I can do."

"I'll be in contact."

The line went dead.

Ally slammed the phone back in its cradle.

It still amazed her how draining a conversation with her mother could be after all these years. Lost in thoughts of her childhood, she jumped when her bag beside the couch vibrated. This time she knew exactly who was calling.

If her mother hadn't already killed her desire for brownies, a conversation with her father would finish the job.

She debated whether to let it go to voicemail. Experience warned her that would be a rookie mistake. Pressing her fingers against the back of her neck, she succumbed to the tension headache.

"Hello, Father."

CHAPTER SIX

"*S*o why can't she hire someone to look after your dad? Or better yet, have him find someone if he's so damn picky?" Maddie pulled over just beyond the large, brick house that sat in the prettier part of Melbourne's suburbia. Lawns were immaculate, gutters gleamed, and the grass was always green—regardless of any water restrictions in place.

The wide roads were lined with gnarled tree branches that extended their arms of welcome across pavement and bitumen. The array of gold, green and brown leaves sat proudly in place —autumn's emblem, a joyful parade of light that would herald the chillier nights to come.

Maddie swivelled in her seat and pinned Ally with an I-can't-believe-it's-not-bullshit look.

"That would be logical and so very unlike my mother. Plus, my father is threatening her out of the will again, and she doesn't want his current girlfriend muscling in, so it's my job to convince him we'll be able to take care of him like a happy family. Oh, and to remind him how magnanimous my mother has been putting up with his affairs."

Sera popped her head between the front seats. "What did you tell her?"

"I said to send through the dates and I'd see what I could do, but that I can't just drop everything simply because they think I don't have a proper job. Or because he's threatening her financially."

"Not a proper job?" Maddie's eyes narrowed.

"Yep. That's Vera McVeigh for you. Not long after that, I got a call from my father about his will. Which naturally leads to all the questions about my inadequate choice of career. As if threatening to withhold money would be an inducement for me to drop my job and do what he thinks is best. My mother falls for this every time."

Sera squeezed her shoulder. "I wish there was something I could do for you, darling."

Ally offered a weary smile. "You are. Letting me rant all morning was exactly what I needed."

"You know that you're within your rights to flip them the bird after the way they've treated you over the years."

"They're just not considerate." Sera shook her head.

Ally knew her friends didn't understand her parents' behaviour. Especially Sera, whose mum and dad were still deeply in love after thirty plus years of marriage.

"I know. I do. In here." She tapped her head. "But in here." She placed her palm flat against her chest. "I still get sucked in. I've kept my distance, but they have a way of worming in and manipulating the situation. Then I end up feeling guilty." Which they both knew. It shamed her even more to think she still wanted to make things right with her parents. She had thought she had given up on seeking their approval long ago. She had, in many ways, forged her own path. But still, she couldn't shake the ten-year-old girl inside, desperate for her parents' love. Desperate for their approval. To make it right.

"It's called mind-fucking. They're world-class manipulators. I'm sorry to trash-talk your folks, but they're awful."

Ally sagged against the passenger window. "I know. It's the truth. I keep hoping that things will change, that they'll change. I just want to stop caring. That sounds awful."

"Not at all. You're getting there, Al." Sera encouraged. "You just have to do what you think is right. Regardless of what we have to say on the matter. Or even your parents. Do whatever you're comfortable with and we'll be here to support you. Now throw me an oop!"

Ally rolled her eyes then made a slam-dunking motion with her hands.

"Show 'em how it's done, girl!" Sera high-fived her. "Right. Time to eat too many lollies and get high on birthday cake."

Maddie raised an auburn brow. "Who are you and what have you done with Miss Health Freak?"

"It's called a 1st birthday party. You can bet I'm getting my sugar fix."

"You okay?" Maddie placed a hand on Ally's arm.

"Yeah, I am. Or I will be. Now let's go eat some cake!"

"Doesn't Irene look fantastic?" Maddie murmured. They had spent the past few hours catching up with colleagues and sampling the gourmet finger food out in the backyard, enjoying the last bit of autumn's warmth, when they had been called inside for the cake cutting.

They jostled through the crowds of people after pictures had been taken.

Maddie whispered, "she always looked fab while pregnant, but wowzers, talk about post-baby body."

"She *is* a gym teacher, ya know…and an ex-body builder." Ally gave her friend a pointed look.

"And a rock-climber," Sera added.

Maddie swatted away their comments. "I *know* that, but my God. Isn't pregnancy the only legitimate time a woman can have an 'excuse' for eating whatever the fuck she wants without arseholes commenting on her figure?"

"Shh," Sera whispered, flapping her hand. "There are children everywhere. Plus, arseholes are always going to comment on a woman's figure."

"True."

Ally noted a line forming for cake. She didn't think it was acceptable to yank little kids out of the way to get there.

Maddie continued. "I would be the first to embrace getting my tub on while pregnant. I mean, you're growing a small human from nothing, for pity's sake. I've seen how much builders eat and they only construct shit from the outside. Imagine doing it inside your body! They're like leeches really. Anyway, it's ridiculous that a new mother has a better post-baby body than I do. No fair."

"No one is stopping you from being a body builder."

"Or a rock climber. Think of all your chipped nails." Ally teased.

"The horror." Maddie jerked her shoulder. "Just sayin'. Woman is fit as fuck." Maddie tugged at her dress.

Despite her friend's bravado, Ally knew she was conscious of her weight. Maddie had her own mother to thank for that. She had confessed to her years ago—whilst very drunk—that her mother's scathing comments about her weight over the years only worsened when she became an adult. Not that Maddie would talk about it now—or ever—it seemed. She had tried broaching the subject a few times, to no avail.

She understood what it was like to shove shame beneath a happy exterior. Never letting others get too close.

"Is that..." Ally frowned at a familiar blonde head by the window.

"Miss McVeigh!"

Holly Fairchild waved her arms excitedly. She was surprised to see her and Charlotte Davies at a first birthday.

"That's my cue. You two go get cake."

She crossed the room to where the young girls stood, arms linked, faces close together and whispering. Friendship. Exactly what Charlotte needed to draw her out. The animated expression on the little girl's face vanished the moment she approached.

"Hello, miss."

"Charlotte. Holly. It's a surprise to see you both here."

"I'd say the same thing." The deep, male voice behind her tickled her spine.

She turned to find Owen balancing a few plastic cups in his hands.

"Mr. Davies."

"Owen."

"Right. Hey."

"Hey, yourself." A dimple winked at his right cheek.

The girls took the proffered cups, giggled and ran away.

"Hanging out with infants this weekend?"

The dimple deepened. Ally returned the grin.

"Irene is my cousin. We couldn't miss Ethan's first birthday. Or more so, wouldn't be allowed."

She gestured to the parents milling around. "Who knew people drank so much at a first birthday?" Not that she was one to talk; she'd kill for a champagne. And perhaps, maybe one day, to be one of the lovely, coupled-up parents cooing and laughing at their own children. Her heart quivered. She was crazy. She'd accepted that a family wasn't in the cards a long time ago. No point wishing for the impossible.

She wasn't cut out for a normal, stable relationship. Her ex-partners would attest to that. Emotionally distant. That's what kept coming back in her face. She didn't know how to be any different. She wouldn't let herself.

47

Events like this were every single, childless woman's nightmare anyway. Or dream, if you were Sera, the positive Earth Mother Goddess beloved by all; her friend would have a baby in each arm before they left. And a grin a mile wide.

"Isn't it just an excuse for the adults to get drunk and the kids to eat cake?"

"Must be."

"Care for a glass of champagne?"

"Love one."

When he returned with two fluted glasses, she tried not to down the champagne in one mouthful. But what was a woman to do when a man who looked like *him*, was looking at *her*, looking like *that*. He was effortlessly masculine, and unbelievably appealing in casual jeans and a navy sweater. Broad shoulders and blue eyes, with a hint of stubble. Jesus. A man like that made any woman thirsty.

She took another swig. Where in the world were the girls? She needed cake. And a chastity belt.

"You here alone?"

"No...I'm with Maddie and Sera. My friends. You met them in my office."

Owen scratched his jaw. "Tall redhead and short brunette."

"That'd be them. How about yourself? Are you with anyone?" Ally gripped her near-empty glass.

"No."

A small group of children eager to play games jostled around their legs. The decibels increased to an indescribable level.

"I got your note. Thanks!" She shouted over the noise.

He motioned to the large patio beyond the floor to ceiling glass doors.

She stepped out into the cool afternoon breeze, grateful for the change of scenery. It was becoming too stuffy inside.

"You're welcome, though I should be thanking you. I've

never seen Charlie click with kids this fast. I know it's because you've made her feel comfortable. She seems to enjoy her classes and answers my questions when I ask her about school. I know you've accommodated us to make that happen and I appreciate it."

"Just doing my job."

He held her gaze. "Somehow I doubt that. But speaking of work, what made you get into teaching?"

Ally shrugged, grateful for the topic but intensely aware of the man standing beside her. She looked out past the potted plants, to the large cubby house beyond it.

"I've always loved school. Couldn't wait to be learning new things and mingling with my peers. When I found out that cooking—baking in particular—made me happy, it made sense to try to share that love with others. I wanted to give kids a chance to experience that joy, no matter what was happening at home, or how bad they thought their life was, they'd have something immediate to show for their effort."

"Not a great home life?"

She faced him, disconcerted. "You're a very perceptive person."

"You're easy to talk to."

"My parents and I didn't exactly see eye to eye growing up. They had certain expectations and as an only child it was hard to dodge that scrutiny. I sometimes wished for a sibling to bear some of the brunt of it all. But…" she shrugged, mortified that she was revealing this to a perfect stranger, "…baking was something I could take comfort in." Ally sipped at the champagne. Her head was considerably lighter.

"And control."

"Yes, I suppose so. All I knew was that it made me feel happy. And I needed that growing up."

What she had needed was a saviour in that household. Ever since she could remember she was the bartering tool, the bait that Peter and Vera McVeigh would use in their game of "poor parent." If Vera wanted to take her away to Fiji on semester break, Peter insisted they travelled to Hawaii. Holidays were painful, especially as an only child.

It shamed her doubly to know that most kids would have dreamed for the wealth that her parents had—the wealth that meant she could have anything she wanted. Except what she craved the most.

Owen's voice drew her back to the present. "I wonder if that's why Charlie took to it so much. Her mother, Rebecca was a keen baker, but Charlie really embraced it after her death."

"That's only natural. It keeps her memory close. It's good she had that relationship. It'll help when she's older, thinking about her mum that way."

"It's the in-between now and then that I'm worried about."

Before she could think, she reached out, squeezing the band of muscle at his bicep, both aware of the man and the plight of the father. She jerked her hand away.

"The fact that she has you to guide her through it all, will be more than enough. It's hard for kids to lose a parent, but you seem ready to protect her at every turn. To fight for her needs. I've no doubt you'll be able to handle it."

"You probably deal with this sort of stuff every day. But I'm still learning how to navigate our lives together without her mum."

Ally nodded. "We have a variety of families at the school. If you're there long enough, it's inevitable that you end up teaching kids from foster homes, kids who've been orphaned, or worse, who are in the system. I've had the pleasure of seeing a few graduate and become stable, independent individuals. We really try to nurture the whole child at Woodbury, and we'll do everything we can to support Charlotte. You have my word."

She stiffened when he tucked a strand of hair behind her ear. "I trust that you will, Ally."

He looked straight at her. Into her.

It was both thrilling and terrifying. She shivered at the loss of contact.

She didn't know how to act around him without the structure of those school walls. There were barriers there. Reminders. Standing close to him on a weekend, drinking champagne, made this all too casual. And casual was bad. Very bad. Like baking bread with a soggy bottom. Not that he had a soggy bottom. Those jeans proved otherwise. Not that she had checked out his butt.

The silence between them was a marked contrast to the cries of small children high on birthday cake.

Owen cleared his throat and stepped closer. "I was actually wondering if you'd like to—"

"Hey, Al!"

Maddie and Sera paused, then began their retreat.

"I thought you girls got lost." Ally finished off her drink, the champagne bubbles flooded her nerve-endings leaving her tingling all over. She crossed the patio, Owen a step behind her.

"You remember Mr. Davies. Charlotte's dad. From school."

Maddie's eyes shone. "Yes. I have to say I do. We were on cake duty," she said, passing her a plate.

"Looks sugary enough to make these kids psycho any minute now." Sera spooned a large dollop of cream in her mouth. "And worth it too."

"I figure the dream will die in about ten minutes. Maybe five." Owen looked at the toddlers rubbing their eyes. "But at least the cake is a winner." Owen motioned to the birthday boy, whose blue and white overalls were coated in frosting.

"That's adorable!" Sera cooed.

"And thoroughly enjoyable from Ethan's glazed expression. I better go find Charlie before it gets annihilated. It was nice to see you, Maddie, Sera." Owen angled his body. "Ally." Those blue eyes pinned her to the ground. "I'll be in touch." The firm

51

pressure of his fingers on her arm, whilst fleeting, sent a jolt of electricity straight through her chest.

Maddie waited a beat, then shuffled them all around the corner. "Well? What happened?"

"Nothing."

"What do you mean nothing? I saw the way he was standing earlier, and that look he gave you just now…" Maddie fanned her face with her empty plate.

Ally shovelled in cake like a woman on death row. "He came over. We had a very pleasant, professional conversation. Then you guys arrived."

"I don't buy it." Maddie sniffed. "I smell a rat."

She swallowed a dollop of cream. "Oh, and he came alone. Which I think means he's single."

"Ah huh! I knew there was something."

The girls cooed and crowed. Ally only opened her mouth to eat more cake. They didn't need to know that he almost asked her out. It would just make matters awkward between them at work. For all she knew, he could have been asking if she wanted more champagne. She didn't want to start making wild assumptions.

Despite her own advice, Ally's lips curved around the plastic spoon. She indulged in the fantasy for as long as it took to demolish the sweet treat.

It was best for all concerned that Owen Davies remained as distant from her as possible. He was a parent. An acquaintance. That was it.

This giddy sensation was simply a reaction to consuming too many bubbles and sugar in a short span of time.

It had nothing whatsoever to do with a sexy single dad who tempted her to break every rule in the damn book.

CHAPTER SEVEN

"You can't be serious, Tony." Ally looked at the Daily Organiser like he was a Year 8 Sport class on a Friday afternoon. "There's no one else?"

Tony Alvarez shoved back his square framed glasses that had slipped down his thin, straight nose. His skin was flushed. He tapped short, bitten-to-the-quick nails along the base of his keyboard in a staccato rhythm. Dark, onyx eyes looked back at her in defeat.

"I'm so sorry. There is literally no one else who is willing *and* available to come along."

Ally whimpered and leaned against his tidy desk. She would not compare it to the mess that had begun to encroach on her own workspace. She supposed it was his job to organise the timetable for the school—substitute teachers, room changes, excursion lists, passes—so she wouldn't sulk at all the colourful stationary and immaculate looking binders. Especially as he was fantastic at his job.

But right at this minute, she was just petty enough to want to mess up the neat vibe he had going on, even though it was a pure Maddie-move. On second thought, Maddie would have done it already, out of sheer principle.

"Are you telling me we've exhausted all options?"

"Unfortunately, we're heading into the busy season of Term Two, Ally. Report writing, PDs, sports days, excursions, exams. All the other CRT agencies that I've contacted have already placed teachers in other schools. We have our regulars whom we use but we need them in the classroom. As it is, I'm wound tight. And no—we can't just make them come on junior school camp."

"This is ridiculous, Tony. If we don't get our minimum number of staff to supervise, we can't let the kids attend. It's not like we're in a cabin in the woods with some organisation running things. It's the CBD for heaven's sake!"

"I get it. Just, take a breath. What happened when you sent out the other email?"

"I had a couple of maybes, but a lot of people have senior classes and just can't take three days off to attend. I get their reasoning, but I'm already across four camps and I have seniors too." She rubbed at her eyes. They were stinging from too many sleepless nights.

Ethan's birthday party and her encounter with Owen seemed like a lifetime ago. It had been three days. At this rate she wouldn't have a weekend free until camp was well and truly over. She was already overloaded and would be working all hours to catch up. It was a good thing she was single, and that Owen hadn't "been in touch." She had no time for dating. Or any of the indulgent fantasies that continued to play in her head since seeing him.

"Ally?" Tony waved his hand across her face.

"I'm here. Look, I need staff and I'm desperate enough to provide incentives."

"Before you start offering to do everyone's yard duty, I'll make a call to some retired staff. You just better hope they're not on some lavish cruise of the Rockies or looking after tiny tots. In the meantime, speak to Gabriel, see what he suggests. But if you don't get your numbers up, then you'll have to cancel the camp. From a legal standpoint, you need to get people on board."

Her blood throbbed in her ears. It was as if someone held the base of her neck in a vice grip and was slowly, by degrees, strangling her.

Everything for camp had been paid for—hotels, tours, transport. All that planning and organisation. All those disappointed kids. She knew that junior school had been abuzz since they had announced the camp dates.

It would be too late to recover costs, not to mention the trust of the kids again. It would be a big strike against her chances of keeping this job. If she couldn't organise a year level camp, why would they think she could plan end of year activities, or sports days, or anything of merit for the Year 7 and 8 students?

She had less than three weeks to make it happen.

"Right, thanks Tony. I guess I better see Gabriel then."

At this point in time, she needed a miracle.

"Knock, knock." Ally tapped on Gabriel Steele's office door. He sat by the window glowering at his computer screen. When grey eyes flashed at her in annoyance, she stiffened. For some odd reason images of Heathcliff on the moors flashed in her brain—minus the wild, unkempt mane.

Gabriel's jet-black hair, a similar shade to her own, was short, unlike his literary counterpart. His usually clean-shaven jaw was dotted with dark growth, offsetting the white of his skin. It made his weary expression even more arresting. She wasn't sure why Maddie found him infuriating. Commanding, yes. Intimidating, for sure. But Maddie could barely tolerate the man.

She bit her lip when Owen's summer blue eyes clouded her vision. This was not the time to get distracted.

"You come all the way into my office for the view?" Gabriel's smile flashed. It softened the straight, stern lines of his mouth.

Ally unlinked her fingers. "As appealing as the senior courtyard may be, I'm afraid not. A lot on my mind at the moment. But I can come back later if it doesn't suit?"

"No, not at all. I'm just working on curriculum issues. It's enough to drive anyone insane. Come in, take a seat."

She was bolstered by the litany of papers, books and folders that lingered in an incriminating mess in the corner of his desk. She tuned out the hum of voices that infiltrated his opened window.

"What can I do for you?"

"We have a bit of a disaster with the city camp." She outlined the problems, keeping the hysteria that clawed at the base of her throat out of her voice. Reason, not emotion, was key.

Gabriel crossed his arms. "When is it?"

"Less than three weeks."

He drew in a sharp breath. "That's tight."

"Tell me about it. Too close to cancel. I had assumed that Davina Lynch had confirmed the list of teachers attending before she retired, but we're still really low on numbers. I can't force staff to attend camp and I don't even want to think about the logistical nightmare for the front office in terms of refunds for parents."

"Then don't. I find dealing with the crisis at hand best, rather than the ramifications. Keeps your head clear for solutions."

Which was probably why he was so effective at disciplining kids and teachers. His direct approach elicited both fear and respect across the school.

"If I don't get staff numbers up, we have to cancel. And that isn't an option. All the kids will be so upset."

Gabriel leaned forward. "Deep breath. We'll figure it out."

"I have no idea how to go about cancelling this if we need to."

"Worst case scenario, parents will be pissed that they don't get rid of their children for three days, but—" Gabriel paused, his eyes narrowed. "What about parents?"

"What about them?"

"Invite them to come on camp."

"I was under the impression that wasn't an option."

He picked up his pen, gave it a few thoughtful clicks. "Not necessarily. It's a school guideline—unofficial—that we don't get parents involved. They had some interesting experiences in the past, but I'm sure Jacinta would prefer that we don't cancel the camp if we don't have to, especially with all the vocal parents on council."

"What do I do?"

"Run it by Jacinta. Hold on, let me call through now." He smoothed down his tie and punched in Jacinta Cavarello's extension. The principal picked up on the first ring. "Hey, boss —got a minute?" He swiftly outlined the problem, tapping his fingers against his desk.

Ally knew that Jacinta was tough, but fair. She had taken over at the helm, at a time of crisis—much to the school council's relief. Their disastrous predecessor had left many fires in his wake, but Jacinta had handled them all like a professional. Staff opinion surveys showed that morale was up, as were student outcomes. She aimed high and maintained that expectation for all staff. Which meant cancelling the camp would be a significant step backwards.

Gabriel glanced at her; his grin flashed.

"Great. Thanks, boss. Right. You too."

He hung up and spread his hands. "You got it."

"So..."

"She's more than okay with parents being involved, provided they have a Working With Children Check."

"What's the probability of that happening?"

"You'd be surprised. You might have more parents whose kids are coming into junior school with that card. But you'll need to ensure that we have it on file. And make sure it's current. You'd be surprised how many teachers on leave might take up the chance to be out of the house."

Ally's shoulders lowered. A flicker of hope eased the pressure in her neck. If she wasn't careful, she'd end up slammed with a migraine and out of action for a week. She didn't have time to be lying in a dark room with a cool cloth over her head.

"Should I just send around an email to all parents, or just junior school?"

"I'd send around an email to junior and middle school parents, but I think you should place a notice in the newsletter, for a general call-out. Done that before?"

Ally shook her head, mind already working a mile a minute adding to the list of tasks she needed to complete by the end of the day. "It'll be pretty standard, right?"

"Yeah." Gabriel ripped off half a sheet of blank paper from the minutes of some meeting. "Tell them the dates of the camps and that they need their Working With Children Check—updated. Give them until the end of this week, maybe start of next week at the latest to let you know. We can post something up on Compass as well. Actually, do that first, it's more immediate."

"Wouldn't this look bad, that teachers aren't contributing?"

Gabriel grimaced. "A lot of schools do this all the time. We're more cautious after you-know-who left. Woodbury High is about community. Parents are an integral part of that, so it'll be fine. Remind them the risk of having to cancel if we can't get numbers up."

"I can guilt-trip like the best of them." She had her parents to thank for that one. "That sounds do-able. When does it have to be in the newsletter by?"

"Tonight."

"Excuse me?"

"Next one is a fortnight away. David needs to finalise the online formatting and send them off tomorrow so that's your window."

"Crap."

"Swing by the front office and let him know to wait for your notice."

The peal of the bell signalled the end of recess. Ally jolted out of her chair. She had a full afternoon of classes and yard duty at lunch. Her stomach grumbled. No chance of grabbing something to eat either.

"We've got the coordinators meeting this afternoon, don't we?"

"Yep."

"I'll have to type it up after then."

"Check with David. He tends to work late, but you can't assume he'll hang around."

"Thanks a lot, Gabriel. You're a lifesaver."

"Glad I could help. And Ally?" She turned in the doorway. "You're doing a great job. In case no one told you."

She half-laughed. "Tell me that *after* I pull this thing off."

But his words of encouragement sat warm with her for the rest of the day. She really didn't know why Maddie found him to be so difficult.

If he had sky blue eyes and dark blond hair, she would have found herself thinking about him in ways that would send them both to the principal's office. She certainly didn't need more complications in her life; she was doing a good enough job of screwing things up all on her own.

CHAPTER EIGHT

*O*wen sipped his coffee. His third for the day.

He re-read the city camp notice in Charlie's school newsletter. He wasn't certain his daughter would be happy to have her dad tag along. Once upon a time—in what felt like a different life—he would have known the answer. Known his child.

Once upon a time, Charlie would have begged him to come along. He rubbed his hand over his face. He'd speak to her this afternoon. She was already growing up and away from him faster than his heart could handle. Her latest fixation was with a two-hundred-dollar cookbook and the need to catch the bus home with friends.

He didn't want her to think he was hovering. But he was reluctant to give a twelve-year-old too much freedom. Not that he didn't trust her. It was all the other psychos in the world that left him wary.

When Rebecca died, volunteering at Charlie's school, attending excursions—just being present—helped ease the gaping hole in their life. He had wanted to be there for her as much for her comfort, as his own. Maybe this camp would be exactly what he needed to see Charlie in a new light. If she could navigate the city, maybe she could handle public transport on her own.

Owen opened his wallet and drew out the rectangular card. His Working With Children Check was still current. He was honest enough to admit that going on camp would be a good opportunity to spend time with Ally.

His initial plan was to drop by after school tomorrow to see if she wanted to grab a Friday night drink, but something told him she'd baulk at his direct approach. He would call her instead, to let her know he was keen to volunteer on camp. It was a good excuse to get in contact. Not that he needed one.

It had been five days since Ethan's birthday. Long enough to give her some breathing space.

Ally interested him in a way he hadn't experienced in a long time, and he wanted to find out what that meant. It didn't hurt that she was hot as hell.

Reserved. Cautious. And surprised when he had shown interest on the weekend. A woman like that surely had guys throwing themselves at her all the time.

Owen didn't know what had compelled him to ask her out. He ran his hand along his chin. His timing probably wasn't great, but she had stirred something up in him. And he was man enough to admit those secretive green eyes had hit a nerve.

He would take his time. There wasn't any rush.

If he wanted to pursue anything, he'd have to run it by Charlie eventually. He wouldn't do anything to compromise her happiness at this new school.

He glanced at the picture of his daughter at eighteen months on his desk. She'd had such a sunny personality. His chest ached thinking about the withdrawn child she had become. He didn't know what to say to her half the time that would bring her out of it. He was painfully aware that he wasn't her mother.

He braced against the familiar sense of dread. No matter

what, he couldn't seem to shrug off the guilt at Rebecca's death. Maybe if he had been more mature, more of a husband, their marriage would have worked.

Realistically he knew that her parents' disapproval only increased the strain on their relationship. They had undermined everything he tried to do as a dad; from how he soothed Charlie to the way he prepared her food. It was their way of trying to break them.

Hindsight made him realise just how much it had eroded his confidence, and his marriage. The pressure of being young parents trying to make ends meet had changed them both. By the time Rebecca had fallen ill, there wasn't much of a marriage left to salvage.

The ache in his chest intensified. He missed his parents. They always knew what to say to put life into perspective. They would have known what to do.

Owen rolled his shoulders and checked the time. He had a child to pick up and errands to run. He would focus on the present. Charlie's happiness was all that mattered. He'd do anything to bring back that carefree little girl.

He had a feeling that Ally McVeigh was just the right woman to help him do it.

CHAPTER NINE

$\mathcal{A}$ s week four of Term Two made its presence known, Ally desperately wished for a decent night's sleep. Life in the junior school office was chaotic at the best of times. It was downright mental now. She was like a tight-rope walker, balancing her way through assemblies, truancy issues and the impending behemoth that was city camp.

She was currently surrounded by two hundred and fifty eager Year 7 students at lunchtime in the hall, all excited to pick their room buddies. After explaining the process to them, Ally and the other coordinators let the first batch of seventy-five students organise their groups. Excited cries filled the room. The cacophony of noise, tears and laughter was not dissimilar to being at the zoo. Her job was more one of hostage negotiator than teacher on such days.

She placed the sign-up sheets along the back wall and seconds later she was surrounded by eager children who jostled for place. Negotiations and alliances had begun—nothing like a camp to test the strength of budding friendships.

She had made sure that all the new and friendless students

were in a group prior to today's sign-up, and this first batch of seventy-five were a pretty low maintenance group. She had checked on Charlotte—who seemed to be happy with her new friends. Ally was relieved to see some of the reserve with her teachers—not to mention herself—starting to fade. Something she'd be reporting back to Owen in her email.

Her stomach pitched up and over like a crashing wave. Now was not the time to think about Owen, or the message he had left on her voicemail last week. She had been so busy with back to back classes and meetings on Thursday and Friday that she hadn't had the chance to call.

She was being a coward. But she had freaked out at the thought of ringing him on the weekend. Too intimate. And her Monday had been just as hectic.

Ally bit her lip. She was avoiding it. She knew this. But the man made her nervous.

She didn't know what to make of his comment about "continuing their weekend conversation." She wouldn't let herself analyse it or she'd drive herself crazy.

She hadn't expected him—of all parents—to agree to chaperone on camp. Ever since his call, her traitorous mind conjured fantasies of stolen kisses in the cover of night along one of Melbourne's city laneways.

Three days. Two nights. Her nerves would be ripped to shreds.

A piercing wail cut through the hall.

"Ms. McVeigh!" Ally turned. "My father's going to hear about this!"

Amber Sullivan stuck her small pug nose in the air, mouth covered in lip gloss. Her round, youthful face was buried beneath an avalanche of concealer. In what was no doubt a practiced move, she flicked back her straight blonde hair, clutching at her friend's arm. The rest of her clique trailed behind her.

"What seems to be the problem, Amber?"

"This is so dumb! Casey doesn't have a group! It's your job to put her in our room for camp."

"Hold on. Casey *does* have a group but unfortunately, it's not in yours. If you remember we planned for her to stay in Vanessa's room? I know you're still upset about it, but it's not possible to add more people at this stage. The hotel has a strict policy on how many students can share a room."

"Mrs. Volero said the same thing," Casey whispered. "I told you, Amber."

She thanked heavens that Barbara hadn't given in to "I know my rights" Amber Sullivan. In her short time in the role, Ally had been lectured by Reginald Sullivan, barrister of some prestigious law firm, on numerous occasions. He thought he could bully the school and its teachers because of his position in society. His daughter thought that gave her clout to do the same.

They didn't realise that she grew up surrounded by entitled bankers and businessmen; their intimidating tactics rarely worked on her. Or the school for that matter. At least not now that Jacinta was principal.

Amber jutted her chin. "Why isn't it possible? You make the rules, so you can change them!"

"You know why, Amber. We've been through this with everyone. You're at a hotel. Those are their rules."

"Well how come the retards get a bigger room?"

"Amber!" Casey gasped.

The girls behind her giggled. It was all the encouragement a mini-diva in the making needed. Amber continued, casting a quick, sly glance at the audience that slowly gathered around her. Defiance dripped off every syllable. "I mean, it's so *stupid* that we let Athol and Dougie and the other *retards*—who are too dumb to know they're even in a room—be together, and we're not allowed!"

Ally's features turned stony. "Amber Sullivan. We do not

speak about others in such a manner at Woodbury. It's disappointing coming from you, an intelligent person who knows better than to denigrate her peers just to make a point. It's bullying behaviour and we will not tolerate it. It's against our school values. You need to apologise, please."

Amber's bottom lip wobbled. Remorse flashed behind her eyes. There was a moment's hesitation, as if she weighed up all options. A sneer replaced any sentiment of contrition. Her shoulder jerked. "It's true. They are retards."

"That's a warning."

An expectant hush fell across the hall. Ally was keenly aware that a small group of children had stopped to listen, and she wished she had handled it in the privacy of her office. But she had been caught off guard. Proof that she couldn't afford to be distracted, especially when certain parents were out for blood.

"My daddy says I shouldn't even have to be in the same class as those *retards*. They're just dragging us down. They should be in retard school. And you're incompetent for not having them streamed in separate classes."

"You're being rude and disrespectful. I've asked you to stop. Come with me. Now, please."

The little girl stood her ground, temper tears finally spilling over.

"Junior school. Now."

Amber dashed away tears and stormed off. "I hate you!" she screeched. "I hate this stupid school. You're such a retard!" she bellowed, before pushing her way past the crowd of students. "Wait 'til my father hears about this! You'll be fired!"

Ally rolled her shoulders and broke up the crowd on her way out.

"Want me to handle it?" Murphey was at her side a second later.

"No, thanks, Murph. I got this one. Could you bring back the sign-up sheets when the rest of the kids are finished? Also, ask around to see that this wasn't filmed. I'd hate to get my fifteen minutes of fame this way."

He squeezed her shoulder. "Will do."

Barbara walked out of the hall beside her. "Best to have a witness with kids like Amber. Sly little creatures," she whispered.

Adrenaline pumped through her body. She knew she would be in for a battle.

She just wasn't sure if she was going to win the war.

Ally's head pounded.

The meeting with Reginald Sullivan, prominent barrister and patron of the arts played in her mind. She walked out of the junior school office and couldn't quite believe that the man was even more belligerent than his almost teenage daughter. What exhausted her spirit more so was the fact that he supported his child, even though she had insulted her coordinator and her fellow peers.

The man argued against her decision to give his daughter a detention saying that his baby girl was not to blame. Amber was merely standing up for her rights, and that of a friend. Honourable really. Ally had clearly instigated the whole incident and needed to learn how to work with children before she stepped inside a school. Naturally Reginald was raising this with the principal and would look to the school council for guidance on this matter.

Oh yes, it was a great meeting.

She disliked the man intensely, but it was unprofessional of her to act in any other manner but cordial. Even when he told her that she was incapable of doing her job. Too young. Too inexperienced. Too naïve.

No matter how many times Ally had heard those comments —or a variation thereof over the past month—it still stung. Not that she gave parents like that the satisfaction of how much his insults hurt. One of the perks of growing up in the McVeigh household was being able to hide her emotions from a young age. After all, showing vulnerability only left one open to attack.

She headed to the nurse's office to pick up some pain relief for her throbbing head. Once sorted, she stood in line at the photocopier trying to avoid small talk. She just needed to make it through this parent information session for camp, then she could go home.

Her start to this new role had been a bumpy one, that was a given. But perhaps if she were a different person, she would be better able to handle the pressure.

Maybe she wasn't cut out for the job after all.

Her temples throbbed. She had the ingredients for a whopper of a migraine. An empty stomach, dehydration and stress. She could sense it creeping up the back of her neck. Emotion tickled the back of her throat.

She blinked back tears and focused on keying the right settings into the photocopier. She would not let them get to her. Crying would only prove that she was weak. She needed to show everyone that she could handle this job, no matter how stressful.

Handouts complete, Ally headed back to her office, cradling the warm bundle of copied paper in her arms.

"Are you sure you don't need us to stay?" Barbara asked the second she stepped through the door.

"We can take the camp meeting," Murphey added.

"Not at all. I'm fine. A bit depleted, but it shouldn't take too long. And it can't be as bad as what we all had to witness. You guys head on home."

Ally waved them off and slapped a smile on her face. She opened one of the classrooms in junior block and placed the handouts along the table, for the ten parents who volunteered for the first camp. It was more than they needed, but experience taught her to be overcautious about these things.

When the first few parents began arriving, she swallowed her turmoil. She hoped she was a better actress than she gave herself credit.

Something was up.

The other parents seemed to buy the warm smile that Ally beamed their way, but every now and then her emerald eyes flashed as turbulent as a rip tide.

It hadn't surprised him that she hadn't returned his call. He wasn't offended by her silence. He got the impression that she wasn't the type to rush into things. And he was a patient man.

It crossed his mind that the quick, hot leap of attraction that seemed to spark when he was in her presence might not be reciprocated. He'd catch her after the meeting for a quick chat. If she wasn't keen, he'd have his answer.

Owen shifted in the uncomfortable plastic chair and willed his brain to focus on the information booklet rather than the arresting woman at the front of the room. He would have begged to have a teacher like Ally as a kid. She was relatable and kind beneath her reserved exterior. Then again, he probably would have failed in a spectacular blaze of distracted glory, but he would have preferred her to the mole-haired, garlic breathing octogenarian he had as his teacher.

Ally outlined the process for volunteering on camp with the efficiency of a woman used to working on the clock. She took questions from parents, repeating information with the patience of a saint. The itinerary looked loaded, but fun and Owen was starting to feel excited about experiencing the activities as much as being a volunteer. It seemed that only a few parents, himself included, would be staying overnight. The others would be attending during the day only.

As the meeting ended, Ally thanked everyone for their time. A few parents asked questions. One stood; arms crossed.

"This is bullshit."

"I beg your pardon?" The easy expression frozen on her face.

"You heard me. This. Is. Bullshit. I took time from my busy schedule to be told that I probably won't be needed. Why the hell am I here then if you have reserves?"

"Sir, I believe I said in the email, those who would be—"

He shook his head furiously. "No. You didn't. You can't just assume that people will give up their free time. This is shit. Guilting parents to go on camp. What do we pay you people for anyway?"

"Look, buddy." Owen stood. "It was in the email."

"Was I talking to you?" The angry father's face was red and contorted.

"No, mate. But I was talking to you. Calm down. We're all here to help."

The father threw down the folder. "I'm not wasting my time on this." He paused before he left. "Next time do your job properly and we all won't have to suffer from your incompetence. And in case you didn't get it, you can count me off the list."

Ally jumped when the door slammed.

"Forget about him, he's an idiot," Owen said.

The other parents agreed. But it was no use. One minute, she was smiling in embarrassed appreciation. The next, tears were streaming down her face.

"I—I'm s-s-sorry," she mumbled to the parents. "I h-have to go. Please email if you h-have questions."

Before he could stop her, she was out the door.

The volume in the room escalated as the parents all spoke at once. It took Owen ten minutes to usher them out of the classroom. Making sure they all left, he walked in the opposite direction to Ally's office.

He didn't know why the need to protect her had come upon him so strong, but he accepted the emotion for what it was; his focus now was to figure out how to make things right.

Ally dashed away the river of tears that blurred her vision. She was stupid. So very stupid for bursting into tears in front of a group of parents like that.

She was a professional, damnit. She should never have allowed that parent to upset her. It was proof that she was too emotional.

Closing the interview room door, she buried her head in her hands. Word would no doubt spread like the plague. She prided herself on being an efficient person; a considerate, hard-working, organised teacher, but she was afraid that it would all be questioned after the mad events of the day. First, Amber and her dad. Now this. It was just too much.

With shaking fingers, she reached for her phone, then jumped.

Her heart thudded at the figure behind the glass. Owen slid the door of the interview room open. It seemed she couldn't even hide in her own office.

Ally bit her lip when he offered her some tissues from the box on the shelf in the corner. Kindness always cranked up her sob-meter when she was upset.

"I'm so sorry for disturbing you, but I had to see if you were okay."

"I—I—I." She hiccupped.

"Hey, hey, take a deep breath. It's okay. Let it out."

Owen ran his hand up and down her arm. The gesture, whilst a little too familiar for acquaintances, was oddly comforting.

She gulped in air.

It was only when her breathing slowed that she noticed that Owen had sat beside her and was rubbing circles against her back. She straightened, sensations of pleasure coursing through her body, awareness lighting up her senses. His hand dropped away.

Ally swayed, once, then stilled. If crying in front of parents was inappropriate, asking a parent to continue stroking her body because it felt so damn good would be scandalous. What had gotten into her lately?

"Sorry. You really don't have to be here. I'm fine."

"I wanted to. For my own peace of mind."

She simply stared. Of course he had to see her when her nose was all red and blobby from crying. He was just so...irresistible. She couldn't think of a thing to say to him. Especially when those blue eyes locked on her in that way. Like he cared.

"So, nasty parent." He leaned forward. "I'm sure you've had your fair share of them in this job."

"Mmm. The waters seem to be infested with them today." Ally gave an abridged version of what happened with Reginald Sullivan.

Owen winced. "Wow. Parents can be real bastards, can't they?"

She laughed. She had been humiliated more than enough for one day. "No comment."

An errant tear escaped. His knuckles brushed against her cheek.

"I wouldn't worry about what happened back there. Seriously. After the day you've had I'm surprised you were able to keep it together for so long."

Ally was grateful for a neutral topic that didn't have her fantasising about his hands. "Those parents don't know that. People talk. And it's going to seem like the new head of junior school cried over some silly parent."

"I wouldn't worry about it."

"It's my reputation," she snapped. "Sorry. I shouldn't get mad at you. I'm mad at myself."

"You're allowed to feel emotions."

"You're not a teacher."

"You're human. That means occasionally getting upset."

Mortification seeped through. "I've never cried in front of parents before. Oh, God." She put her head in her hands. "I'm so embarrassed."

Owen shifted closer. "I know you probably don't want to hear this right now, but my mother was a teacher. And she told me the story of a horrible Year 8 class she had one year. She had just come back from maternity leave and felt the pressure of a full-time load. It took that class three days before she snapped. Said she broke down like a blubbering baby. Right in the middle of class. In front of the rat-baggiest group that ever came through those doors."

She lifted her face, feeling the horror of such a scenario deep in her heart. "Your poor mother."

"Yep."

"What did she do?"

"She sat down on the steps outside the classroom and cried and cried, until one of the boys came outside and pleaded with her to come back."

"And did she?"

"Wiped her eyes, and fragile as glass went back in. Told them she was human too and they'd hurt her feelings behaving that way. Then she continued on with the lesson."

"What happened?"

"Next day the boys left a note on her desk, apologising. I

think she petrified them with the force of her emotions. They were still rat-bags, but it never got that bad again. My mother was certain she lost control over the class for good, but they surprised her."

"She would have been so embarrassed. I know I would."

"She was. But she moved on. Got over it. Got through."

Ally sniffed. Her mouth wobbled even as she smiled. "She was a brave woman."

"Yeah, she was. But also, human. It was her best and worst teaching moment. She had loads more stories like that to share. But she tells me *that* story—or told me that—when I was feeling down about losing face, or if I made a fool out of myself over a girl. I guess what I'm saying is, don't assume that you'll know how others will react. You're a great coordinator and you've made Charlie feel good about school again. Take the wins for what they are."

The pressure on her chest abated. She breathed in. "That's lovely."

"Glad I could be of service."

"Seriously, though, thanks." She paused. "About your call. Sorry I didn't get back to you."

"Don't worry about that right now. I apologise if I crossed—"

"I freaked out." She blurted. "About your intentions." She didn't think she could humiliate herself in front of this man any more, but here she was, doing just that. In spectacular fashion. "Truth is, you make me nervous. I…"

Owen's eyes held hers. "Feeling's mutual." His gaze skimmed her lips, and her chest tightened. "I'll call you, Ally. Then maybe we can make plans to be nervous in the same room together. Over coffee…I'll let myself out."

She nodded, watching him leave.

She didn't know this guy at all, but somehow, he managed

to comfort her in a way that only her close friends could. It left her a little disoriented.

Despite her looming doubts, the anticipation of hearing from him again made her smile.

She hugged the warm sensation to her chest and packed up for the day. It was well and truly time to go home.

CHAPTER TEN

*H*e rang her the next day to see how she was feeling. Ally had been caught up in a lunchtime meeting with her senior students and had missed the call. Along with four others from staff and parents.

She had finally listened to her voicemail after school, just as the package arrived in her office.

Barbara's face was glowing when she placed the chocolate bouquet on her desk.

"Sweet treat for the lady."

"Me?"

Ally hung up the phone. Her mind was so preoccupied with Owen's voicemail message that she had to blink a few times to focus on the note attached to the large bundle.

On it was a single line.

Take the wins.

She knew exactly who had sent it and was touched that he wanted to remind her of the good things she was able to achieve in this job. Owen's advice the previous afternoon had hit the mark. The message wasn't flirty, and she appreciated it, given she was at work. But it was sincere.

The pleasure shot through her and try as she might, she couldn't hold back the grin.

"Secret admirer?" Barbara threw her a sly wink.

Paul and Murphey looked up from where they were working on the centre table. A few of Barbara's middle year students made cooing noises.

"A friend."

Her cheeks burned. She tucked the note in one hand and placed the bouquet in the centre table.

"Feel free to take a chocolate, team."

They didn't need to be asked twice.

When her office finally cleared for the evening, Ally dialled Owen's number.

She had just begun to leave a message when he picked up.

"Ally!"

Behind the surprise at hearing his voice, was a current of delight. She fought against the silly grin that would no doubt travel down the line. Professional, Ally. For God's sake, you're still at school.

"Did I catch you at a bad time?"

His breathless voice held humour. "I just about broke my damn neck to answer your call. It's perfect timing. And really good to hear from you."

Butterflies. Hundreds of them fluttered across her chest.

"I called to say thank you for your message. And the bouquet. The staff in my office were grateful for the sugar rush this afternoon."

"And what about you? Does *Ms.* McVeigh have a sweet tooth? Or did I get it wrong?"

"Take the win, *Mr.* Davies. I can confirm I thoroughly enjoyed them."

Ally rolled her eyes. Why did she sound like a robot? She caught herself tapping her fingers on the desk and stood up. She would not let him affect her so much. It was stupid. She didn't even know the guy.

"I'll make a note of it."

"Are you keeping tabs on me, Mr. Davies?"

Great. Now she sounded breathless. If she wasn't careful the phone call would turn into something else entirely. *Reel it in, McVeigh.*

She was saved by his next question.

"I'm feeling much better, thanks. Sorry you had to witness that, but I'm grateful for the advice, so...thanks again."

"No need to thank me. But I do have a bone to pick with you."

"Okay...I'll bite."

His low rumble of appreciation sent a delicious shiver down her spine.

"I think it's only fair, given that you have access to all my details, that I get to have your number."

"Is that so?"

"It's a fact. I have a delivery of baked goods to send over soon."

"Baked goods? Aren't I getting spoilt."

"Charlotte insists on making something for her friends and her teachers. Your name may have come up...I think I'm making it clear that I want any excuse to contact you."

Hello? Middle ground, where the hell are you? The reins were slipping from her fingers, as was her sense of control when it came to this man.

"Got a pen?"

She heard him grin. "Two seconds."

She hung up the phone a few minutes later and succumbed to the rolling waves of nausea.

What the hell was she doing? She turned around to look at

the bouquet in the centre of the room. Getting involved with a parent...had she lost her mind?

Ally rubbed her eyes, tired now that the exhilaration had begun to ebb away.

Something had begun. She was letting herself get caught up in this man when she knew it was a mistake. This wasn't like her at all...problem was, she had no idea what to do next.

That scared her more than she cared to admit.

Weekends for Ally meant juggling marking, prepping curriculum and baking up a storm. She had been warned when she applied for the job that running a sub-school meant she would have zero time during the week to spare on prepping and planning. That had been a gross understatement. She never stopped working.

Which was fine by her. It meant she was able to ignore the fluttery sensation that danced across her chest when she thought about Owen. She hadn't heard from him for a few days, since she had given him her number. Which was more than okay.

She didn't know what she would say to him if he did call.

Ally focused on her laptop screen and sent her grocery order to the school's food assistant, Cassandra, so that she could do a shop for her classes. She couldn't imagine having to do that herself on top of everything else. She just wouldn't have the time.

She glanced at a parent email next, wondering how best to response. Whilst she once had the luxury of replying to emails during school hours, doing so now would give her more time to chase up student welfare and prep with her team during the week. Win/Win.

Take the wins.

Ally shook her head to clear her thoughts.

She had so many initiatives that she wanted to implement in her very limited time as coordinator; one being to tackle the end of year program—a current lead weight that loomed on the horizon, feared by all and loathed by some. Even though December was light years away, she knew just how quickly a few terms could fly. They were already in the middle of May, yet she was still treading water. If she wanted to implement all the changes, she needed to work a bit harder.

She was about to send an email to the school counsellor regarding another self-harming fourteen-year-old when she swore.

The fucking pamphlets. She forgot to drop them off to her parents. It had been two weeks since she spoke to them about her father's surgery. And even though it would be months away before he actually had the hip replaced, she wanted to give them all the information she had found so they could handle it themselves.

Barbara had recommended a private nursing service that had cared for her mother at home when she had Alzheimer's disease. She was grateful to her colleague for the small mountain of booklets. She trusted Barbara's judgement and could only hope it met with her parents' approval. Not bloody likely.

She squeezed at the bridge of her nose. Her parents had already rejected the first nurse she had found, all because she worked at a public hospital and had wanted to book in the dates in advance. Her father kept delaying the process, claiming the merger needed to happen before he set a date for the procedure. If she didn't know him better, she'd say he was afraid of the surgery. Not that her father seemed capable of such emotion.

She shouldn't be surprised by his sheer arrogance in thinking a surgeon could be available at a moment's notice. These operations were booked months in advance.

Ally contemplated sending the information to them in the mail. She glanced at the small square clock on her living room wall. It was almost midday on a Saturday, which meant the post office would be closed by the time she arrived.

She cringed when her mobile buzzed. Her mother.

Ally shut down her laptop and dragged out the pamphlets from her bulging chronicle. She stripped off her pyjamas and threw on her favourite hoodie and tracksuit pants from the washing pile at the foot of her bed. She added a scarf for good measure and flew out the door before she could change her mind.

The quicker she delivered it to them, the sooner she would be able to come back home and continue working. She enjoyed having an uninterrupted Saturday to herself so much so that she toyed with the idea of throwing the bundle at her mother's front door—paper boy style.

But she wasn't a coward. She would make it a quick visit.

It was the only kind she could tolerate these days.

Forty minutes later, Ally parked a few doors down from a beautiful French-style townhouse, complete with colourfully potted plants, despite the autumn chill. She parked her slightly beat up Hyundai Accent down the street, not wanting another reason for her mother to admonish her financial state. Best not to provoke the Bear when she was on a time limit. She ran up the steps and rang the bell.

Her mother's eyes widened.

"Allyna McVeigh, what on earth are you wearing?"

Ally bit her tongue. She would not get into a battle over her Saturday dress code. She would not rise to the bait.

"Please tell me that's not what you wear to work. Though I suppose it *is* a public school. I know they're very casual, but had you taught at Childawn Grammar you'd be expected to dress the part. No doubt the salary would be much better as well."

"Hello, Mother."

"Come inside! For pity's sake, I don't want the neighbours to see you dressed like that. They'll think you're a beggar."

"Just fitting the part."

"No self-respecting person stands at the front step and conducts a conversation. I won't have it."

Ally crossed her arms and stepped inside. "Well maybe I don't want to be self-respecting." She tried not to pout. Why did her parents always manage to bring out the sullen fourteen-year-old in her? She hated who she was around them.

Vera McVeigh shot her an icy stare, out of eyes a few shades lighter than her own. Her mother's fair hair was turning silver, but she wouldn't dare let anyone know that, feigning perpetual youth to her social circle. It was a world of status. Appearances. Make-believe. Nothing was sincere. It made her skin itch.

"Too much time teaching in that public school. I don't understand why you won't teach at Childawn. The McVeighs have a reputation to uphold, and it is your responsibility to ensure that you do so at all times. It's not becoming of a woman of your background to teach riff raff."

"The 1830's called, Mother. They want their ideology back."

"Don't you mock me young lady. You don't know what it means to be a McVeigh in society, the—"

Ally held up her hand. "I need to get going, so painful as it might be, I have to cut this visit short. I'm just dropping the pamphlets. As requested."

"If your birth hadn't been so horrific, we would have had more children. Someone who could have taken over from your father and—"

"I'm leaving." She rifled through her handbag, picked out

the bunch of pamphlets and plonked them down on her mother's antique side table in the foyer.

"What would you have me do with it, Allyna?" Her slightly wrinkled face—thanks to her cosmetic surgeon—shifted slightly. "I don't need these."

"You asked for them."

"Give them to your father."

"I'm not your messenger, Mother. You need to sort this stuff out between yourselves. I'm sick of being your go-between."

Her mother's mouth pursed in displeasure. She never approved of confrontations. Unless she was the one leading the attack.

For the millionth time since she was a small child, Ally wondered why her parents didn't get a divorce. The "separation" was beyond the point of ridiculousness.

"We don't ask anything of you, Allyna. You've made sure of that. This is the least you could do for him."

"Still wants to change his will, huh?"

For a small, slim woman, Vera could intimidate. Back straight, large eyes icy and slightly narrowed, she opened the door with the cold detachment of a bitter rival. "We are terribly sorry to inconvenience our *only* child. But that is quite alright, my dear. We want nothing from you."

Guilt, the incredible, narcissistic friend that wanted only its voice heard, made Ally speak. "I already spoke to Father about this a few weeks ago. Look, I have to get back to work. I have a job, remember?"

Her mother lifted her nose and spoke right through her. "That will be all, thank you."

Dismissed like a servant. Or worse, a stranger.

Ally wanted to scream. Instead she forced herself to sever the poisonous words like a gangrenous limb. Even as she looked into her mother's detached eyes, she knew that it was too late. The infection had long ago entered her bloodstream. If she wasn't careful it would blacken her own heart.

The door closed, not with a slam, but with a forced click. That restrained anger, the cold disdain, was exactly how her mother treated her for as long as she could remember. Vera McVeigh's demeanour was so frigid it could chill the most hardened criminal to the core. As a child it had been distressing. Soul destroying.

Ally gulped in the cool autumn air in an effort to cleanse herself and wished she had worn her fluffy slippers. Just out of spite.

She stomped towards her car, shoulders hunched, eyes downcast. She was a grown adult for pity's sake. She refused to feel guilty just because she lived her own life. Yet the heavy, churning sensation persisted.

She was proud of what she'd achieved, damnit. She was able to support herself and would, hopefully be in a leading teacher role permanently by the start of next year. Maybe then she could finally prove that she was able to succeed on her own merits.

She wrenched open the passenger side door and flung her purse on the seat.

"Ally?"

She froze, staring at the roof of her dirty, beat-up car. She knew that rich, smooth voice. She had heard it too many times in her dreams. Knowing that *he* would be standing behind her, when she was looking so...so...Ally briefly closed her eyes. She wanted to bury herself in the dewy grass.

She'd have to die of embarrassment first.

Slamming the car door, Ally turned. It was even worse than expected.

He was immaculate. The thick, V-neck sweater, clean blue jeans and scuffed boots were perfect against his rugged frame. It was a far cry from the "down-to-my-last-dollar" look she had going on.

Owen stood on the pavement; a look of disbelief plastered across his attractive face. One hand was on Charlotte's shoulder, the other tucked into his pocket.

Oh, if her mother could see her now. Ally gritted her teeth against the image of Vera's smug, know-it-all face.

Why was he constantly catching her off guard? It made it hard for her to keep those much-needed boundaries in place. Hell, she'd need an electric fence to keep herself in check. She was painfully aware that she looked like someone in need of a GoFundMe page, whilst he looked like some rough and tumble, sexy as sin, lumberjack. It just wasn't fair.

"Guilty. Hello again, Mr. Davies. Charlotte."

Ally's fingers twitched. She fought against the urge to brush at the stain on her hoodie. Her tatty tracksuit bottoms, wild hair and un-made up face provided very little in the way of a confidence boost. A perfect outfit to piss off Mother Dearest, a perfect nightmare to scare off a potential suitor. She frowned. Not that he…

"*Ms.* McVeigh." He raised an eyebrow. "You can just call me Owen."

"Right."

She was clutching at the loose threads of professionalism. Not that she could lay claim to it with her hair looking like a bird's nest. She lifted her chin, noting the glint of humour in Owen's eyes. Head held high, she stepped onto the footpath.

"What are you doing in this area? Do you live here?"

Ally's eyes popped. "Here? In Somerset Village? Hell, no. My mother lives a few doors down." She gestured to her left. "I was just dropping something off in my Saturday best." She motioned to her outfit.

Charlotte's giggle somehow made the mortification worth it.

"We're visiting my grandparents," she supplied, holding on to her book bag.

"That's pretty cool."

"They're mum's parents."

Ally caught the grimace that flickered across Owen's face. Had she blinked she would have missed it.

"Do you visit them often?" She looked down at Charlotte, pleased at the forthcoming chatter. In all her talks with the girl, she had never been very animated. The four weeks of counselling seemed to be working well. Ally was hopeful she was coming out of that shell.

"Every second weekend. Sometimes every month."

The front door of the house behind them opened. A woman with ash blonde hair stood on the porch. Unlike her own mother, this woman had no qualms raising her voice to be heard.

"Owen!" She waited until he turned. "You should have the presence of mind not to loiter out on the footpath, especially in this weather. Charlotte could catch her death. Inside now, please."

He stood behind his daughter, hands on her shoulders. The statement was clear to Ally, despite the casual way in which he moved.

What was more interesting was the way the little girl seemed to shrink before her. Like a turtle retracting into its shell. Something to pass on to the school counsellor.

"In a minute, Anita. We're just finishing up here," Owen called back.

"What are you going to do at Grandma's place today?"

Charlotte shrugged her shoulders. "I'm not sure. Grandma usually has a schedule. We paint sometimes."

"Oh, do you like painting?"

"Not really. But mum was taught, and she was accomplished. I also have to play the piano. Grandma pays for lessons."

"Well I'm sure you're great at it." Ally injected cheer in her voice, even though her stomach pitched. Memories of being forced to play an instrument that made no sense to her clouded her mind.

"We have a keyboard that Dad bought me at home. Grandma says it's not the same thing."

"Charlotte!"

She looked up at her dad, and he nodded. "It was lovely bumping into you, Ally, but we're being summoned." Whilst his voice was jovial, his face was a complete mask.

"Yes. Well, it was nice seeing you both. I'll catch up with you next week on camp."

Charlotte waved, walking past the black gates and up the steps.

"You wouldn't happen to be free for a coffee now, would you?"

The expression on his face was inviting. Tempting.

"Actually, no. I can't. Sorry. I do have to go, but I'll see you both at the train station on Wednesday."

"Ally?"

She scampered around her car, knowing she was handling this all wrong.

"Next week, then." He eventually turned and followed his daughter up the steps.

Ally looked through her side window just in time to see the front door slam in Owen's face, swallowing his daughter behind it.

Definitely something to follow up next week.

CHAPTER ELEVEN

*A*lly walked through the crowd of seventy-five animated school children huddled in the local football field. Their excited chatter—visible wisps of smoke—surrounded them as the morning fog skimmed through the trees, settling on the rooftop of the adjacent train station.

They completed a preliminary roll check, but there were still a lot of absences. Droves of students, laden down with their luggage had rung saying they were going to be late, others simply arrived bedraggled, with mussed hair, having slept in.

She bounced on her colourful blue and green trainers, excited and petrified of what lay ahead. It was the first of many camp groups that would take place over the next few weeks. She wanted it to be enjoyable for all the kids and staff. Hell, she wanted to knock it out of the park.

"Has anyone seen Tyler?" Barbara asked 7A. "He's still not here, and I've phoned his mother, but there's no answer."

"Tyler is with his dad on Tuesday nights, Mrs. Volero," Amy Dappelou offered. "We texted him, but I don't know whether his phone is charged."

"So much technology, such a nuisance," Barbara muttered.

"Well we're catching the 9:02 train, so if you manage to get through to him, please tell him to hurry."

"Everything okay, Barb?" Ally handed her a first aid kit.

"Just Tyler Banks M.I.A. I reminded him the other day, rang his mother about it too," she lowered her voice, moving them both out of earshot. "But honest to goodness, that boy could get lost in his own bedroom. His mother is heavily medicated, so that makes it difficult at the best of times."

"What about the father?" She attached her own first aid kit around the strap of her backpack.

"He's on the DNC list. His choice. Doesn't want to get involved in school issues. Mr. Banks says we can contact Tyler's mother who is the primary caregiver if we have any problems. It's...complicated."

"But we probably should contact him if we have a number?"

"I'll ring the front office."

Before Barbara could pick up the phone, Amy called out, "Tyler's here!"

Ally breathed out a sigh of relief, then stifled a giggle.

Amy stood, arms akimbo, berating his arrival time. She stepped back suddenly, questioning Tyler's outfit. "Wait a minute—is that a tent?"

Tyler shoved aside the messy mop of hair behind his ear. "We're going camping, Aims." He waved the tent that sat around his shoulders.

Amy slapped her hand against her head, shaking dark, braided locks. "You idiot, Tyler! We're going to *city* camp!"

His eyes lit up. "I didn't know we could camp in the city!"

Ally bit her lip. Hard.

"Tyler!" Amy giggled. "We're staying in a *hotel*."

She walked over to them. "Good to see you, Tyler. Are you planning a tent-style sleepover in your room? How inventive."

Blue eyes stared owlishly back at her. "Yeah. Yeah, I am. I like that, miss."

"I bet you do."

"I even bought marshmallows." He said proudly, holding up the packet. As Tyler's friends gathered around him—Ally was sure he needed them as much as they did him—she raised her voice signalling for everyone to follow her to the station.

Five minutes later, they were on the platform. She made sure the teachers double checked the consent and medical forms, as well as the camp itinerary. Students were placed in their groups, mainly ten to twelve students for every two teachers or guardians. She could only imagine looking after a bunch of high-energy students all day, for three days in the city would be an exhausting feat for the parents who were volunteering. Not to mention just a little scary and out of their comfort zone.

She was about to check on her group when Owen walked up to her.

"Ready to report for duty, miss!"

Those blue eyes were warm and a little too inviting for her liking.

"Glad you could join us. Here's a first aid kit. Strap it to your bag so you have it when you need it."

"I've never seen the station so full."

"There's a lot of us. I just feel sorry for commuters. How was Charlotte feeling?"

"Really good. Excited about the week and happy in the friendship group she's made. I think she's starting to relax. I have to admit that I'm surprised at how fast she's adjusted."

"It's amazing what good friends and a shrink can do."

"I'm man enough to eat crow when I'm wrong. Mr. Taylor has been great with her, so I apologise for jumping the gun."

"It's understandable after what you've been through at her last school. But that's the beauty of starting fresh. You can re-invent yourself to some degree."

He assessed her face. "I never thought of it that way. Are you okay?"

"Yes." She didn't want this to be awkward, but her nerves were shot to shreds. Ugh. She sounded like her mother. "How does she feel about having her dad tag along?"

"Surprisingly, fine. Probably because she'll have a portable 'tap and pay' in her group. She keeps harping on about finding baking books with Jeremy."

"They've formed a good friendship."

"They talk on the phone for hours about baking. When I ask her why she can't just chat to him the next day at school, she gives me that look." Owen mimicked the exasperation of a twelve-year-old.

"That's really sweet."

"Mmm. Anyway, it's a relief to be in your group as some of the other parents are a bit..." He raised a brow.

She pressed her lips together. She knew exactly whom he was talking about. Once they got word that he was a single dad, there would have been many covert pictures taken and sent off to single sisters across the school network. Especially with that face. Not that she was paying too close attention.

"Intense? I can only imagine."

The way Owen was looking at her made her feel like a summer heatwave.

Danger! Danger! squeaked the Dalek inside her brain. Their robotic arms waved in front of her eyes, demanding that she abort the mission. Immediately. She unfastened the buttons of her green jacket, glad for the gust of autumn air.

If she wasn't careful, she would let something stupid slip and that was not allowed to happen. She channelled Miss Rachel Lynde From *Anne of Green Gables*. It was simply out. Of. The. Question.

Ally shifted the folder with the itinerary and all her student contacts in her hand. Time to change the channel in her MA 15+ mind.

"More like vultures. I take it this morning went off without a hitch?"

"So far. The first camp is always a tester of sorts. We can use it to iron out any potential glitches for the rest of the camp groups."

"Don't be afraid to lean on other people's shoulders. That's what all great leaders do."

"Is that right?"

"So I'm told."

"I'll keep that in mind."

His grin was a combination of charm and sex appeal. And she'd be surrounded by it for three whole days.

When the train blared its horn, Ally herded the children, teachers and parents onto the last carriage. The commuters, she was certain, wouldn't know what hit them.

CHAPTER TWELVE

*I*n the heart of the bustling Melbourne CBD, the Queen Victoria Market sparkled from the rain the night before. Brisk and crisp, the cloudless blue sky teased busy commuters who embraced the last few weeks of autumn, and any vestige of warmth with it. The first day of camp had so far proved a success.

They had taken the kids on a cultural tour of the NGV and Immigration Museum, then stopped by the Victoria markets for a late lunch. The colourful stalls and the gaggle of voices thrilled the wide-eyed kids.

"Right, you all have to be back here in an hour and a half." Ally rubbed her slightly numb hands together and addressed her group. "This is your free time, but you can't go beyond the market. Always walk in pairs and make sure at least one person in each group has a mobile phone. We'll meet you here." She pointed to the doughnut stand. "If you forget where it is, just follow your nose." The cinnamon sugar drifted along the breeze. She noted the children's big eyes and eager grins. "And even though there's a Maccas on the corner, try out some real food at the market. You'll thank me later. It'll be something you can include as part of your assignment. Don't forget to take notes!" She waved them off.

"Got enough money, Charlie?" Owen called out. She nodded and raced off.

"Then there were two." Her heart raced a little at being alone with him. She wanted to talk about whatever it was that was happening between them, but she didn't know what to say. Or where to begin.

The girls had flipped when they saw the bouquet, and again when she told them about bumping into him on the weekend. It made her even more self-conscious.

"Lunch?" He gestured. "Whilst it isn't a coffee in some cozy cafe by ourselves like I had planned, it's a half-way point to a first date."

"Is that what's happening here?"

"I have a feeling you'll frown at the idea of considering this a date, especially surrounded by children and parents on camp. I wouldn't say it's the ideal setting either. But yes, dating you, seeing you outside of school hours is my end game, Ally. Right now, I'll make the most of any time I can get."

"No beating around the bush is there?"

"Not when I know what I want."

She absorbed the warmth in his gaze and let it settle close to her heart.

"So. A half-way date."

"Consider it a trial. If you like what you see after these three days, then you can take me out for a real test drive." He wiggled his eyebrows. "I'll make it worth your while."

How could she resist when the man made her laugh?

"Sounds like a deal. Do we get to eat on this half-way date? I'm starved."

"You bet. I hear the *gozleme* is killer."

"Oh really? Familiar with Turkish cuisine?"

"I am. Charlotte and I go to Goz City down on Cavendish street."

"The one on the corner? I love that place."

"Turkish then?"

"Read my mind. Though I'm more of a *borek* kinda gal."

They bustled in amongst tourists with their cameras, worming their way through the crowds, vying for a spot in line.

Finding a dry bench, they sat out in the weak sunshine. Ally kept the conversation casual, nothing too personal. Too revealing. She was still technically at work.

"It's good to see Charlotte finding friends with similar interests."

"You mean Jeremy?"

"You don't approve?" She hid her smile beneath her pastry.

"Of boys in general? What father would?"

"They're both keen cooks."

"He's a Heston wannabee and she's already pestering me to have a sleepover so they can try out a recipe."

Her eyebrows rose.

"I know, I know." Owen placed his fist against his chest. "My heart can't take it."

"What did you say to her?"

"When he can pull off a particular Heston dish in under three hours, I'll consider it."

"How long does it normally take?"

"Sixteen."

She laughed. "Harsh."

"Necessary. The kid's already started time trials. I may be eating my own words."

"When you're not protecting your daughter from budding chefs, what do you do for work?"

"I run my own data consulting company."

"Right. What does that mean exactly?"

"Lots of talking." He rolled his eyes. "Working with clients

IDA BRADY

of big and small businesses to ensure their systems run better. Collating their tables and troubleshooting their programs. Boring stuff."

"Not to one who loves tables and graphs."

Owen bit into his *gozleme*. Steam rose from the paper wrapping and Ally had a moment of envy that she didn't get the spinach and cheese filling. "Now you're just humouring me."

She wrinkled her nose. "Maybe. But in baking I need numbers to make recipes work so I've had to negotiate with my inner math-phobe. Plus, Maths gets a bad reputation these days. Have you been in business for long then?"

"Nearly five years. I decided to start out on my own when working for others became dissatisfying. It was tough going but it meant I could have flexible hours. Picking up Charlie from school, working from home when she's sick. It has its perks."

"Do you travel much for work?"

"I try to limit it. A pitfall of the job, but a necessary evil when you're starting out. I thought about calling it quits a few years ago, when things were tough, but then, what would I be teaching my daughter?"

"It shows her resilience, to not give up when things are difficult. That's admirable."

"Thanks. It's hard leaving her."

"She doesn't come with you?"

Owen's mouth tightened. Whatever warmth lingered there moments before was gone.

"No. I leave her with her grandparents. Mine passed away a while ago."

"I'm sorry to hear it."

"Let's just say when it comes to Rebecca's parents...well, we don't get along."

"I got that vibe on Saturday actually."

"I'm not surprised. It's...messy."

Ally couldn't imagine ever leaving a child alone with her

96

mother and father, let alone having a child of her own. Her stomach rolled. She wouldn't daydream over the fantasy of "happy families;" she wouldn't be the kind of mother a child needed—not with her parents' DNA running through her veins.

His gaze roamed across her face.

She sipped at her lemonade. *Rein it in, McVeigh.*

"That must be hard for you not having your parents around. For all the little things."

"For Charlie, more so. She loved them, and they were great, but they died when she was just a baby. It was harder back then, as a teenager taking care of an infant. We relied on my parents a lot, and then we lost them in a car accident. My brother, Jack was a few years younger and still finishing off school when he moved in with us. It was a lot to take in."

"I can imagine. And a ton of responsibility on your shoulders. Most teenagers are getting wasted at university parties and backpacking through Asia after they finish school. Hardly any would be managing a family. That says a lot about you to have juggled it all, Owen."

He shrugged. "It was a comfort to have Jack around those first few years, but he left for university not long after. Life was hectic in those days and he learned to be self-sufficient faster than most. But he's found his feet now."

"Does he live in Melbourne?"

"No. He's in L.A. The last time I spoke to him, he was wrapping up some film and living the rock star lifestyle. He's an actor, slash photographer, slash model. Successful too, but never in one place for too long."

"I bet Charlotte loves that."

"When she gets to see him. There's not much incentive to stay here anymore. He was only sixteen when my folks died, and it hit him hard."

"That's a lot to go through."

"It is. I feel guilty that I couldn't do more when it all

happened. But that was a long time ago." Owen looked around them at the bustling crowds, but his eyes were distant. He blinked a few minutes later, shutting out the past. "You know the only reason my brother got a modelling contract is because I couldn't bust his pretty boy nose first. He was always a quick bastard." He rubbed at the slight bump on his nose, eyes warm. "He still reminds me of it whenever I rip into him about his career."

Ally laughed. "I think it suits you. Character building, and all that."

"Yeah?" His lips curved. "Think so?"

"You have an interesting face."

Earth to McVeigh, shut the hell up.

"Tell me more."

"You're not pretty enough to be a model anyway."

"How to damn with faint praise."

"Sorry, I didn't mean it like that. I meant, you're not a "pretty boy," you have a handsome face. A manly face."

She needed a gag order on herself.

"I believe you're paying me a compliment."

He made flirting too easy. In this case, easy was dangerous. She couldn't trust herself to say anything more. She wasn't sure what else would come out of her mouth if she did.

The second day of camp had proved equally hectic. That was why Ally hadn't mentioned anything about going on a real date with Owen.

It wasn't because she was running scared. He made it very clear that he wanted to see her romantically. After lunch yesterday, she could see how easy it would be to go out on a date with him. But with that very thought came the white-hot fear that she was making a mistake.

For now, she would see them as friendly acquaintances.

Not that she had much time to ponder over the state of her relationship. Their day had been filled with activities and requests from the kids to stop into this shop or that.

After a morning filled with team-building activities, they had taken the kids to The Shrine of Remembrance, enjoyed lunch along Southbank, then walked up to the Melbourne Cricket Ground for a guided tour. Jeremy had been chosen to touch the grass on the grounds and had picked Charlotte to accompany him, much to the awe of the other children.

"And what football team do you barrack for, young lady?" their elderly tour guide, Redmond Barry asked her.

"Me?" Ally's eyes flew open. "Oh, well. I never...I don't follow AFL."

There was an uproar from the students.

"Well, I'm sure you've seen a game, or two, at any rate. The 'G is the finest stadium in Australia. Home to many legends."

She managed a weak smile.

"You have watched a game haven't ya, love?" Red prodded. His brown eyes twinkled but never left her face. A gnarled hand tipped back his cricketer's hat. He was making her sweat.

"Well. Technically..."

"Miss! How could you never have watched a game?"

"It's the footy miss!"

She caught Owen attempting to stifle a grin at her interrogation. Red had somehow made her feel very un-Australian.

"I've seen snippets. On telly?" she offered.

Red roared with laughter. His thin frame shook with the force of his amusement. Ally wanted to justify her response, then decided it was best not to argue with an eighty-something M.C.G volunteer. When he wheezed out his last laugh, Red straightened and turned to the kids. "What do you lot reckon? Shall we treat your miss here to a game of footy, on the house?"

The betraying twelve-year-olds cheered and whooped.

"There you have it, miss." Red turned back to her, "It's settled. You're going to see a match. I don't suppose you have a team you like?"

By this stage Owen had sidled up next to her. "Essendon's always good," he whispered.

"Essendon then," Ally proffered, only to have Red's eyes light up.

"And you sir, you follow football?"

"Religiously." He nodded.

"Well, that's it then, tickets for this weekend's pre-season charity match—Essendon versus Collingwood. It'll be a rippa'. For two. You, miss, and this fella' here—"

"Owen."

"Owen. You beauty."

The kids looked at Red in awe.

Recovering her words, Ally intervened. "Honestly, Red, you don't have to do that."

"Nonsense. And just because I hate to see an opportunity wasted, you can come up to the members stand. I'll meet you here myself and show you around some."

"Really, you don't—"

Red waved off her protests and talked to someone on his two-way radio. The kids clambered after his retreating figure, firing off questions.

She turned to Owen. "Why didn't you save me?"

"Save you?" His eyes danced with humour. "From 'lil ol' Red? Why would I do that?"

"Because I hate football."

"How do you know if you've never seen it?"

"I just do." She crossed her arms.

"Ah huh." He ushered her along, a safe distance behind the children. "Look, Essendon and Collingwood," he whistled, "it's a big game. Draws tens of thousands of crowds. You don't turn down free tickets to the 'G for that."

"Well if you're such a fan, why don't you go? Take Charlotte and have a daddy daughter day at the football."

"First, Charlie—to my great disappointment—is one of those girls who hate football. Second, why are you afraid of coming to a game with me?"

Ally lifted her chin. "First," she repeated dryly, "you can take someone else, and second, I'm not afraid."

"Ah-huh. That settles it. We'll go to the footy." His eyes danced with glee.

"But—"

He held up his hands. "Think of Red. He expects us both to attend and he'd be pretty let down if you didn't. Plus, I'm not giving up tickets to see the mighty bombers thrash the 'pies at the G. Members stand to boot!" Owen turned and gripped her shoulders. His grin was a mile wide and way too infectious. "Now let's get those tickets from our good friend Red, hey?"

Ally whimpered and trailed behind them. She wasn't certain what frightened her more: spending one on one time with Owen or watching a football match.

Walking back from the M.C.G. with Ally and their group of camp kids, Owen was buoyed. It wasn't because he scored tickets to one of the biggest matches in the footy calendar—that was a bonus—it was because he hadn't felt this happy in a long time.

Getting away with Charlie for a few days and being in Ally's company had been exactly what he needed to clear his head. Especially as his lawyer had called him earlier in the week to talk through the initial process. Not that he could do much for the time being. Marcus was in the middle of a big case but reassured him he'd handle it.

He had tried to get in contact with Jack before they had left, but it had gone to voicemail. He wanted his brother's advice about everything.

It had been on the tip of his tongue to tell Ally about it yesterday, but something made him hold back.

He wasn't even sure the school needed to know. It was a family matter. A personal problem that he would handle. Plus, it wasn't going to affect Charlie as their claims for custody were ridiculous.

So why did he feel guilty?

"I thought you'd be skipping back to the hotel after that big score." Ally's green eyes teased. "You look concerned."

Owen caught himself and grasped at the happiness that had stolen over him only moments before.

"Essendon vs Collingwood is an important match. Lots at stake."

His silent request for privacy was met with understanding. He was grateful she didn't pry.

"I'm ecstatic."

He nudged her shoulder. "That's the spirit. C'mon, did you see how the kids' eyes nearly fell out of their heads? This is an honour to be chosen."

"I'm reserving judgement on that one. But yes, I did see how excited they were. It's nice for them to see kindness in action. Some of those kids have it rough. You always hope that you can help ease some of their distrust and wariness of others."

"You mentioned you've taught a lot of kids who've struggled."

"I find myself drawn to them. I know that sounds mental, but I was very lucky to grow up with privilege, and I want to help those kids who really need it. I didn't realise how much until I started teaching. I still remember one child who snuck back into the Foods cupboard when I was finishing packing up after class. He was so hungry he was eating handfuls of raw spaghetti and butter from the fridge."

"Wow."

"Yeah. I found out he had a drug-addicted parent and often-times he'd give the little food they managed to have to his baby brother and sister. Poor kid was starving."

"It's no wonder you're in Coordination."

"I felt helpless. I wanted to really do something. A lot of the time when you're a classroom teacher, you pass the welfare—the major issues—on to the sub-school. There was only a limited number of things I could do as a teacher, but in Coordination I can do more."

"My mother used to say teaching wasn't a job, it was a vocation."

"It's true. And even harder when you lose kids in the system."

"Welfare system?"

"Mmm." Ally's eyes clouded over.

"Does that happen a lot?"

"More often than you care to think about. One day you're teaching a child, and the next they've been taken away or put into foster care over some nasty custody case."

The quick jab of pain lanced through his chest. He absorbed it and any fear from her words.

"Does the school get caught up in those?"

"We try to do what's best for our students, and sometimes that means making recommendations to social welfare about what the child has revealed to us and letting them, and the courts decide what's in their best interest. Nobody wins in a custody battle."

Owen wouldn't let his imagination run away with him. Charlie's circumstances were a far cry from dispossessed children from broken homes.

"Anyway, we can do only so much in the school system."

He opened his mouth to tell her about the Langdon's claim. His fears for Charlie. But as he glanced at Ally, the weak sunlight deepening the green in her eyes, the cold slapping colour against her smooth skin, he wanted to just be in the moment. He didn't want to think about court dates or custody hearings. He didn't want to be consumed by heartache and fear. He just wanted to enjoy the few days of camp getting to know this woman and seeing his daughter act like the carefree child she hadn't been in a long time.

A part of him knew that if he told her, he'd have to tell Charlie. And he didn't want his little girl to lose that sunshine just yet. Not when she was starting to let down her guard.

He didn't know if it was the right decision. But it was one he was making anyway.

"I think you're doing a hell of a lot for those kids. A lot more than anyone else in your position."

"You should see Sera. She teaches some of the poorest inner city kids every weekend in her spare time. Then treats them to a game of basketball or some sport as a reward. Every month she helps her mother cook and bake up a storm and feeds the kids and any of their families in need. Her mother was a refugee, and it means a lot to her to give back."

"And now that you're head of junior school, I'm sure you're thinking about all the ways you can add to that."

The surprised warmth that blossomed across her face was worth it.

"You're a very perceptive man, Owen Davies."

"A stunning woman once told me that not long ago."

He had the pleasure of watching her blush deepen.

"I've helped Sera's mum with the baking a few times. Occasionally, Maddie and I will go down to help serve the food or teach a weekend session. But it's Sera's mission. Her mother's legacy. I'm just a helper."

"I think you're a lot more than that, Ally. But if you ever need another set of hands, I know Charlie would be keen to offer her assistance."

"That's very generous of you."

"What you do is important. You might downplay it but you're a formidable woman. If you haven't realised, I'm impressed. Not just by those looks of yours. Though, I suppose you're easy on the eye." He held her gaze. "You intrigue me...I'd say Charlie is damn lucky to have you as her teacher. And I'm feeling pretty lucky to spend a little more time with you, too."

He tugged at the long braid that ran down her back, pleased by the shy, bewildered look that had crossed her face.

"I—I don't know what to say to that."

Owen grinned. "Caught you off guard, eh?"

Ally managed a gurgled assent, a small smile playing at her mouth.

His laughter rang out through the gnarled trees. Unlike the cold, crisp afternoon, his chest was warm, his step light. He forced himself to focus on the children a few meters ahead of them, but he was mesmerised by the woman at his side. Whatever this spark was, he wanted more.

Whatever she would give, he would take.

It was as good a beginning as any man could hope for under the circumstances.

CHAPTER THIRTEEN

$\mathcal{T}$hat weekend Ally stood at the entrance of the football stadium and studied the stream of people milling about. She had been so exhausted upon her return from camp that she rebuffed Maddie and Sera's offer of a Friday night movie and pizza. She had fallen asleep on the couch before she had a chance to eat her dinner.

When she woke this morning, her body stiff, but her mind refreshed, she was able to tackle the marking that sat on her kitchen table before she got ready for her...what was this anyway? Surely not a date, despite Maddie and Sera's insistence.

She hadn't really confirmed their status on Friday. She had been too depleted to think and Owen hadn't prodded. They were in a limbo state. Uncertain of whether she was making a mistake, she hadn't said anything. Which left an uncomfortable itch between her shoulder blades when she thought about what was happening between them.

Ally took off her jacket, suddenly overheated. She glanced at the fans that gathered around the M.C.G trying to spot Owen in the crowd. Some fans held banners with catchy slogans, others wore face paint like battle armour. Excitement rang in the air as clear as the boisterous cries from the two rival teams.

She waved at him through the throng a few minutes later.

"Hey! You weren't wrong," she said, gesturing to those around them as he drew closer. "I can see what you mean by the atmosphere. Is it always so...charged?"

He stared at her in horror.

"What?" She looked down, afraid that she had a coffee stain on her top.

"What are you wearing?" he whispered out of the corner of his mouth.

"A very cute, stripy top that I got on sale last winter. Are you the fashion police?"

Owen shook his head, shifting them both away from the turnstiles. "You can't wear that."

Ally huffed, already uncomfortable. "Well, I hate to break it to you, sunshine, but I can't exactly take this off, unless you want me to flash the whole stadium my bra."

His eyes raked down her body, mouth curving in a wolfish grin.

She wanted to bite her tongue for being so careless. She needed to try and keep things friendly. Light.

She was such a coward.

"As appealing as that thought is, if you're taking an item of clothing off, it sure as hell won't be in front of a 100,000 strong crowd. I don't like to share."

He was unashamedly flirting with her. Damn it if she didn't like it. A lot.

"Your point?"

He turned her around to look at the football fans streaming past. "Notice what they're wearing?"

"So?"

"*So?*" he spluttered. "We're sitting with the mighty Bombers...the *Essendon* section." He gestured to his black and red jumper, then to the opposing supporters who were wearing black and white colours. "You don't want to be caught in the Essendon camp wearing Collingwood colours."

Ally rolled her eyes. "It's no big deal. It's just a game."

"It's just a—" Owen looked appalled.

"Well there's nothing I can do about it now, is there?" she huffed, feeling like even more of an idiot. And so very out of place.

"Here." He pulled off his jumper, handed it to her. "Take this, at least it will cover what you're wearing."

"I don't need—what is that?" Ally gestured to his shirt.

"My Bombers jersey. Got it autographed as a 30th present." He turned around to show her the signed names. "I wear it to every live game I get a chance to see. My brother and I used to love going to the footy as kids."

"Right, well, I don't need to wear this." Wasn't it too inti-mate to wear a man's clothes? They weren't even friends or anything. She blamed old Red for getting her into this mess in the first place. She blamed herself for looking forward to it.

He held his jumper in outstretched hands. "Please?"

"This is utterly ridiculous, you know that, right?" Ally muttered, shoving her bag at him.

"Ah huh."

It must be football fever. She yanked on his jersey.

Then regretted it instantly. His scent infiltrated her defences. Firewood, bark…and something else surrounded her; a smell that was so essentially male it made her yearn.

She would not allow herself to be enticed by it. By him.

She flopped the arms of the sleeves up and down, comically.

Owen shifted closer. The combination of his oversized jumper with those summery eyes looking down at her, made her feel deliciously feminine. She understood now why Maddie had a complex about only dating guys who were taller and bigger than she.

"May I?" He held her arm and gently rolled back the sleeves. His fingers brushed against her wrist. What would it be like to have those hands on her body? Stroking her, holding her.

Ally shivered. It was only a few seconds, but she didn't want the delicious stretch of sensations to end. He made her want to curl up on his lap and purr.

Big no, no.

"Thanks." The length of the jumper skimmed against her thighs but covered her outfit. "I look ridiculous, but I guess I won't seem like the enemy."

"Exactly. The last thing you want is for a bunch of Essendon fans booing you for the whole match."

They both stepped back.

"Shall we get our seats?"

Owen rubbed his hands together. "Not before we get a pie and hot chips. You can't go to the footy without over-priced, over-nuked footy food."

Ally didn't know why something so unappealing whetted her appetite. She supposed hunger was the best sauce. It wasn't that the company made the meal.

Allowing herself a chance to indulge, she nodded. "Lead the way."

By the end of the game, Ally's voice was hoarse from barracking, her cheeks sore from laughing. They left the stadium a few hours later buoyed and sated. Owen's passion for football; roaring at the half-time goal, cheering when the final point shot through at the siren, was infectious. She could now appreciate the camaraderie of watching a game live. But the thrill of watching it with a fan as earnest and enthusiastic as Owen only heightened her pleasure.

She supposed she had that thrilling win at the end to thank

for the loud, lip-smacking kiss he planted on her. Not that she minded one bit. They had hugged and cheered as if she were a veteran fan.

She'd never had such fun at a sporting event—ever. She knew it was all because of him.

"What d'ya think?" He nudged her shoulder. They walked out of the stadium amongst the throng of people jostling out to the station, others to their cars.

"It was surprisingly great, actually." Her body was still humming from the post-game high. "I'm the first to admit that I never thought that I—Ally McVeigh—would ever be so interested in a football match."

"Does that mean you're a convert?"

She chuckled. "Not a chance."

"I'm glad you had a good time. I enjoyed initiating you. I think Red's eyes nearly came out his head at your half-time barracking."

"It was infectious. Though I'm blaming all the champagne in the member's stand for that one."

"Pretty sweet, wasn't it?"

"It's a comfy way to watch footy, that's for sure."

"Care to grab a post-game drink? Celebrate the win?"

Ally fought against the large part of her that wanted to. "I should probably get going. Sorry."

"No problem. We'll catch the train back together. I left my car at the station."

They crammed in on one of the carriages, talking of the match until they reached their stop.

"This is me," he gestured to his car. "I had a great day. Thanks for letting me tag along."

"So did I. Thanks for convincing me to try something new."

"You have Red to thank for that one. Sorry if I was too enthusiastic back there."

"You mean the screaming, the hugging..." she teased.

"And the kissing."

Her body responded even before her mind registered his intent. It was as if he had plucked the strings of a violin; she vibrated with intensity.

Owen's eyes locked on hers. "To be honest, I don't think it was my best work. I wouldn't want to leave you with the wrong impression of my abilities. Especially as I have that date at stake."

Despite all reason, Ally stepped in, tilting her head back in invitation.

He closed the distance. Cupping her face, he brushed his lips against hers, teasing her mouth by degrees, beckoning her to open. To surrender. She hummed in appreciation, pressing her breasts against him, yearning for more contact. He sampled her, slowly, as if savouring the kiss. There was only need.

The pressure increased; his tongue stroked, dancing with her own until she was floating along a sea of sensations. His hands at her waist were firm, anchoring them both in place. The drumming of his heart against her chest echoed her own.

Her appetite for him scared and thrilled her.

Like a persistent alarm in her brain, the sounds around them sliced through the spell. She realised it was the peal of her phone, left on loud from the game.

Ally broke away. She had just kissed Charlotte's dad. The after-shock—like the remnants of an earthquake—left her unstable.

She should regret it...*would* regret it once she got home. Maybe. She touched her lips and stepped back.

Owen's eyes were dazed. His hair was mussed. She was woman enough to find some satisfaction by it. But she had given in to temptation, when she had no place to be tempted. She held up a hand.

"I—"

"I wanted to kiss you, Ally." He held her shoulders, moving

closer. "I wanted to kiss you because I find you ridiculously attractive, sexy as hell, and God-knows what else."

"But I'm—"

The phone was a shrill warning between them.

"And from your response I'd say you wanted to kiss me too."

She lowered her hand. He had her there. Not that she was going to deny it, but it didn't make it right.

"I didn't plan to kiss you, just in case you were wondering. I knew it was coming…since that birthday party, I knew," he continued. "We're not going to apologise. Or say it was a mistake. It wasn't."

"But we can't—sorry I need to answer this." She muttered a curse when the phone rang again.

Ally heard Sera's voice at the other end. It took her a good thirty seconds to register what she was saying. She could only hear the blood rushing in her ears.

"Sorry, say that again?"

Owen hadn't taken his eyes off her face. His expression was calm. Open. Inviting.

"Oh no! Is she okay?" She frowned, brought back to Earth. "Yes. Consider it done. I'll come by tomorrow and give you a hand as well. No way, you can't manage that all alone." She looked up at Owen. "I'll talk to you later about it." Her cheeks bloomed.

She could hear Maddie in the background shouting obscenities. She'd tell them about the game—and the kiss—tomorrow.

"Everything okay?" He murmured.

She put her phone in her bag. "I've gotta go."

"What's happened?"

"You know how I mentioned Sera and her mum cook for the South Row kids once a month? Well, Sera's mum is sick and she can't manage the cooking for tomorrow. As Sera can't bake to save her life, she's taken over the cooking but needs someone for all the sweets."

"And she called the best."

"Hardly. Look, I hate to cut our...conversation short, as I think we need to talk about this, but I have to get to the shops. I need a ton of ingredients so I can bake my butt off tonight."

"Then don't."

"Pardon?"

"Don't cut it short. I can take you to the supermarket, we can pick up everything and I'll get Charlie dropped off by Holly's parents, so you get an extra helper."

Ally was overcome by his generosity. "I can't let you do that. Thanks for the offer—"

"Afraid we'll out-bake you?"

Owen's grin cut through her defences. She didn't have time to argue with him. And, more to the point, she didn't want to.

She'd spend just a few more hours in his company. After all, it was for the greater good. The more help she had, the more baked goods she could produce.

A few hours. To get it done. Then she'd go home.

Where was the harm in that?

CHAPTER FOURTEEN

*S*he had lost her mind.

Ally convinced herself of all the reasons why she shouldn't be standing barefoot in Owen's kitchen with a litany of ingredients spilled across the marble countertops. But none of them stacked up against the very base desire she had to simply be with him a bit longer.

She rarely gave in to indulgences or impulses. At least not the male kind.

She had failed at too many relationships to bother trying to make it work. And the men she had dated only confirmed what she always feared. She wasn't relationship material. She was great for first dates, for those few giddy months of getting-to-know-you, but when push came to shove, she wasn't warm enough, soft enough, loving enough for them to stick around. Or for her to keep trying for that matter.

It had been far easier to succumb to a Friday night bake off than to scroll through yet another dating site to begin the process all over again.

But Owen...she swallowed the saliva that pooled in her mouth. The man made her want things she had no business wanting. To indulge in something that wasn't ever going to amount to anything.

Emotion, that giddy, gooey sensation that swirled around her stomach had nothing to do with the way the man had kissed her. The way he made her feel. She'd only met him a month ago. Hardly enough time to *really* get to know him. Or to develop feelings.

"Tell me this." Owen leaned back against the counter, arms folded against his chest. He still wore the Bombers shirt, which sat a little too appealingly against his body. Ally's throat was dry, from all that barracking they had done at the match. Obviously. "Do you always bake in your bare feet? Not that I mind—that shade suits you." He glanced down at her toes, painted a bold, hot pink.

"I find socks are a slipping hazard in the kitchen. It's shoes or bare feet." She couldn't dismiss the very male, very appreciative stare.

"I find a barefoot woman in my home, wearing my clothes, a very sexy, very appealing thing."

She was about to take off the sweater when Owen caught her against him.

"I find kissing said woman even more appealing."

His words slid past her defences. When his mouth lowered to hers, she tilted her chin up, accepting the kiss, accepting him, even for the briefest of moments.

When the pressure on her mouth increased, she folded her arms around his body, savouring the sensation of the hard planes against her chest. His tongue stroked hers, igniting the quick burn of desire, demanding that passion she normally held in check.

She craved more. To lose herself for a few hours of frenzied pleasure in his arms. She broke away, legs shaking, body straining.

She could get drunk on the way he looked at her. Which is

exactly why she needed to step back.

"I think that's a dangerous way to start this evening."

"But pleasurable all the same." His eyes darkened.

There was such lightness; an easy, playful manner about him that made resisting more than difficult.

"You promised that you'd help me bake. Kissing me isn't helping me bake. It's also something we shouldn't be indulging in."

"Why not?"

"Because I teach your daughter and don't want things to get messy."

"Messy is good."

"Owen—"

"It's like baking." He said, stepping closer. "You get your hands dirty…"

Ally arched her neck, unable to stop the smile from forming. He spoke against the curve of her shoulder, planting small bites along her collarbone, up to her ear. "There's all that kneading, and mixing, a hell of a mess." He nibbled at her earlobe, and she grasped his arms. The pleasure shot straight to her belly. "A lot of foreplay if you ask me." He kissed her jaw now, hovering above her lips. "But the result, is something to be devoured. Something good, and pleasurable." His mouth was a whispered promise above hers. "Why can't this be the same?"

"It's moving too fast."

The slamming front door cut through the shimmering spell. He was seducing her, and she was stupidly allowing it to happen.

"Your little helper has just saved the day." He planted a quick kiss on her lips before leaving the room.

Ally smoothed back her hair and schooled her features. She had to keep a distance between herself and Owen. Having Charlotte helping them bake was the perfect distraction.

After tonight, she'd make sure to steer clear from him and his kisses. She'd lose herself if she wasn't careful.

The commission flats of South Row were a far cry from where Ally had grown up. It was even a stark contrast to the modest suburb in which she currently lived. Because of it, she knew that even her simple jeans, sweater and thick wool coat would make her stand out.

On her first trip out to help Sera and her mother, she had felt like a fish out of water. It had been eye-opening to see just how destitute some of the children—and their families—were, not to mention how difficult it was for them to access basic amenities.

Some of those kids were caught up in an endless cycle of starvation, stealing and sentencing; and they were barely in their teens.

She wondered if Casey would be there today. A woman her age, whose face spoke of hardships and turmoil that made her appear twice that. Casey had finally managed to get herself away from an abusive relationship and was looking forward to quitting the cleaning job she had to start her own small business. It was more than many could hope for in such situations. More than many could dream.

"You okay?" Owen's hand on her arm was beginning to feel familiar. Welcome even. Because of it, her guard was up. She wanted to shake herself out of it, but she couldn't escape the gnawing fear.

"Miles away. Yes, I'm good. Thanks again for coming along today." She turned to face Charlotte in the backseat. "I really appreciate your help, and no doubt Ms. De Lotto does too."

She could just imagine her friend's expression at seeing who was with her.

They unloaded the boxes of baked goods and crossed the

street to where the large, grey block of commission flats stood, plain and yet as glaringly obvious as a neon sign. Whilst the street cleaners must have been there in the early morning, remnants of the night before sat amongst the bark of the dilapidated playground; empty beer cans and takeaway wrappers coloured the drab landscape. But what pervaded the area was a distinct tang of urine. It crawled inside her nostrils and stung her eyes. She wondered how Charlotte would react.

They walked to the large, rectangular area where Sera had already set up tables—the only undercover space across the whole block—it was a walkway to the rear of the building, but its open space served many functions to its residents. In the winter, kids would huddle beneath it in groups, smoking and drinking to keep warm. In summer, they'd lay out flat under the concrete shade, lying as still as possible.

There were a few kids there already, milling about, others helping Sera unload the steaming hot food.

"We come bearing sweets." Ally set down the first box on the nearest table.

Sera whirled around, her colour fanning out across her cheeks, brown eyes bright. She knew from experience that her friend had been up early reheating food and loading boxes.

"You're a lifesaver!" She beamed. "Oh! You have helpers."

"We were there when Ally got the S.O.S."

"We helped bake." Charlotte piped up.

"Fantastic. We can always use more people. It's a chilly day, so I'm sure we'll get a good turn out."

Ally was grateful for her friend's subtle look a few moments later. She'd be spilling the goss to the girls before the evening was out. She'd bet her life on it.

"Maddie has drama rehearsals so it's just us. Dad is nursing mum. She's got a raging fever and can't get out of bed." Sera placed food on the tables.

"We got this. Charlotte can hand out paper cups and plates and we can do food."

"I take it the footy went well?" Sera winked, unloading a tray of saffron rice pilaf. The aromatic scent went straight to her belly. Whilst her friend wasn't much of a baker, growing up the only girl in her mother's home meant she had learned how to cook like a pro from a young age.

"Kicking goals as you'd say."

Before they could continue, Owen and Charlotte returned along with a steady stream of locals. Caught up in the organised chaos of feeding the masses, Ally didn't even have a chance to see how they were handling the crowd.

Not that she had to worry.

Stealing a glance at the two, she wasn't surprised to find them in their element. Owen was chatting to a group of boys who devoured their food and spoke about the weekend footy match, and Charlotte was already making friends with a few kids, explaining the ingredients of the muffins she had made with enthusiasm.

When everyone had been fed, some twice over, Ally milled around with a tray of baked goods offering it to those who hadn't yet had a meal or wanted seconds.

That's when she spotted Casey. The woman had dyed her hair red—last time it had been bleached blonde.

"Hey, Casey! I wasn't sure if I'd see you today."

"Likewise." Her lined face glowed. The bruise she had sported on her cheek a few months before had healed. She looked lighter. More carefree. She told her so.

"Thanks, love. Got meself a makeover. Celebrate the first paycheck."

"It suits you. I take it the business is off to a good start?"

"It's slow. But word of mouth is getting me through. I got me a few clients and it's better than working for that stuck up cow. I get me whole paycheck to spend hey, love?"

"Sounds great."

They were deep in conversation when Owen stepped up beside her. His hand landed on the small of her back.

Casey's missing teeth flashed. A knowing look passed over her face.

"You brought your fella here today, Ally?"

She tried not to squirm. "Oh, Owen is here with his daughter, Charlotte who actually helped with today's baked treats."

"Love, I may be poor as dirt, but I ain't blind. I know a couple when I see one. I'm Casey."

"Owen. Good to meet you." He shook her outstretched hand.

"You sweet on our girl, 'ey?"

"Guilty." He threw his hands up.

"Been on a date yet?"

"Not a proper one. The footy doesn't count."

"That was *not* a date. Owen is a parent at the school," she began to explain.

It was like she was invisible.

"You gotta take her to some nice place. Bit of food and dancing."

"That's the plan. Though I need to convince her first I think."

"With a face like yours? Jesus, she'd be right stupid to not enjoy that company."

"Keep talking, Casey. You're doing wonders for my ego."

"Oooh, he's got a mouth on him too. Love, you'd be a fool to pass up on that. Let the man take you out. Have a bit of a laugh. Don't think too much or you'll spoil yer own fun."

Ally turned to him when Casey winked and wandered off.

"Care to explain that to me?"

"Hey, I'm just taking her advice."

"Owen, we can't get into this."

"Why?"

"Because I teach your daughter. You're a parent at the school. It's unprofessional."

"Lots of people date their co-workers."

"This is different."

"How?"

The anxiety rose up her throat. "It's unethical."

"I'm sure there isn't an ethics department at the school frowning on teachers' private lives. It's not like you're dating a student."

"We're not dating."

"Semantics."

"We can't date."

"You haven't given me a good enough reason."

"I just did. It would be unprofessional of me, just starting this role, to be dating a parent. And while it's none of the school's business, I don't think it's a good look. I didn't want to have this conversation here. Owen, I've enjoyed your company, but I'm just not sure this is a good idea."

And it's something her father would have no hesitation in pursuing. Something she hated about him as long as she had become aware of what he was doing in his office with his secretaries and employees.

There were boundaries.

"What are you afraid of?"

Ally took the hit before she had time to lift her shield. It was unnerving to stand opposite a man whom she was wildly attracted to and have him know her. See her. It meant admitting to all the things she couldn't face—to risk falling for him when she didn't trust herself to be better than her upbringing. Better than her past relationships. Or herself.

He had a child. The stakes were higher just on that basis alone.

"I can't get into that."

"You won't because you know you're using work as an excuse."

"So what if I am? That's my business."

"Ally, when you kiss me back like that, you make it my business. I like you. I want to see you. Not just at camp or in a parent meeting."

She could see it. The carefree weekends. The fun. But she was so afraid she'd not be enough. For the both of them. Not to mention Charlotte.

"I think I made my case. I won't push you. That's not my style. But I want to understand why you're using this as an excuse. Especially when you've just told me you enjoyed spending time with me. If you want to talk about this all you need to do is call. And Ally, I really, honestly hope that you do."

The rest of the afternoon was a blur of activity. Even though she kept busy, rejecting Owen had left a heavy, weighted pressure on her chest. She told herself it was the right decision, that the feeling would pass. She just needed a little time.

Owen dropped Ally home that afternoon, trying to keep the conversation light for Charlotte's sake. They had both tried, but failed, to convince her to come along with them for some ice cream. He knew it was a long shot after her rejection. She was running scared. Far be it from him to ever force a woman to give more than she was willing.

She had convinced herself that it was the right decision; had all but let the axe swing before they had even stepped into the forest. No matter how many times he tried to see it from her perspective, to convince himself that it was perhaps for the best, he knew something was missing.

Over the past month he caught glimpses of her personality, of the emotions that simmered beneath the surface, and he wanted more. He had an inkling that what she felt wasn't just attraction.

But she had to want it too. Just as much as he did.

His gut urged him not to give up.

"Regretting your choice already, dad?" Charlie looked at his untouched ice cream, having annihilated half of her own.

"Don't think you can weasel two cones out of me, kiddo. I was just thinking."

"I thought you had brain freeze."

"Brain freeze is for suckers."

Huddled over their cones in their woolly jackets, Charlie looked him dead in the eye. "I really like Ms. McVeigh." She contemplated her triple chunk rocky road. "Does that mean she's going to be my new mum?"

Owen let the ice cream dissolve on his tongue before responding. He shouldn't have been surprised by the line of questioning. Charlie was bright and seemed to take in a lot more than she let on. "We went to the football and baked cookies, kiddo. I'm not sure if doing that makes us an instant family." Though it'd be a hell of a bonus. "Relationships between boys and girls don't always end up in marriage. Sometimes you can just be friends. Like you and Jeremy."

She shrugged. "I don't mind if you do like Ms. McVeigh like that. Lots of boys do. I think she's really nice. And you know, pretty and stuff. I know that single parents have *needs*." She raised her eyebrows in a pointed look. One that had no place on the face of his innocent twelve-year-old daughter.

His ears were on fire. He was equally proud and bemused by his child. "Really?" He sampled another mouthful of caramel swirl. "And how'd you figure that one out?"

"Jeremy told me. His mum is divorced, and she started dating a few years after his dad left. Something about tinder box losers or something."

Owen swallowed his laughter. "Right."

"I know that's what adults do. I don't mind, Dad. I don't think Mamma would mind either."

"You think so, kid? If I decide to start dating Ms. McVeigh, we'll have a chat about it."

He watched her demolish her ice cream. It was a good sign that she was talking about her mother more often. If there was one thing he knew since Rebecca's death, it was that he didn't want Charlie to ever forget her.

But there were some things you just couldn't tell your own child. Kissing her school teacher was one of them. At least, for the time being. She was whip-smart and apparently more clued in than he suspected. He didn't need to fuel that imagination.

He could see where a relationship with Ally would lead. But he needed to slow things down a little. The spark between them was so strong it almost scared him. Almost. It was no wonder the woman was petrified.

But he had more pressing matters that he had to fix if he ever wanted the luxury of having a future with her. He would make sure that his daughter's welfare was secure. Which meant going head to head with the Langdons and hoping they could come to some kind of amicable resolution.

For Charlie's sake.

CHAPTER FIFTEEN

Owen gripped his mobile. Looking out from his study room door, he saw Charlie across the hall, glued to the T.V. screen, with a few of her friends from school huddled around a bowl of popcorn. The noise of some after school kid drama was loud enough to carry across the large rectangular space. Far away enough that he wouldn't be heard.

Rather than close the door for privacy, he lowered his voice.

Even though his daughter was one of the most well-behaved children he knew, he had three other girls and one wide-eyed boy in his lounge room that he would keep an eye on. Twelve-year-old girls were still a foreign entity. Boys however...well, he knew *exactly* what went on in their little prepubescent minds.

"You're telling me they're seeking a court order because they don't think I'm a fit parent, is that correct?"

"I can hear you're frustrated, Owen, but you've got to bear with me a second here."

He studied the picture of Charlie on his desk and forced his jaw to open.

"Explain this to me, Marcus. I still don't understand how this is possible."

"They want to apply for a court order, so that they can be the sole guardians for Charlotte, in the absence of her mother, due to her passing."

"She died years ago. Why now?"

"I'd say this has been brewing for a while. In answer to your question, yes, they want to prove that you are an unfit parent, but before they can do this, they need to make an application to the family court, which might lead to mediation. They want full custody."

Fear, no matter how unfounded, had him kicking up, away from his desk. He paced the carpet. Hadn't Charlie been through enough?

"So just by the fact that they have some crazy arse claim, I'm being dragged into this mediation bullshit. Do I have it correct?" He paused. Waited. Then recognised when the tightly wound cord around his patience snapped. "How the fuck is this possible, Marcus?"

He kept his voice low when he wanted to howl and rage. The animal instinct that lay dormant was straining against its leash. He wanted to protect his child from all the bad in the world. It hurt knowing that he had failed already. Supporting her through the death of her mother, dealing with the bullies at school, and now this?

"Unfortunately, they have rights as well."

"But they see Charlie. Every second weekend, on school holidays. Whenever they fucking like, they get to see her. I'm not keeping her away from her grandparents. No matter how they treat me, or what they think of me. She needs them in her life."

"I hate to remind you of this, but it seems you had signed paperwork agreeing to give Henry and Anita Langdon some power of guardianship of Charlotte, if I'm not mistaken?"

Owen's mind reeled. He could feel the threads of the carpet rug beneath his toes, he could hear the distant chatter of Charlie and her friends, but his body may as well have been carved out of stone.

The cold, clammy hands of dread brushed against his skin. His hands shook. This was all his bloody fault.

"I signed an agreement when Rebecca was sick, only because she wanted her parents to have access to Charlie, to see her grow up. We agreed to every fortnight, and time on the school holidays, but not this."

"You're lucky that the document hasn't been formalised by the court, so as Charlotte's legal guardian, you have the final say in this matter. However, that doesn't mean they can't go to the courts and argue their claim." Marcus paused. "The fact that you've given them some authority in raising her makes them think they have a leg to stand on."

"This is bullshit."

The only reason he had agreed was because he made a promise to Rebecca.

She had requested it in those final six months of her life, at a time when she had been so very sick that caring for her at home had no longer been the safe option. Palliative care was the last bastion of hope; her comfortable death had been more important than some naïve pretence of life. He hadn't the heart to refuse her. More than anything, he had wanted her to leave this world at peace.

He knew her parents would have been in her ear. Manipulating her in the only way they knew how, through fear and guilt. But he hadn't wanted to argue. No matter how deep his dislike for Henry and Anita Langdon, they were still Charlie's grandparents. Their hatred for him didn't extend to his daughter. She was happy there, happy with them, and that's the only reason he had agreed to it.

He wasn't stupid to think they would ever accept him, but he was hopeful that his daughter could have a relationship with her grandparents. It was the only connection she had left to her mother. He wouldn't be the one to take that away.

He never dreamed it would come to this. The pain in his chest radiated up to the base of his skull. The threat of losing his daughter was now as tangible as the frantic rhythm of his heart.

"Owen? You there? Look, you have to take the emotion out of it. Especially when dealing with them."

"What the fuck?" he yelled, then bit down on his lip when five little heads turned in his direction. He gave them a tight smile and a wave and turned his back to the open door, grateful for the distance of the corridor. "Tell me," he murmured, "how in the hell I'm supposed to be *emotionless* when it's about my kid. Huh? Tell me that, Marcus."

"Owen—" his sigh was audible over the phone. "I never said it was easy. But we're in preliminary stages. It's early days yet and their claim is just that. Calm down and listen to me. You calm?"

He grunted in assent.

"From what I can garner they say they have proof that you're an unfit parent."

"Proof? What kind of crap is this?"

His lawyer cleared his throat.

"Continue."

"Let me repeat. They think they have a claim because you agreed to them being a part of Charlotte's life. Albeit it was in a limited capacity, and remember, not finalised by the courts, but still an agreement."

"But they have no legal power of attorney now."

"As her parent, you are responsible for her. Without a doubt. That document does give them a foot in the door, however."

Owen continued, mind reeling. "Plus, we never got the divorce. Rebecca got sick."

Something which Henry and Anita believed to be his fault at the time. It had devastated him to think that filing for divorce had been the catalyst for her decline. But logically, he had known the reality of their marriage. Choosing between her parents and being his wife slowly ate away at Rebecca's spirit until she began to look at him though their eyes. Eventually their communication had broken down to a point where not even reconciliation was possible.

They had both known where it was heading. They had spoken about it at length. But it was Owen who had taken that decisive step and filed for divorce, unable to watch their family unit suffer any longer.

And then she had fallen ill. And none of it mattered. Rebecca needed the support. And Charlie needed the stability of her parents together in crisis. No matter how fractured their relationship had become.

"They're maintaining that they were co-parenting already, and that, ah," Marcus cleared his throat, "you wanted the divorce out of mercenary motives. That you still do."

"Screw their money! Christ, I raised that child, Marcus. I barely slept trying to be everywhere at once. Sure, I gave them the right to have a say in some of the parenting decisions, but that was at Rebecca's request. I've kept them informed about everything when it comes to her welfare. They can't do this."

Not now. Not when Charlie was finally beginning to settle.

"They have money and the means. They can do whatever they like. Not that it's likely to stand up in court, but they're trying to make your life difficult. I get that it's a blow. I'm going to give you time to let it settle. I've still got this case to finalise and then you and I will make an appointment to sort out the details. I just wanted to call to keep you in the loop. Okay?"

"Sure. Fine."

"Owen?"

"What?"

"Don't contact them about this no matter how much it eats

at you. Don't mention it in a text, over the phone, in person. Nothing. Nada. Zip. Got that?"

"Yep."

"I'll see you soon and we can talk through proceedings."

And eat through what was becoming Charlie's college fund money he had been saving. He thought they had moved past the drama and heartache. How much more was his little girl able to take?

She was slowly getting comfortable with her friends and her new school. His baby girl was laughing again; a sound he hadn't heard in a long time.

He'd be damned if he was the one to burden her with all this right now. He just wanted to give her the comfort of innocence. For a little while longer at least.

"Fine. But, Marcus, mark my words, when it comes to my daughter, I'll fight. You understand me? Grandparents or not, I'll fight."

He rang off on an oath, then jumped at the tentative voice from the doorway.

"Is everything okay, Dad?"

Charlie looked up at him. He had seen that weary expression on Rebecca's face towards the end of their marriage. It was enough torture to know that he had failed her mother. He wouldn't make that same mistake with his child.

"Everything is fine, honey. I'm a bit frustrated, but nothing for you to concern yourself over."

Her eyes narrowed. "Okay." The word was drawn out.

He didn't believe it himself.

"How's the show going?"

Charlie shrugged. "Good. Hey, Dad, can I have a sleepover?"

Owen checked his calendar, surprised by her eagerness. "You can't this weekend, but we're free the next. Yeah, why not."

She offered him a rare smile. "Really?"

He nodded.

"Cool!" She ran off, then skidded to a halt, turned. "Thanks, Dad!" She raced across to the waiting hoard.

He watched their excited chatter and ignored the stabbing sensation in his chest. He would fight for her alright. He'd do whatever he needed to make sure she was happy.

Whatever it would take to make it right.

CHAPTER SIXTEEN

O wen figured he'd let the dust settle before contacting Ally. It had been ten days since they had baked up a storm for the residents of South Row. He figured she'd appreciate the space. After his conversation with Marcus last week, and the long hours working to secure this new deal with a company in Sydney, he had needed a little time to himself to process everything.

But he didn't want to wait until parent-teacher conferences —that would be too far away—so when he managed a spare moment, he decided to test the waters. It gave him something good, something happy to think about in amongst the shitstorm.

Having told Charlie to wait in the car, Owen approached the junior school office. It always amused him at how fast school emptied of kids at the end of the day. Knocking on the door, he waited a beat and entered. There was no one there. He checked his watch. 3.30pm. Maybe she'd gone to a meeting?

He turned to leave, when her friend—the fiery redhead, Maddie—walked through the door.

"Oh, hey!" She placed the tub of materials on Ally's desk.

"Owen."

"I remember. How's Charlotte going?"

"Good. Yeah really good, actually. She's enjoying your classes, and the creative writing unit. She's coming up with lots of crime stories around food. I don't know if I should be worried or impressed."

"Cozy mysteries are all the rage."

"Good to know it's a thing, and I don't have a budding serial killer living with me...I actually wanted to know if Ally was about, but it seems I've missed her."

"She was at camp today. Third round. We've barely seen her; she's been that flat out."

"Completely forgot." His head had been filled with mediation drama, business demands and bad dreams.

"Thanks for carrying that, Madds." Ally walked in carrying the cool breeze with her.

Owen simply stared. It was hard to think when a woman looked so damn good in a pair of jeans. Her hair was bundled up in a ponytail. What would it look like, unbound in his bed?

No doubt about it. He wanted to kiss her again.

She tugged off her coat and shot him a quick glance.

"Mr. Davies. Good to see you again."

"Ms. McVeigh. Slightly formal today."

She made a noise in the back of her throat. He barely registered when Maddie left. He anticipated what was coming and wondered why.

"I was at camp today." She gestured to her clothes.

"I meant your address." He stepped closer. She inched back. Interesting. "I stopped by to get my Working With Children card?"

The look of relief across her face should have been warning enough. "Yes. Let me grab that for you." She darted past him and rifled through a stack of folders on her desk.

Taking the card from her outstretched hand, Owen tilted her chin up. Her mouth was set in a thin line.

"To be perfectly honest, I came by to see you."

"Owen—don't."

Her green eyes darkened.

"I think we need to talk about this properly. What's going on, Ally?"

She huffed. "I've explained why I'm just not ready for this. We can't be..."

"What? Kissing? Dating? Sleeping with one another?"

"Yes, yes, yes." The storm began to swirl in that green ocean now. Tumultuous and violent. But contained. Some perverse part of him wanted to see her lose all control.

"Yes, we can't be, or yes to all of those things?"

Ally stepped back. Crossed her arms. Amusement tugged at the corners of her mouth. "I'm sorry, Mr. Davies, but I don't date parents."

"As a rule?" His lips curved.

"Ever!" She all but ran across the office to the interview room. He followed.

"Let me get this straight. You've never dated a parent."

"No."

"Then how do you know it can't be done?"

"Just because I haven't gotten a speeding ticket, doesn't mean I don't know it's illegal to speed."

"That's because you've never gone for a ride with me." And what a ride it would be. He paused, catching up. "Wait. What? You've never gotten a speeding ticket?"

Ally tilted her chin. "No."

"As in, ever?"

She shrugged her shoulders. Despite her best efforts, her bottom lip curved down. She somehow looked hotter when she pouted, when those big eyes snapped with annoyance. Oh yeah, he was starting to crush on this woman pretty damn hard.

"You really are an angel."

She laughed. "Look, Mr. Davies—"

"Ahh, c'mon, Ally. The least you could do after I've put my hands on you is call me Owen."

She lifted one dark eyebrow, and he straightened. That got her fired up. How much more to really let her lose her temper?

"Let's be clear. I owe you nothing."

"True. But I'd be a liar if I said I haven't stopped thinking about you for the past ten days."

She had the sexy, mad teacher thing going on and it made him want to do a lot more than kiss her. He never had any teacher fantasies before. Not surprising given that all his high school teachers were dragons.

The thought of her giving him a detention in an abandoned classroom didn't sound so bad.

"Owen. I won't put Charlotte or myself in that situation, no matter how much I may have enjoyed kissing—spending time with you." Her eyes were saucers.

He hadn't meant to tease her like this; he had come to have a serious conversation about why she was running scared. But he'd be a damn liar if he said he didn't enjoy their banter. He'd be a fool to miss the opportunity for a bit of fun.

"You enjoyed kissing me, eh?" This woman was too good to be true. "How much did you enjoy it? On a scale of one to ten. Was it A+ standard?" He inched closer. He could just shove the pile of papers aside right there, take her on the table. But that wasn't his style. A woman like Allyna McVeigh required a hell of a lot more. He wanted to be the man to give that to her.

"That's beside the point. And I'm not rating our kiss. It's juvenile."

"But good enough in your book?"

Ally rolled her eyes. They sure were pretty eyes. A man could lose himself in them. Especially when they sat so perfectly on that stunning face. She was positively edible.

"I'm not answering that."

"Pity." Owen sighed dramatically. "You could have given me pointers on what I could do to improve. For next time."

Ally's heart rate soared, and beads of moisture gathered under her arms. Why did he have to stand so bloody close? She cursed her woollen sweater. She was swimming in her own pond. No doubt she smelled just as bad.

Someone could walk in any minute. Not that it was likely, as the others were on the Wednesday to Friday camp, but still. A student. A teacher. The principal!

"Owen." She gently laid a hand on his chest. Big mistake. He was warm and hard, and she wanted nothing more than to gather him up against her and kiss him senseless. But she had made her decision. With good reason.

His fingers held hers in place. It was strangely romantic yet absurd to be standing in her office, the afternoon sun filtering through the windows, with a handsome man trying to...what? Woo her? How very 19th Century of him.

"Yes?"

"We can't."

"We can. We already have. Look, I told you in South Row that I wouldn't push. But you've been on my mind since then. Hell, since we met. That says a lot about what's happening between us. I'd like to think you feel the same way...Tell me you want me to kiss you. Touch you."

She slowly shook her head, even as her lips parted.

"I need to hear you say it, Ally."

Say it! her body screamed. *On behalf of every single, sexed-up woman out there, just say it!*

On a choked murmur, Ally looked up at him. "Like I said, I

may have enjoyed spending time with you, but we can't. *I* can't."

He stepped back. "Then we can't. I'm not a man who throws his weight around. But I am a man who gets what he wants. Everything tells me that I want you. When you're ready, you let me know and you can bet we'll make it happen. Because I know that these reasons are excuses. You said so yourself. I don't know why you're running from this, but I'm going to wait until you feel comfortable to have that conversation with me. In the meantime? I'm gonna enjoy watching that pretty face of yours."

She opened her mouth. Closed it. She'd never met a man willing to wait for her. A man so determined to date her.

Date! Jumper!

"Your jumper. I forgot to return it."

"Next time." The look he sent over his shoulder was hardly that of a rejected male.

She started to protest then stopped. It dawned on her that she was clinging to these excuses not because she didn't want to see where this was heading, but because she was afraid that it had already started. And there was nothing she could do to stop it.

She wanted more. And that scared the hell out of her. But she wasn't certain she could take that first step. Not when there was so much at stake.

CHAPTER SEVENTEEN

*O*wen wished he didn't have to fly out to Sydney on such short notice. He knew that if he wanted to really be financially secure, that he would have to take this business dinner with the new energy company that was on the rise. Offers like these didn't come around very often. And now with potential legal costs on the horizon, his business, and family, could do with the money.

Charlie sat in the front seat, arms folded, a determined look on her little face.

Now that she was making friends, Owen would have preferred that she stay with any one of them this weekend. But given the situation—and his conversation with Marcus over lunch—he couldn't be obstreperous in any way. Bloody lawyer speak. It was the Langdons' weekend after all.

"I'm sorry you couldn't go to see Holly after school. Are you angry about cancelling your play date?"

"What am I? Two? It's fine, Dad. I don't mind changing plans. But I don't know why I have to stay with Grandma and Grandpa. I'm old enough to stay on my own."

"Any particular reason for not wanting to go there?"

"No." She retreated further. He saw that stubborn look, identified it as his own. Didn't prod. She was already in a mood when he picked her up from school. Only two months in at Woodbury and she had the brooding adolescent thing down pat. He dreaded to think what would happen when those hormones really kicked in.

"Alright, kiddo. I'll be back on Sunday morning to pick you up. We'll do a special movie night."

Owen smoothed down the tie of his business suit as they opened the gate. A minute or two later, Anita swung the door open, her cold eyes assessing him. It took every bit of strength not to say anything to her.

"Have a great time, Charlie. I'll see you Sunday."

She hugged him tight then ran inside.

"You best enjoy your time with your daughter whilst you can. For all you know these little visits might not be for much longer."

He clenched the car keys in his pocket. "Is that so, Anita?"

He wanted to ignore the smug expression on her face. To walk away.

"Your time with that child is ticking. We know what's best for her and will do everything in our power to ensure she gets the life she deserves. Without you in it."

"I'm going to keep this straight and simple," he murmured, voice controlled. So much for keeping his mouth shut. "You do not get to play with our lives like this. Is that understood?"

Her eyes narrowed.

They thought they knew what was best for his child? He'd see about that.

He looked over her shoulder to make sure Charlie wasn't lurking. "Do you even care about what your grandchild needs? I'm her father and I will continue to be so whether or not you want me in the picture. You can't change that fact, Anita. What kind of grandmother is willing to put her only grandchild through this pain? This isn't what Rebecca would have wanted."

"I don't care for being spoken to in this manner. You were an unfit partner for Rebecca and an even more useless father to Charlotte. What sort of society will she be brought up in? We had agreed to send her to Bridgefield Academy, not for you to pull her out after only a term."

"She was miserable at that school. The bullying was debilitating. How could you forget that? Charlie was barely able to function."

"You made the decision to put her in Woodbury High and it's the worst mistake you've made to date. Who is she socialising with at that school? What sort of person will she marry? Trash, if you had your way. No—you've brought nothing but suffering to this family, Owen, I will not allow you to ruin that bright girl's future as well. It seems Rebecca at least had the presence of mind to be persuaded of the truth before she died. What court will give you rights knowing your own wife thought you useless?" She called out to her husband.

"Trouble here?" Henry opened the door a little wider and stood in front of his wife.

"You're despicable. You know that?" Owen looked him straight in the eye. His body stood stiff and imposing. A man used to getting his way. "Whatever you have against me is one thing, but I at least give you a chance to see your grandchild. You wanna play hardball, I can make sure that never happens."

"You threatening me, boy?"

"Just stating facts." He crossed his arms. "You could have had the decency to talk this through with me. Outside of the court system. But you chose to be a coward."

"I won't have some nobody speak to me like this. We'll see you in court."

"I'm picking up Charlie on Sunday morning. I'd appreciate it if she was ready by 10:30 a.m."

The door slamming in his face wasn't unusual. He banked down on any desire he had to storm inside and take his child with him. It's not like he even had relatives in Sydney whom he could leave her with when he was with clients.

Owen pounded down the stairs and jerked open his car door. Marcus had been right. The battle had only just begun.

CHAPTER EIGHTEEN

*E*ven in the comfort of her own home, Ally couldn't relax. It may have been the weekend, but she had an eye-watering amount of reports that she needed to begin, especially as parent teacher interviews were on the not too distant horizon. After spending a few hours barely making progress, she had given up.

Even though the junior school camps were over, work was manic and unrelenting. Her senior students were busy with their folios, and life in coordination was filled with one drama after the other. Yet every time she walked into her office, images of Owen flooded her senses.

When thoughts of him began keeping her up every other night, she was convinced she was going to go mad. She'd never had this problem in her past relationships. The more she tried to distract herself, the worse it became, until she couldn't seem to get him out of her head.

Maddie and Sera said she was insane to fight it, but were, surprisingly, leaving her to make the decision on her own. As requested.

The only way that she could calm the tangle of nerves that

wreaked havoc on her insides, was to bake. The simple, soothing action of assembling ingredients, playing with recipe ideas and focusing on the process of adding and mixing, helped to ease her troubled mind. The yoga DVD that she had naively played earlier had done absolutely nothing to 'clear her thoughts.'

He said he would wait. For how long? It had only been a week and a half, but it felt like a lifetime.

She rolled another chocolate ball in her hands, enjoying the sensation of all the blended fruit and cocoa in her palm. The combination, once coated in desiccated coconut, would be little balls of bliss. Sera had given her the tick of approval when she had made it for their Christmas in July party last year.

She was developing a crush on Owen.

Ally cursed, inadvertently mushing a perfectly round ball out of shape. She shoved it in her mouth instead of attempting to rearrange it. So what if she had already snacked on three others whilst making this batch? There was plenty of it. So what if she needed to write reports? She'd get to it eventually.

It bothered her that she found him not just attractive, but interesting. Every time she thought about pursuing the hot little fantasies that had bounced around in her head, she stopped short.

Charlotte was coming out of her shell. To disrupt that would be cruel. After two months of counselling, Mr. Taylor had reported her improved outlook—a large part of that due to the friendships she had made. Even though she was still reluctant to talk about her mother or her grandparents, the SCC believed that would happen soon enough.

She was making excuses. Hiding behind those old fears.

Pursuing a relationship with Owen petrified her. It wouldn't be just a casual fling. Being with him would be life-changing.

Something she just wasn't prepared to accept.

But running away from her problems was the coward's way out. Ally McVeigh was no bloody coward.

Owen's visit to her office had stirred the pot. If she wanted something to happen, the decision was up to her. It had been for quite some time now. She picked up the phone and did what she should have done when she had returned from camp.

The dizzying relief at hearing his voicemail almost left her weak at the knees. Maybe she was gutless after all.

"Owen...hi. It's Ally. I've had a think about what you said the other week, and you're right. I am afraid. I'm terrified of starting something with you, but it's complicated. Not really a voicemail kind of chat, either. Give me a ring when you can and we can set up a time to talk. Hope you're well."

She hung up and waited for the sense of dread to wash over her. She was pleasantly surprised when it didn't happen. She had ignored his offer to talk things through, but since South Row, everything had shifted. If this was going to work, they needed to slow down. But that meant she needed to be open. To communicate.

Her shoulders lowered. Her breathing deepened. She was feeling better about her decision already.

Any sense of calm was quickly thwarted when her phone rang seconds later.

Her father's name flashed across the screen and a small part of her was relieved. A distraction was exactly what she needed until she had the chance to talk to Owen.

God, she must be desperate.

"Hello, Father."

A pause.

"Ally, Ally, Ally."

What? What? What?

"Yes?"

"I don't need some stranger nursing me in my home."

"I take it you got the pamphlets?"

She had given them to her mother a month ago. The depths of their dysfunctional relationship still amazed her sometimes.

"I have them, yes."

"And do you have a date for surgery?"

"This merger has taken longer than expected."

Ally wandered around the apartment. She couldn't sit still when she spoke to her parents for very long. Thinking the better of it, she went to find her trainers.

"I don't see why I need to be given home care like some invalid. I should be kept in a private wing of the hospital considering how much I pay for insurance. As family you should be seeing to that. Or at least taking the time to care for me personally."

She shoved on her shoes, not bothering with the laces. What she wanted to say was that he already had a wife, and many other women whom he dallied with on occasion to see to his needs. Surely they would be able to find time in their non-working schedules as ladies of leisure to nurse him.

What she actually said was, "Is that what Mother told you? That I'd be taking care of you personally?"

"She may have mentioned something along those lines."

Unbelievable. Her mother would stop at nothing to butter her father up. All in the hope that he wouldn't take his money to the grave. What else had she promised?

"I'm aware of your hip operation, but as I told Mother, it'll be difficult to take a lot of time off in this role. Especially this time of year."

Before she could change her mind, Ally picked up her coat and let herself out of the apartment. Her legs itched to run off the frustration that was building. She welcomed the smack of cold winter air on her face.

"You know that your talents are wasted in that job. Now, I understand that you're young and you want your own space. I was the same. But I soon learnt the importance of building an empire. A family business that I took over once I realised the value of money. You've yet to see that."

"Trust me, I understand the value of money." And the pride of having accomplished something by herself.

"I don't think you do. If you did, you would have come and worked with me. It's never too late to do a business degree. Cooking is what you pay servants to do. It's not a profession."

Ally was accustomed to such comments from a young age. It never failed to annoy her. "I have a proper job. I'm a teacher and now the head of a sub-school. It's a busy role, and a busy time of year."

"No need to get defensive. When the money runs out don't come crying to me."

"I manage my money just fine, thanks." She made sure never to have to ask them for a cent.

"Tell your mother I don't need a nurse. I will get on well enough without any assistance."

"I'm not going to pass on messages between you. If you tell me when your surgery is, I can come over and take a few days off. But I can't take more time than that."

Why she had to when she was planning around the clock care was beyond her, but it was far easier to give in than fight sometimes. She was picking her battles.

"I'll have my new secretary contact you."

"You've *another* secretary? What happened to the last one?"

"Young. You know these things. Happens unfortunately."

She stopped mid-stride. She'd heard that line before. It either meant that the woman didn't take his shit, and left, or that he had slept with her and decided it was too awkward. Or she was too clingy. Or after his money. His list of reasons ran ridiculously long. It made her stomach pitch and roll to think of the way he treated women. He always flicked off her protests with a disdainful hand, or a condescending remark.

"It's called boundaries, Father. You need to learn some."

"Now now, you just play school, and I'll let you know when your opinion is needed. Have to run, Ally. Call around and I'll set you up with our financial adviser. Might stretch that purse of yours further."

She stared at her phone until the screen went dark. No good-byes, no endearments. Just talk of the superficial things, and an unnatural obsession with money. She didn't matter. It was all about her reputation and income. Not once had he asked after her wellbeing. She could have been married with six kids and he wouldn't have known.

Rubbing her neck, she pocketed her phone and wandered down towards the oval, a fifteen minute walk away.

As a child, she hadn't known parents could be any different. As an adult, she had realised that her desire to be loved wasn't a weird aberration. That there wasn't something wrong with her to crave cuddles and attention.

She had seen what a real family was like when she had been invited to the De Lotto's Easter feast all those years ago. Sera's parents held large, boisterous family gatherings where everyone spoke at unnaturally high volumes, but they actually listened. Asked questions. Cared. It was such a stark contrast to her own upbringing that it had taken all her effort not to burst into tears at their genuine concern for her wellbeing.

Everything about Peter and Vera McVeigh was cold, so very cold.

Yet they were her parents. It was their DNA that ran through her veins.

She shivered.

Past recriminations circled in her head. Maybe she was the product of her environment? She bit back the tears. It wouldn't do to cry. Didn't she learn that early on? Not to let others in, or show you were vulnerable? To place a mask on her face even when she was hurting the most.

Ally hugged her arms tighter to her chest, braced against the chill that seeped far beneath her clothes.

Maddie's voice lurked at the edges, faint but firm. She needed to stop being an idiot. Stop focusing on her fears.

But lately it seemed like everything was teetering on the edge. Nothing was clear.

What she wanted more than anything right now was to talk to Owen. To see him again and have him look at her in that knowing way of his. To give her a reason to hope.

But more than that, beneath it all, she wanted to feel whole.

She had been broken for so long, she didn't even know where to begin.

CHAPTER NINETEEN

*T*he dull thud of a migraine lurked at the base of Ally's skull all day. She didn't think it would be that bad, but she never knew if the headache would morph into a giant ball of pounding pain. She'd been caught out a few times and vowed since to be vigilant. She wasn't nauseated, which was a good sign, but she really needed to get away from the fluorescent lights of the Foods kitchen. She'd pop a few Panadol before she headed to the staff meeting and see if that did the trick.

The one thing that kept her going was the date she had with Owen this evening. He had called her back briefly on Saturday night from Sydney to let her know he was eager to talk. It was her idea to make the catch-up a mid-week one.

Less pressure. Less intimate.

But she couldn't contain her excitement even through the pain.

Wednesdays were always manic, and once again, today proved no different. She was just coming out of the pantry storeroom when one of her top senior students came in sobbing.

"Penelope, what's wrong?"

Mascara ran down her flushed cheeks. Her eyes, normally a

bright blue, were bloodshot. The sobbing soon turned into wails.

"Deep breaths. That's it. Here take a tissue and tell me what's going on."

Ally guided her into the adjoining classroom used for their theory lessons. She turned on the bright overhead lights and winced.

She was not getting a migraine. She didn't have the time for one.

The young girl gulped in air, hiccupping after her sobs. It took her several minutes to calm down.

As the crying subsided, Penelope opened a mouth painted dark as midnight and started again. "My—my p-p."

"Take your time."

"Port-port-f-folio. Gone m-m-missing." The breath whooshed out of her lungs as if desperate to escape the vice it was in.

"You've lost the design portfolio with your food briefs, is that right?"

She nodded, pressed her chipped black nails against a mouth that continued to wobble.

"C-can't f-find it a-a-anywhere," she wailed.

"Alright. Keep breathing. It could be that you've placed it somewhere without thinking?"

She shook her head. "I c-checked at h-home."

"Okay. That's fine. Here." She offered her a bottle of water from the cabinet. "Take a few sips. Good." She tried to think desperately through the pounding in her neck. "You've checked at home, and in your locker again?"

Another nod.

After reeling off a list of places, and still not dawning on a new idea, Ally changed tack. Penelope's face started to crumble in despair again, and it had taken a good ten minutes just to calm her down initially.

"I've an idea. Let's send an email out to the class and ask them to check their folios. Sometimes these things get mixed up and someone might have them or have seen it?"

"But I asked a few people already."

"Yes, but a few isn't everyone, and it always helps to be thorough in these situations."

Penelope looked down at her hands in despair. "But what if I don't find it, miss? All my designs! All my work for the S.A.C's and the ideas for my final piece—"

Ally held up her palm. "Stop. Breathe. There's no point getting yourself worked up over it until we've exhausted every option, and we haven't done that yet."

"But—"

"Penelope." She met her gaze square on. "I know it's difficult to be positive when you feel like you've looked everywhere, but you need to hope for the best until we send out an email to the class. I'll also email the staff in case someone has seen it."

"But there's nothing in lost property."

"We'll find it."

Penelope slouched, a sulky pout sitting stubbornly on her lower lip. "And if we don't?"

"If we don't, then we'll figure it out. Yes, you'll have to start again with your designs, but it isn't the end of the world. Did you take those photos and upload them to the network for our peer critique?"

The teenager sat up a little straighter. "Yeah."

"You've got the basics of your designs all online then. I'm certain I have some photos of the ones I really thought were striking when I was proofing it, so all isn't lost."

She nodded slowly. "Yeah, yeah I suppose. Brad has a few copies 'coz he wanted some inspiration off my drafts."

"There you go. Yes, it'll be a lot of work, but you still have that same brain on those shoulders that thought of the ideas in the first place. If we can't find it, you can re-create it. Perhaps sketch out the ideas you were having for finals over the next week, so you have it fresh in your mind. Might make you feel better while you're waiting for a response."

The hope that sprang into Penelope's eyes was a win in Ally's book.

"Now hang tight, I'll just grab my laptop."

By the time she had sent the emails, shooed Penelope out of the classroom and made it back to her own desk it was 4:15 p.m. She had fifteen minutes left of the staff meeting, then she could go home, grab a shower and finally see Owen.

She grabbed her planner off her desk, then jumped a mile when her office door slammed open.

"Owen!" she grabbed at her chest. "You startled me...and you're two hours early."

The smile died on her lips; that quick jolt of pleasure at seeing him soon dissipated. The stark expression on his face left her cold. Something was wrong.

"What's happened?"

"Where's Charlotte?"

"I beg your pardon?"

"She's usually home by now on a Wednesday. She wasn't there when I arrived, and I haven't seen her at the bus stop, either." His chest was heaving, eyes wild.

Ally ignored the trickle of dread in her stomach. Teachers were always receiving coded alerts based on incidents outside school grounds. Thankfully none of the children who ever reported being followed or chased had been abducted. She tried to think back to the last alert. It would have been months ago. Before taking the new position.

"Explain this to me. Charlotte takes the bus on a Wednesday, that right?" Facts, not emotion would get them through.

"She just started last week. She was supposed to catch the bus today with Holly and Jeremy. It drops her down the road at the shops and she walks five minutes home. We went through it together, damn it."

"Alright." Ghastly scenarios played in her mind.

"What if something has happened to her?"

"You don't know that."

"Neither do you."

Ally raised her eyebrows. "Point taken, but you need to stay calm."

"Calm. Christ, Ally, Charlie is missing!"

"You don't know that for sure. She may have stopped at a shop or gone to Jeremy's or Holly's house to play. Kids do that without thinking sometimes."

He shook his head. "Not without telling me. Charlie knows the rules."

"It may have been impulsive."

"Not Charlotte. I thought she was ready. I thought after seeing her at camp that she was more than capable...I should have listened to my gut. I knew she was too young to take public transport."

"Does she have a phone?"

"I gave her a spare one but it's not on."

Her stomach quivered. "Alright. I'm going to call Jeremy and Holly to find out when they saw her last."

"I called their homes. No answer."

"I have their mobile numbers from camp. Just, come with me to the interview room. Take a seat. Five minutes isn't going to change much."

Owen bunched his fists, eyes turbulent and distant. "Fine." He sat down then sprang up again. "What if she was taken."

"Then, we'll deal with it. Please, just give me a few minutes to concentrate." She rifled around the folders until she found them. On slightly unsteady feet, she ushered him back to her desk and into her chair. The pounding in her temples had begun.

She dialled Holly's number first. After a few failed attempts she shoved the office phone back in its cradle.

Owen started pacing again.

"Let me put an announcement over the loudspeaker. She may still be at school?" Ally called reception. She waited until she heard the announcement over the speakers before picking up the phone again. "Let's see if Jeremy knows anything." She prayed that he answered. Relief poured through her when he did.

"Jeremy! Hello. It's Ms. McVeigh, from Woodbury High School calling." She paused. "No, no. You're not in any trouble. I'm calling because we have Charlotte Davies' father here. We were wondering if you've seen her. She usually catches the bus with you, is that right? Ah-huh. Right." Ally looked at Owen, shook her head lightly. "And did she come back? Right. What did she say? Mhmm," she pressed her lips together. Waited. "Yes, I'm here. Can you read it out to me? Sure." She waited again. "Did she say why? No, no, it's fine. Just a misunderstanding. If you do manage to hear from her tell her to call her dad or school reception. You have a good night."

Owen's shoulders were hunched over. "He hasn't seen her?"

"According to Jeremy, she walked with him to the bus bay then realised she didn't have her phone, so she went back to her locker. About five minutes later he got off the bus to find her when she messaged telling him to leave without her, that she'd see him tomorrow."

He stilled. "She didn't say why, did she?"

"No. He said he was going to go back to check but assumed that you had called her and changed plans. He hasn't heard from her since."

"I knew it was too soon. She begged me. Said she was responsible. But where the hell is she? A twelve-year-old girl doesn't just go missing out of the blue! Unless something has happened to her."

"Let me put another announcement over the P.A. again." She did so, and then fired off texts to Sera and Maddie. "Calm down. I know this isn't good. But she'll turn up. Kids have a way of doing that."

"She's not the type to wander off. Not even as a toddler."

"Owen. Stop." She grabbed his arm. "I know you're scared right now, but you have to think clearly. Is there anywhere that Charlotte would go to? A favourite place of hers?"

"No—nothing around town."

Ally bit her thumb nail, tapped her foot. "Could she have gone to the library? Forgotten her house key and waited at a local cafe?"

"No. I checked with her this morning. Especially because she was catching the bus."

"Alright. What about a sweets shop? She loves baking. Could she have gone to pick up something?"

"Not without telling me. We had a deal. Any change of plans and she contacts me."

"What about family? Her grandparents? Could she have gone to their place, or called them?"

Owen's head shot up. His eyes bore through hers. "Son of a bitch."

"Owen? Hey!" She stepped in between him and the door. "What just happened?"

"They wouldn't..."

"Wouldn't what? Tell me."

"Her grandparents. Rebecca's mum and dad. She may have gone there. But that's miles away."

"Okay, we'll look. I'll go back to your place. You go to her grandparents' place."

He looked furious. "Call me if you hear anything." He texted her their details before barrelling out the door, just as Maddie and Sera came in.

"What's going on?" Sera demanded, "we got your text."

"No time to properly explain, but could you do a check of the school before you go—see if you can find Charlotte Davies? She's gone missing. Call me if you hear anything?"

Ally winced.

"You okay?" Maddie squeezed her shoulder.

"Headache." She picked up her handbag. "I'll be fine."

She only hoped that Charlotte would be too.

Ally parked in the driveway of Owen's two-storey home. The gates had been left wide open in what she could imagine was his earlier haste to leave. Idyllic and quiet, the neighbourhood was inviting, and the neighbours she suspected—friendly. Surely someone would have seen a schoolgirl in the area if Charlotte had come back home? She toyed with knocking on doors, but that somehow made the situation so much more dire. She wasn't quite ready to face that.

She turned off the engine and shivered. The thought that something—or someone—had been responsible for taking the little girl kept her adrenaline pumping.

They always taught their students to be vigilant and mindful when they were out in public. She thought that being on camp in the city had provided them with a greater awareness of "stranger danger." But it only took one moment, one lapse in judgement for everything to change. Ally could only hope that she was with her grandparents. Regardless of whether they had a good relationship or not, it was safer than being taken by a stranger.

She rolled her shoulders. The Panadol she had taken—dry—on the way over seemed to have dulled the pain. For now.

She focused on their house, admiring its facade. Potted flowers hugged the porch, where a Hamptons style swing chair sat nestled to the side. She could imagine the two of them

BEFORE YOU WERE MINE

working out in the yard on a weekend, making the place not just a house, but their home. There was something inviting about the rich, red brick and charming blue shutters. A place where a family could settle down and build happy memories.

Ally walked up the stairs to the porch, which offered a good view of the street. She would be better able to see Charlotte from this vantage point. Her phone volume was on maximum so she wouldn't miss a call.

With nothing left to do, she sat down on the chair and blew hot air on her frozen fingers. She hoped the cold would clear her head.

She jerked when her phone buzzed. Sera and Maddie hadn't seen the little girl, and neither had anyone else that had been lingering around the school.

When nerves threatened to overwhelm her, she wandered towards the driveway. She needed to keep moving.

Twenty minutes later a car pulled up just outside the house. She wouldn't have noticed it, the engine barely purred.

Ally almost cried out with joy when Charlotte poked her little head out of the latest model Mercedes.

"Charlotte!" She waved. "Thank goodness you're home!"

"Ms. McVeigh? What are you doing here? I thought you were coming over later?"

The car sped away just as they met at the bottom of the driveway.

"Change of plans. We've been looking all over for you."

"But why? I was with my grandparents. We—"

"Hold that thought. I have to call your dad." She shook off the lingering adrenaline. "Owen, Charlotte's home. She's fine. Yes, they just dropped her off. Okay, will do."

"What's going on?"

"Your dad has asked me to stay with you until he gets back."

"Why are you here?"

"We…" Ally bit her lip. "We couldn't find you."

"But I was with my grandparents."

"Did you have a nice time with them?"

"Yeah. I saw them on my way to the bus. They wanted to take me out for ice cream as a treat for getting an A on my Maths test." Charlotte's voice pitched; tears swam in her eyes. "Is Dad mad at me? I got a take home tub of his favourite too."

"No, not at all." Ally followed her through the front door, past the hall to the kitchen.

"But they said they'd text dad and tell him. Did he check his phone?"

"Hmm? I'd love a cup of tea if that's okay with you?"

"I'm in trouble, aren't I?" Her blonde head ducked down.

"Listen here, it was all a bit of a misunderstanding. I'm sure it'll be cleared up once your dad gets home, okay? You've nothing to worry about."

A pair of knowing brown eyes looked at her in disbelief.

"Alright if I make us some tea? It's so cold to be having ice cream and I'm frozen through."

"Mamma and I used to like ice cream in the winter. That's what Grandpa and Grandma said."

Ally's heart squeezed. Charlotte wanted to be a part of something that connected her to her mother. And her grandparents had used that fully to their advantage. She wanted to wring their necks for the stunt they pulled. They knew what it was like to lose a child in the cruellest of ways. It was thoughtless and underhanded of them to put Owen in such a position. And spoke volumes about the nature of their relationship.

She was just pouring the hot water into the colourful blue and yellow tea pot when the front door slammed.

Owen picked up his daughter, hugging her tight. The relief that washed over his face shook something loose within her.

"What did I say about texting me?" He kneeled in front of her. "I've been worried sick."

"But Grandma and Grandpa said they texted you already and I should save my credit. They were at the gate when I went to get my phone back from my locker. You always say to not leave school without it."

"I know, baby."

"Why didn't they tell you?" Charlotte frowned from her father back to Ally. "They said they would. They said you knew they were taking me for ice cream."

"I must have had my phone off or not in reception when they did. You know how this winter wind can affect the signals. I'll check it now and see." He unlocked his phone. Slapped his head. "There it is. They did. They texted me and I didn't see it."

Charlotte's eyes narrowed. "I'm not stupid, Dad. You're also a really bad actor. What's going on?"

"Nothing, kiddo. Everything is fine."

"Why do you treat me like a baby? I'm not a kid! You always think I'm stupid but I'm not!" She raced around him. Seconds later they heard the slam of the bedroom door upstairs. Owen ran a hand over his face then leaned against the kitchen counter.

"Sorry about that."

"Don't apologise. She's just trying to make sense of it all. It's a normal reaction."

"That's what scares me. I really appreciate you helping. It means a lot."

"I'm just glad she's safe."

Owen's face should have looked relieved. All it held was concern.

"Are you okay?"

He made a non-committal sound and gestured to one of the stools in the breakfast bar. "Take a seat. I know this isn't exactly how we planned this evening to go, but I'd kill for a cup of tea. No, I'll do it. You've done more than enough for the evening." He held up a second cup.

"No, I'm right, thanks." Her body vibrated, as if she had low blood sugar and needed a hit. The throbbing in her head had started again. All she wanted to do was curl up on the sofa with some chips and maybe a Snickers bar.

"I probably should have told the school earlier. But I don't really want Charlie having much contact with her grandparents outside of the times we agreed upon."

"Okay." Ally's mind began firing. She had a duty of care to keep her safe. "Is this something they do often?"

"No. It's a first." He carried his cup over, placing it carefully on a coaster. "Things are bad between us right now, so they probably thought they were being harmless."

"You don't believe that and neither do I. You can bet that smart little girl upstairs doesn't buy it either. Can I ask why they did this? It's classic passive aggressive behaviour to me, and quite destructive from the looks of it if they're telling Charlotte one thing and acting in a totally different manner."

Owen sipped at his tea and considered something before answering. "I'm the guy who knocked up their daughter in high school and had the gall to marry her instead of encouraging her to get an abortion."

"Ouch."

"To say they don't like me, or my parenting style is an understatement. You caught a brief glimpse of that before camp." He looked at her over the rim of his cup.

She knew there was more to it, more that he was keeping back. Not that she could judge. "Should we be worried about them, from a school welfare perspective?"

"I'll handle it."

Something wasn't right here. "That's not an answer."

She studied his expression. The look in his eye told her he had made up his mind.

"You're right. It isn't. The truth is Henry and Anita Langdon are trying to get custody of Charlie. I've received news from my lawyer that they're going to do anything they can to prove that I'm an unfit parent."

Ally processed the news. What kind of grandparents did that to a child? She didn't want any ugliness to affect Charlotte at school—the one place she should always feel safe. Her mind whirled with possibilities. She had to brief her staff and make an official note of it in her file. She told him so.

"I know. I guess I didn't want to escalate things. Or for Charlie to feel different at school."

"She won't. But I must keep staff informed in case they do something like this again. Custody battles can get ugly, and this little stunt they've pulled has already taken it to the next level. You should have told me, Owen. I could have helped prevent it."

"I wanted to handle it. I thought I could. I'm trying to keep the unpleasantness between us away from Charlie for the time being. She doesn't need to know right now."

"How is that working out for you?" Ally stood. "As you can see, kids are perceptive. Your daughter more so than others."

"Very. She's a smart girl. But the problems I have with them shouldn't be ones that she has to face. She doesn't need to know about it. For now, at least. I don't want her to retreat again."

"I think she's already clued in, to be honest."

Owen straightened. "I've made sure to keep her out of it and I'll continue to do so."

Defensive. Protective. Underlying both was blind fear. The topic of parenting was clearly a sore spot. Not that she could blame him. He was facing a custody battle where he very well might lose his child. Her focus was keeping Charlotte safe and happy. Lots of families had dysfunctional dynamics. So long as it didn't jeopardise the young girl's welfare, she had no choice but to let him handle it.

She took a step back.

"From a school perspective, we need to ensure she's safe.

Her grandparents pose a risk, so they'll be placed on a watch and act alert."

Owen's shoulders lowered. Crossing the breakfast bar, he stood before her. "I'd appreciate that. I apologise for not telling you."

Ally shrugged. "I haven't exactly been spewing my secrets, so I understand."

It was ridiculous to be upset when she would have likely acted in the same fashion. She ignored her bruised pride. It had no place here.

A relationship was a two-way street, wasn't it? He had given her every indication that he was ready for more. If tonight had gone to plan, she would have...what? Told him she wanted more, too?

"You're her father, you have her best interests at heart. As do I. She's a bright girl, so half-truths won't work. I get that you're trying to protect her. The school is in the exact same position. But I have a duty of care to that child and if I believe Charlotte is in any way caught up in an emotionally damaging situation, then I will be forced to act. We're both on the same side here, Owen. But you need to let us know if things get worse so I can do my job."

"We're in agreement then. Hey—" he caught her arm. "I'd move heaven and earth to keep her safe."

Those bright blue eyes exposed not only the fear, but the promise in that statement. He meant every word.

"I know this...Look, it's getting late, and after the events of today, I think we need a rain check on our chat." It wasn't the right time to get into it. Though a large part of her was suddenly impatient to move things forward. "Owen, I've m—"

She swallowed the admission.

"Ally." Her name was a caress on his lips. She was drawn to him in every way. "What are you holding back?"

He stroked her cheek. The tension in her neck craved what

those strong, capable hands could do. When he found the knot at the base of her head, she succumbed to his hypnotic pressure.

She didn't want to imagine those hands on her body. Or the way his lips would cover hers. He would be a slow burn, a fissure of arousal that became a gaping chasm of desire.

"I better leave."

"Ally—"

"Or I may start something I can't stop."

She witnessed the moment when understanding bloomed across his face. He looked shocked by her admission. She was equally so. But damn him, he had infiltrated her dreams at night. He tempted her on so many levels.

The pressure on the back of her neck increased. A delicious spark radiated down her spine. She moaned, her breath trembling in release.

The air between them was charged; if either moved, she was certain they'd see the current, heavy and heady between them.

It was there in his eyes. The hunger, the need. For her.

"Make that noise again," he whispered.

Her mouth parted. His hands travelled from the back of her neck, stroking down the column of her throat. The slow, seductive teasing mocked the frenzied beat inside her chest.

"More." Her voice was strangled, strained by her own need. "I want more."

"Christ, you're gonna be the death of me."

She stepped towards him, desperate to feel his chest against her breasts. In a heartbeat, he drew her in.

Her body rejoiced at the pressure of his hands on her hips. She kissed him with abandon, allowing every fantasy to play out behind closed eyes. Oh yes, she wanted more. So much more it frightened her.

She held up a hand, breaking the kiss.

A small smile sat at the corner of his mouth. "I can give you more, Ally. If you're telling me you want to take this further, that you want to give a relationship with me a shot, then I can give that to you. Is that what you're saying? Is that what you need?"

She traced his jaw with her finger. "I'm afraid of what I need. But yes, Owen. I want more. I don't know if it's right, but I want it."

His hands held her gently. "Stay. We can talk. Salvage the evening?"

She shook her head. "I don't know where this will lead. I don't understand it." There was so much more they needed to share. More that he needed to understand.

"That's okay."

"Is it?" She kissed him softly, once, before stepping back.

"We'll take our time figuring it out. We need to talk about this, Ally. But for now, let go of those fears. Trust me. Trust yourself."

"That's probably what we should discuss. But not tonight. Charlotte needs her dad, and you need to process what's happened. I'm really relieved that she's safe." She kissed him again, a balm for them both. "I'll see myself out."

When it came to Owen Davies, she didn't think she could trust her judgement. The problem was, she wasn't entirely certain that it was a bad thing.

CHAPTER TWENTY

"*Y*ou're kidding me, right?"

That Friday evening Ally watched her two friends lug their suitcases through the doorway of her tiny apartment.

"What's with the last-minute sleepover? And why in the world are we having it here? My apartment sucks in comparison to yours, Madds."

"We're not."

"Correct me if I'm wrong, but my superpowers tell me that there are clothes in those square cases. Many clothes in Maddie's one. You realise you'll both have to share the sofa bed, right?"

"Oh, go on and tell her for heaven's sake!" Sera's eyes were bright.

She sniffed at the air. "What are you two up to?"

"Oh, nothing much." Maddie sing-songed, stretching out across the couch.

Ally came up behind her. "What are you cooking, woman? That innocent look doesn't work on me."

"For heaven's sake, Madds would you just tell her?" Sera

bounced. "You said you didn't have plans this weekend, right, Al?"

"Uh huh." Ally looked back and forth between them. "What are you two up to?"

Maddie lifted her hips and drew a white piece of paper out of her back pocket. She kneeled up against the back of the couch to face Ally. "The question is, Ms. McVeigh, are you ready to have some fun?"

She rolled her eyes. "I'm always up for fun, Ms. Fitzgerald."

Sera shook her head and laughed. "The two of you drive me nuts. *Tell* her!"

"Well you better pack a bikini and your contraceptive pills, coz." Maddie opened the paper. "We're going to Sydney!"

"What?" Ally looked from the two maniacally grinning faces to the printed out boarding pass. "We're going to Sydney? Why?"

"Why not?" Sera countered. "It's the long weekend, reports are pretty much done, and we've got a twelve week term that we're still trudging through—I say we need a vaycay."

"But of course," Maddie put on her best British accent. "This weekend is to honour our Lady Mother—the Queen."

"Is that so?" Ally smirked.

"Indeed, child." Maddie shoved the documents in her back pocket. "In light of the fact that we live in a Commonwealth country, we're going to party hard in honour of a woman thousands of miles away."

"That's the only reason why you like having a ruling monarchy...for the holidays?"

"Hell yeah...and Prince Harry is hot. Anyway, you need to pack."

"Tonight? Wait—when do we leave?"

"At un-God o'clock in the morning. You can thank sweet, thoughtful Seraphina for that."

"Hey." She nudged her leg. "It was the only way to keep

costs down. And it'll make the most of our stay. You'll be happy to know we leave Sydney Monday evening. To maximise party awesomeness."

"Brilliant." Ally high fived her. "I suppose proofing all those reports will have to wait until we get back to rainy Melbourne then. Shit. I better go pack."

The girls followed her to the bedroom.

"Please tell me you've already waxed. I've seen the wilder beast in its natural element."

Ally threw a sock at her. "Be nice! I got a Brazilian last week if you must know, Miss Nosey."

Maddie wiggled her eyebrows at Sera and picked up Ally's comb. "A Brazilian you say." She adopted her posh English accent. "And why, in winter, pray tell, would our gel get a Brazilian?" She swatted the comb in her hand and paced the small room. "Unless there may be a gentleman of fine breeding and good carriage come to call at her door. Or—calamity—hiding in her bed!" She swatted Ally as she bent to pick up her suitcase.

She began packing and tried to ignore her. She was disappointed that she wouldn't have a chance to see Owen this long weekend—not that they had made any plans—but after the events of Charlie's disappearance on Wednesday, she knew everything had changed.

Something was beginning between them and it left her a little giddy. They had spoken on the phone last night for a few hours. It had given her an opportunity to explain her reticence at rushing headlong into a relationship. Not that he held it against her. The man had the patience of a saint.

Maddie swatted her butt. "You won't need those in Sydney."

Ally looked down at the slippers she held in her hands. She hadn't yet told Maddie and Sera the full version of events after

Charlotte had arrived back home. Or yesterday's phone call. Only that their date had been postponed.

She turned towards them. "So…"

Maddie's jaw dropped. "You bagged a shag with sexy single dad Davies, didn't you?"

Ally picked up a pair of jeans and folded them with exaggerated care.

"What?" Sera screeched. "But that was two days ago! She would have told us if she had sex with Owen!"

"I did no such thing…but, I also haven't told you all the details of what happened when Charlotte came back."

"Tell us everything!" Sera flopped on her bed, helping her fold her clothes into the suitcase whilst Maddie peppered her with questions.

Ally filled them in on her conversation with Owen, and their kiss. She covered her ears at the two high pitched squeals.

"Shh! The neighbours will think I'm getting murdered. And before you ask, the closest thing anyone has been to this lady garden is Gerta, my beautician. We didn't do anything else. Honest."

Maddie squinted at her. "Okay, keep the juicy details to yourself. We won't prod until we get you to Sydney and ply you with gin."

She made a face. "Vodka, please, you heathen."

"Give me a good red any day." Sera's tone was wistful. "I wish we were going to Tuscany instead. People living in Europe have it so good."

Maddie flopped on the bed beside her. "Yup. Cheap tickets to Sydney will have to do for now. That is until we all make a mint on some reality TV show and cash in our winnings. How does that sound, ladies?"

"Excellent idea," Ally said in her best Queen Mother impersonation.

"Undoubtedly," mimicked Sera.

As they dissolved into fits of hysterical laughter and excitement, Ally stealthily packed her lacy red bra and matching underwear.

It didn't mean a thing that she had Owen in mind when she did.

CHAPTER TWENTY-ONE

"Welcome to sunny Sydney!" Maddie threw her arms out.

It was a Saturday afternoon in the middle of winter, but Sydney had been hit by a dry spell—twenty-five glorious degrees saw locals and tourists flock from all over to take advantage of the unseasonably warm weather.

"I wouldn't have packed my parka if I knew it would be this toasty." Sera waved a hand over her face. "I forgot how humid Sydney can get."

"We just won't talk about what it's doing to my hair right now." Maddie rolled her eyes. "I have a date with monsieur hair straightener this evening."

No matter what delights Sydney had to offer, Ally never tired of looking out over the glistening water to the Harbour bridge. Whilst Maddie and her artistic sensibilities cooed over the Opera House, it was the delicately curved metallic behemoth that time and again captured her attention.

"Can you imagine how difficult it was to build it so many years ago?"

"Didn't a few people die in the making?" Sera asked, tipping her face up towards the sun.

"I think so." Ally stretched out.

"Would you two history geeks shut up a minute and enjoy the sights? This is supposed to be a light-hearted weekend." Maddie had her eyes set on a group of guys in t-shirts that showed off their effort at the gym. "We have one mission and one only this trip and that's—"

"To have fun?" Sera quipped.

"To have fun *and* get some action." Maddie winked. "I haven't had me a man in a while and that dark headed one over there looks yummy."

"He's a complete stranger."

"He's a dream."

"Alright, Madds, simmer down." Sera shook her head, then took a closer look at the guy in question. "Let's go get some drinks, see a bit more of the sights and hit that bar the hot concierge mentioned."

"Ooh I forgot about him. And his friends."

"We can see where they're hanging out?"

"That's one of your better suggestions on this trip so far, Sera. I thoroughly approve."

They walked by the water, stopping to watch a street artist every so often on their way back to the hotel. Sera sidled next to Ally. "Didn't that guy remind you of Gabriel?"

"Gabriel…as in Vice Principal Steele? You read my mind."

"Interesting, no?" Sera wiggled her eyebrows.

"Very. But we'll keep that observation to ourselves. Not sure how keen she is to be told that."

"I'm pretty sure she'd go all exorcist chick on our arses."

"Would you two stop gossiping and check this performer out?" Maddie dragged them closer to the crowd.

Ally watched the singer belt out a power ballad, but her

thoughts—no matter how carefree—cartwheeled over and over to a certain single dad with expert hands and kissable lips.

A girls' weekend away was exactly what she needed to take her mind off Owen. But she'd be lying if she said she wasn't excited about going home and spending time with him.

To finally begin this new chapter in her life. To see where it would lead.

The bar was heaving with skimpily clad bodies, all out to enjoy the heat that blanketed the city's pubs, clubs and restaurants.

Owen had every reason to celebrate.

He had signed the contract that afternoon and his analytics company now had another big client on their books. Which meant a lot more revenue with the potential to expand his business. All of which made him a very happy man.

He couldn't remember the last time he went out for a celebratory drink. Or been out on his own. A lot of his life before Charlie had seemed dull and boring. Then again, he was just a teenager. That attitude went with the territory.

A child having a child, his mother had said. Not that he regretted the decision one bit. Respect led him to ask for Rebecca's hand in marriage. But it was love that made him want to have a baby.

Owen gulped down his lager and remembered the day Charlie was born. Pink and curious, with the squished red face that all startled newborns had when they entered the world—she was the most wondrous person in the universe. Whilst not a man to believe in love at first sight, the moment he clapped eyes on that tiny face, with her ten little fingers and toes, he was struck.

That love, the constant weight of it in his gut had only intensified as the years passed. It made him laugh in joy at her first wobbly step, tear up on her first day at school and vow to fight away the demons at her mother's death. He had promised Rebecca—despite the strain of their marriage before her illness —that he would always protect their daughter. However difficult their marriage had been, he made sure Charlie knew she was loved.

He wasn't okay with leaving her in Melbourne so soon, especially after the stunt her grandparents pulled just that week, but he knew that this deal would give them a lot more financial freedom. Which meant less travelling and maybe even a business partner to share the load.

Not that Charlie had objected to having a sleepover at Holly's place. He had called to check up on her on Saturday morning, then again in the evening. They had a quick video chat this afternoon when he told her the good news. She had looked happy and carefree. Even happier at the prospect of ice cream and pancakes for brunch tomorrow to celebrate.

Even though he wanted to protect his child, he knew the best way to do so was to keep everyone informed. Telling Ally had lifted a weight off his chest. She would do everything in her power to keep her safe at school.

He had been surprised by her call on Thursday evening. Though relieved to hear that all the staff had been briefed about Charlie's situation. They ended up chatting on the phone for a few hours, which they had both needed to clear the air.

He'd send her a bunch of flowers to show his appreciation. Something delicate yet bold. And fragrant.

His fingers itched to call her. He drank the last of his beer instead and leaned back from the bar. It was 11pm on a Sunday night. A little late for a chat, even if it was a long weekend. He had an early flight to catch in the morning and was already planning on surprising Ally with the offer of dinner and a movie at their place tomorrow night. He'd run it by Charlie first just to make sure it was okay.

With images of Ally teasing his senses, Owen turned.

Across the crowded pub, wearing an emerald green dress that made every man praise God for womankind, was the woman of his dreams. A ball of lust punched through any remaining defences he had in place.

All he could see were those red lips. And miles of leg.

He wanted to brush his fingers up along her thigh, tease those breasts in his hands until they both went a little mad. The need had been there for months now.

She laughed at something one of her friends had said—as did the bevvy of men surrounding them.

Owen knew only one thing.

He had to have her. Tonight.

CHAPTER TWENTY-TWO

*A*lly nearly choked on her cocktail. She had taken the last sip of her long island iced tea, which sent her from not quite tipsy to hello drunk when she spotted Owen walking towards her through the throng of bodies. Not that it was hard to miss him. His six-foot frame made the man easy to spot in most situations.

But it wasn't the broad shoulders that caught her attention, or even the curl of muscle at his biceps that made her stop. It was the pin-me-down-and-lick-me expression in his eyes that had her instantly aroused.

Whilst there was a prim and proper school teacher scolding her somewhere in the recesses of her mind, the vixen wearing the scandalous red lace lingerie underneath all that would win the day. Or night.

Maddie squealed. "Mr. Davies!" She threw a joyful arm around his shoulders, silver bangles jangling in mad exuberance. "Why, hello, friend! What are you doing in Sydney?"

"Business deal, actually."

"A successful one?"

"Very." Owen's eyes never left her face. She couldn't seem to tear hers away either.

"And not once did our sly little fox here mention it...Never mind, not important. Have a good one!" Maddie mumbled, shooing Sera and the rest of the male harem further down the pub.

"You look stunning."

Ally was suddenly sick of being cautious. She didn't care if she hated her hypocritical self in the morning. Tonight would be pure indulgence.

He looked at her like she was the last slice of chocolate cake. It unleashed a bold and reckless part of her that had been straining for release.

"Hello to you too, Owen. You look pretty edible yourself."

His grin was slow and sure. Game on.

"The pleasure is all mine."

He stepped in. Soap, sweat and some earthy cologne sealed the deal.

"Girls' weekend away?"

"Something like that." She didn't turn. She didn't want to see the expression on her friends' faces right now. She just wanted him.

A drunken hoard of girls jostled past them. Owen's hands were on her waist in an instant. She revelled in the sensation.

"I wanted to thank you properly for Wednesday. For helping out with Charlie."

Ally found her voice. "You did. Numerous times on the phone if you remember."

"I meant something a little more...intimate. Then I realised I didn't know what kind of flowers you liked."

"Chocolate ones."

He laughed. The sound was rich and full of appreciation. "Can I buy you a drink?"

The sweeping caress of his thumbs at her hips teased her.

She wanted to wrap her body around his and enjoy the hard length of him.

"A drink would be nice. But not here."

"My hotel isn't far. It has a nice rooftop terrace. You can invite the girls if you want to move."

She understood what he was doing. At a different time, on a different night she'd have appreciated the 'out'—tonight it almost annoyed her.

"Just us."

The pressure on her waist increased.

"You know that if we leave this place together, I'm going to kiss you again."

"I'm sorry to disappoint, but if we leave this place together, *I'll* be doing the kissing."

She had the satisfaction of seeing those blue eyes darken.

"Perfect."

"Give me a minute."

She was back in half the time and took his arm.

"Lead the way."

The walk to his hotel was just enough time for Ally to start having second thoughts. They flittered across her mind, only to drift away just as quickly.

"Where's your room?" she blurted before she could stop herself. She felt the heat of him at her side, and her body throbbed in anticipation.

Owen's eyebrows rose. "I thought I owed you a drink."

"Later."

Ally waited until the lift door closed before she was in his arms. It took less than a second for her to wrap her legs around him, before he devoured her. His mouth was firm and demanding. He stroked and teased, torturing her. Arousing her.

He gripped her butt and groaned in appreciation. The sound shot through her, stroking every nerve in her body, until she arched against him, demanding more.

She almost whimpered when he pulled away.

Owen wiped at his lips, motioning to the open lift doors. She tugged down her dress and scurried through them to the corridor. Her blood roared in her ears as she followed him to his room. A part of her was terrified that she could lose herself with such abandon. He only had to look at her for her to want it.

He yanked her against his chest, then backed her up against the door.

The urgency was real. Tugging down the strap of her dress, he needed no prompting. He devoured her breasts like a man starved. She cried out.

She knew it would be like this. The sexual tension had been brewing; the way he looked at her only confirmed that when the time came, he would brand her to the core.

When he circled her nipple, grazing at the sensitive peaks, she shuddered.

"Ally. Christ." He shoved up her dress, took her mouth in his, in a kiss that branded as much as it begged.

Having denied herself this pleasure for months, she craved every inch of him. She fumbled with the buttons of his shirt, desperate to feel his hard flesh against her own. More than anything she needed the heavy weight of him on top of her. She gripped the rope-like muscles of his arms. His broad shoulders kept her trapped against the door. Exactly where she wanted to be.

Ally's hand shook as she popped open the button of his jeans. Her lips curved when she found him hard and pulsing.

Owen bit the side of her neck, wrenching down the red lace panties so they pooled against her stilettos. She gasped when he slid one finger inside her, stroking his way up to her aching clit. Her hips jerked against him.

"I want you, Ally. I need to have you." He nibbled on her ear, his breathing erratic. When he grabbed both her hands and pinned them above her head she growled.

"Owen. Please. I..."

Her body screamed for release. She already anticipated the thick, hard length of him. She yearned to be filled, stretched, pounded. The need was as basic as any other primal urge. But the power of it had them devouring one another in greedy bites.

She cried out. The tip of his cock rubbed against her, lighting up every nerve-ending. She strained against her bound hands; itching to grip his broad shoulders, to stroke the ridges of muscle down to his waist. Her vision wavered, and in one step she was out of her underwear with one leg hooked on his hip.

"Don't. Stop."

Ever. She hadn't wanted to admit how much she had craved this. Him.

Owen obeyed, his body straining as he slid his cock back and forth against her throbbing clit. She wanted to come.

He released her hands only to knead her breasts.

"Ally. If we don't stop, I'm gonna explode."

"Do it. Come with me. I'm so close."

"Ladies first," Owen muttered, gripping her waist, determination darkening his eyes. The sensation of his chest brushing against her sensitive breasts heightened her arousal. He rocked against her, faster now. She wanted to taste him, to savour his length in her mouth.

"Fuck, Owen. I—I'm, I can't hold..."

She came hard against his cock, caught in her own pleasure. Owen's guttural cry a second later only sharpened her release. Her body vibrated in satisfaction when she felt the silky, hot beads drench her clit, and cling to the curve of her waist.

They held each other and in a tangled heap of limbs and clothes, slid to the floor.

"Best. Foreplay. Ever."

Ally laughed, heart racing. She lay beside him with her head propped against his outstretched arm. She still yearned to take his semi-hard length inside her.

"Hell yes." His grin was every bit the satisfied male. He shifted closer, thumb caressing her cheek. The gesture was tender.

Her eyes stung. She was furious with herself and him for drawing this out in her. He kissed her gently, savouring her lips, slowly building up her need once more.

"You're gorgeous. Every part of you is beautiful." He brushed back strands of her hair that had fallen loose. "I want to make love to you with your hair down. It's so long, so thick. It fascinates me." He twirled one strand around his finger. "*You* fascinate me." His gaze was direct, consuming.

Her lungs seized.

The pressure in her chest was overwhelming. Crushing. She pulled away, shifting up. What was she doing? She had wanted to ease into a relationship with him. Go on a bloody date first. Get to know him.

Where the hell was her bra?

"Owen...."

He took her chin in his hand. "Ally. Talk to me. What's going on?"

She was afraid to look at him. Afraid of what he would see. "I need my bra."

"Understandable given the circumstances. Though highly overrated. The bra, that is. Not what's in them. You've got fantastic..." he gestured. "Hmm. I'm rambling. Christ, you make me nervous sometimes."

His genuine bafflement touched her. She paused, kissing him softly, then continued her search.

"Wait." Owen shifted. "I was sitting on it."

"Thanks." She reached for her panties next, slid them up and under her crumpled dress.

Owen found his jeans and slid them on. Both stood at the same time. A web of longing weaved itself around her heart. She could see how easy it would be for her to fall, to take that step and lose herself in him. She had lost control tonight. With a parent. Charlotte's dad.

Old fears swirled through her mind. The panic clawed at her throat, leaving her voice hoarse and bruised. It was so much more than that. He was so much more than that.

She was freaking out. She knew it, but couldn't seem to rein it in.

Ally tugged down her dress and re-arranged the straps. Focus on the normal. The basics.

"What's happening in that head of yours?"

"We can't do this." She gestured between them.

Owen crossed his arms and casually leaned against the door.

"I hate to break it to you." He motioned to his half-naked state. "But we just did."

She trembled, voice thick with emotion. "I'm petrified of what this means."

He stepped towards her, carefully, and held her in his arms. She could hold back the tears. She didn't bother trying.

"Being with you is the most glorious and frightening thing. What just happened tonight was…"

"Amazing? Incredible? Mind-blowing?"

Ally laughed, sniffling. "This…" she clung to him. "This meant a lot. Being with you means a lot to me."

"And that's a hard concession for you to make."

He guided her to one of the armchairs and knelt down. He held her hands, offering her comfort, giving her strength.

She nodded. "It is. I've been making these excuses because, well…I'm not sure I'm enough. I—my parents aren't good role models. I'm scared of screwing this up."

"For what it's worth, this thing between us means a lot to

me too. I don't want to make a mistake either, but I know I probably will. That's what happens in relationships."

"I'm not good at relationships."

"Then we'll learn. Together. How about we start small? Ease into it."

"I can work with that." The fear, the blind panic that gripped her moments before had released its hold some. She breathed a little easier.

"*We* can work with that. You're worth the risk, Ally. Whatever it is that makes you want to run in the opposite direction isn't true. I'll be beside you for as long as it takes for you to see that. Part of that is opening up. Talking it through."

Her smile was one of relief. "We take it slow?"

"Like a tortoise."

The laugh chased out any residual fear that echoed in her chest.

"C'mon, I'll walk you back to your hotel."

Ally placed her hand in his. "I'd like that very much."

Thirty minutes later, Owen walked back to his own hotel. He welcomed the balmy breeze on his overheated skin, wandering past the swell of revellers taking advantage of the long weekend.

He hadn't expected to end the night like this. He wanted Ally to share his bed, to wake up beside her in the morning and spend a bit of time together before his early flight. In some ways, her outburst was surprising. But it had allowed them to set some parameters in how they approached this relationship.

He meant what he said. He was all in. Whatever it was between them was important enough that he would wait a lifetime for her. Owen wasn't a wide-eyed schoolboy learning what it meant to love this time. He knew that whatever this was had the foundations to last generations. To leave legacies. If only she would let it.

If he hadn't seen the hurt, the sorrow behind those lovely green eyes, he would have pressed her further. But there were scars there that hadn't properly healed.

He wanted to be the one she confided in. To make her laugh. To win her affection. She was so much more than she feared. He needed to show her that. To prove it to her so she never looked at him with such trepidation again.

It hit him then. The answer. He would woo her over. Properly. Show her everything that was good about relationships. Convince her that a relationship with him was worth a shot.

It was just a matter of time. And trust.

He would happily do this for her. So she could understand her worth.

Owen let himself into his room and paused. Her floral perfume lingered in the doorway. Walking to the mini bar, he selected a scotch, took it to the balcony and stared out across the city landscape.

For a woman like Ally, he'd give all the time in the world.

Ally was grateful that the girls weren't home yet. She fumbled around in the bathroom, set the shower to scorching and stood beneath the spray, processing the events of the past few hours. She began to wash, analysing it from every angle.

The loofah against her nipples was rough. She dipped her hand inside her vagina; she wasn't surprised to find herself wet. She couldn't quite believe what she had done. One look at him at the pub and that was it, all her inhibitions seemed inconsequential.

She pressed her head against the cool glass. She didn't know where all that emotion had come from; it embarrassed her to recall it.

Setting up boundaries tonight was important, she just wished she hadn't freaked out. Stupid, really, to think tonight wouldn't affect her. That he wouldn't cause a tumult in her system. Starting something with Owen was big.

Knowing it, accepting it, didn't make living with her fears any easier.

But she trusted him. She let the feeling settle her over-wrought emotions. Towelling off, she wrapped herself in her nightgown and snuggled under the covers, nerves abating.

She'd take comfort in the fact that he wouldn't rush her. That whatever was building was a step in the right direction.

Her stomach quivered. For the first time in what felt like forever, Ally was excited about a relationship. She pulled the duvet closer, hugging the warm sensation to her chest. She drifted off to sleep hopeful for the future.

CHAPTER TWENTY-THREE

*A*lly woke up just before 6 a.m. and couldn't for the life of her fall back asleep. She padded out barefoot to the bathroom. Then yelped when Sera's tired voice called out from the lounge.

"You don't need to creep around silently, I'm up."

She clutched at her chest. "You scared the crap outta me!" Rubbing her face, she sat on the edge of the sofa bed. "Can't sleep either, hey?"

"Nope. Too much booze, and we got in late. You were fast asleep though. What happened?"

Ally stood. "Let me go pee first."

"Uh oh."

"What?"

Sera raised her eyebrows. "I know that look."

When she returned, Maddie was sitting on the edge of the sofa bed, her auburn hair knotty, eyes half open.

"What are you doing up?"

"The devil incarnate woke me." She jerked a thumb at Sera. "Not that you were asleep."

"Well I was trying to get back to sleep after Sleeping Beauty screamed."

Sera rolled her eyes. "We can sleep in later. We have a late check out. Plus, I ordered room service when I got up. You'll get your caffeine fix soon."

"Coffeeee. Nowwww, woman. I'll be your best friend."

"You are my best friend."

Maddie swiped the hair out of her eyes. "I'll be an even better one!"

Sera huddled under her covers. "*You* have to wait. And *you*, have to tell us every steamy detail about what happened last night." She pointed her water bottle at Ally before taking a swig.

Ally pressed the heel of her hands to her eyes. "I think I made a boo boo."

"How could sleeping with dreamy dad Davies, be a boo boo?"

"Did you just make that up?" Sera made space for Maddie under the blankets.

"No, actually. It was the by-product of my drunken genius when he stole our darling girl away. I really should write school plays while drunk...that'd totally work."

"Right. Back to the important matter at hand. Why was it a boo boo?"

"Was he terrible in the sack?"

"We...I..."

"Spit it out girl. Did you, or did you not see him naked?"

Her look said it all.

"Hello!" Sera whooped.

Maddie threw her a high five. "Why, oh why do you look like the man has given you genital herpes, instead of an orgasm?"

"You just assumed he gave her an orgasm."

"Uhh. Hello? Naked...of course he did! Didn't he?"

Ally bit the bullet and in a rush of words, told them everything. She had to pause for their questions: was he cut? Did you do it more than once? Before she got to the end of it.

"You what?" Maddie spluttered.

"I kind of got scared by it all and burst into tears."

"Yowzers."

"But then…we had a quick chat about it and decided to take it slow…"

"Finally!"

Sera pumped a fist in the air. "I love happy endings!"

"Ally-oop, I say you slayed this girls' weekend. Not only did you get some action, but you've come away with a hottie boyfriend. I salute you, girl." Maddie's tired eyes were bright with this newfound information.

The bell rang. "Food! Don't say anything more. I don't want to miss out."

"Girl, we have to talk."

"There's nothing to talk about, Madds."

"When you have sexy times with a man who is as fit and kind—" she raised a finger, "*and* interested in more than just sex *and* is willing to take things slow, you should not look like your budgie just died."

"I'm not upset by it, I'm just—"

"I told you not to talk about anything!" Sera wheeled in the tray of food.

"I was trying to convince Ally here to feel buoyed by this new relationship. Aaaand, that there isn't a sane reason why she shouldn't call up Owen, tell him she's coming over, and bag that boy and his morning wood."

Sera coughed on a grape. "Gutter talk this early in the morning. Someone woke up."

She stood—restless—and poured out the coffee. "First, I'm not unhappy about starting something with Owen. I've been making excuses about why we shouldn't date, when every part of me wanted to see him. But that doesn't just mean I can ride off into the sunset and play happy families. The fears that I have are still there. I don't want to mess this up, you know? I feel like I already have by freaking out last night."

"Life isn't neat, hun." Sera passed her a croissant. "You of all people know that. Worrying about messing up a relationship that has just begun is only going to drive you insane."

"I know that. I do, but he's got a lot going on—"

"If you mean the custody crap, then yeah, he does. Which is why he needs something good. You're that thing, Al." Maddie patted her leg. "Don't let anything ruin it."

Her stomach jumped at the thought. She couldn't stop herself grinning. "It's nice to feel special. And he's been nothing but a gentleman. But I've never dated a man with a child, let alone one whom I teach. I don't want our relationship to be fodder for the school gossips."

"Screw 'em."

"I have to agree with Madds here. He's the one with the daughter. He seems to think she'd be fine with it otherwise he wouldn't be pursuing a relationship with you. As for parents, what you do in your own time is your business."

"Ideally yes, but you know what they're like."

"We do. But that doesn't mean shit if you're happy. And, girl, if you don't look like the cat that ate the cream, I'll eat my own words."

Ally place a hand against her fluttering chest. "I am. I'm just not used to it. I haven't been in a relationship for a long time. He makes me feel things I didn't think I wanted. Or deserved."

Sera gave her arm a squeeze. "You do deserve it. And he's got our tick of approval if that matters."

"You're family. You know it does."

"Good. Speaking of family." Maddie batted her eyelashes. "I need an extra pair of hands for the set design in our play. A night this week and a couple next?"

"Is this why you spoiled us with this weekend away? To butter us up?"

"That's what alcohol is for."

"Sure. I'm in." Ally bit into the pastry.

"I bet you are, you saucy sex goddess."

Sera shooed Maddie's comments away. "I want to get to the good stuff. Don't scrimp on the details. How exactly did the delicious Owen Davies give you the big O. And, more importantly, when are we going back for round two?"

"We?"

"A single girl's got to get her kicks somehow. And, honey, right now I'm living vicariously through you."

Owen stepped off the plane Monday morning having slept for only a few hours the night before. He picked up his car and a double espresso on his way to get Charlie. Despite his fatigue, he was buoyed. Light. Last night had been…

His mouth curved.

She was more than he'd expected or imagined. Those cat-like green eyes turned bright when she was aroused, and who knew those lips would be the colour of a rose when he kissed her? There was so much he'd yet to explore. Not just her body—you'd be dead not to want that, but all the little things.

Owen rubbed his jaw, then scratched at the stubble. But how did you woo a woman who was terrified of relationships? There was a lot of fear and self-doubt there. The last thing he wanted to do was move too fast.

He also didn't know what he'd say to Charlie. Even though she gave him the green light to date her teacher, he didn't know whether she'd be okay with the reality of it. What the hell would he say to her anyway? *I nearly had sex with your teacher but we're taking it slow?*

Hell no.

He drummed his fingers on the steering wheel. He'd tell her that he bumped into Ally in Sydney, and that they were interested in each other. Vague, but good enough.

He liked her. Enough to know that he didn't want to screw it up.

He toyed with the idea of calling Jack for some brotherly advice. It took him all of two seconds to kibosh that plan. His playboy brother would offer him advice that probably wouldn't work for wooing a woman the old-fashioned way.

Jack was used to women throwing themselves at him that he was certain he hadn't even needed to perfect his pick-up lines. And the sort of women Jack dated weren't ones that attracted Owen. They certainly weren't comparable to Ally. How could a woman be demure and sexy all in one go? She was Marilyn Monroe and Audrey Hepburn and…

Regardless, he wasn't giving up on her, or whatever it was that had begun between them. Deep down he knew she was someone with whom he could have a family. Provided all this bullshit with the courts didn't drag out.

His trip to cloud nine spiralled back down to Earth.

He wouldn't be comfortable until all the legal crap was over. Mediation was looming like a dangerous smoke-cloud on the horizon.

A blunt arrow of fear pierced through his reverie. The actual idea of losing his child, the very possibility that this could happen wasn't a thought that he'd really entertained up until this point. It wasn't like Henry and Anita had any legitimate legal claim. Nothing had been finalised all those years ago.

Owen stopped at a red light, sipped his coffee and willed his heart to slow down. He couldn't think about it for too long or he'd drive himself mad.

He was betting on them working out some kind of arrangement at mediation. Maybe they could take her for a bit longer on the school holidays—not that he was under any prerogative to do so. She was his daughter after all. But he knew that Charlie needed grandparents. That family was important. If they could stop playing games long enough to see that, then maybe they could negotiate.

Owen cast aside the gloomy thoughts as he pulled up to Holly's house. He wouldn't focus on the negatives. It wouldn't help his daughter, and it sure wouldn't help improve his mood.

He'd take what was left of the long weekend and spend it with his baby girl. They both would need it.

CHAPTER TWENTY-FOUR

*T*he noise that reverberated around the draughty auditorium had an echoey, distorted quality to it; the babble of voices travelled across the large space in unrelenting waves. Ally tugged her Tokito jacket closer and admonished herself for not wearing a scarf. The lancing edge of a migraine stabbed relentlessly at her temples. She struggled not to cry out.

She had woken that morning with the tension already squeezing the base of her skull. Aspirin hadn't dulled the pain, which only increased in severity throughout the day.

It had been brewing since they returned from Sydney on Monday. Working late to mark her senior's work hadn't helped. Neither had the sleepless nights.

Every time she closed her eyes, her mind replayed her hot encounter with Owen. All that foreplay left her unable to think about anything else but sex. It was as if what happened on Sunday had been an entree. And here she was four days later gagging for dessert. Her body was on high alert knowing she'd be seeing him for an interview.

Whilst they had spoken during the week, she was eager to spend time with him.

She had arrived at her apartment Monday night to find a second bouquet of chocolate flowers on her doorstep. Whilst she had to turn down his offer of dinner to finalise reports, she had enjoyed talking to him on the phone the following evening. It had been comforting to just chat about normal things.

Like his favourite ice cream: caramel swirl. Or his favourite hobby: hiking.

When he could recite lines from one of her much-loved comedy series, she hadn't been able to hide her pleasure. Or spend the next hour caught up in quoting lines from their favourite episodes.

What surprised her most of all was how easy it had all been. As if they had known each other for years. Not mere months.

She recalled the cheeky text he had sent her this morning, asking what she was wearing to their interview. She hadn't been able to resist flirting with him, which naturally led to a volley of texts, so much so that she had arrived a little late to her first appointment.

Pain surrounded her head, killing any joy she had. She squinted at her watch then back to her laptop screen. She had twelve more parents to get through—over an hour left of the all-day parent/teacher conferences. It may as well have been a life sentence. It seemed everyone had wanted an interview with the new head of junior school today. Any time she had a brief reprieve there had been a parent waiting to swoop in with a question.

She reached down for her handbag only for the room to spin. Pressure mounted behind her eyes. She closed them against the bright fluorescent bulbs and stole a shaky breath. Any movement made her want to scream.

She tried to squint, searching for the packet of paracetamol. Her fingers shook when she found it. Opening her eyes a fraction, she cursed. Empty. She had taken the last one the afternoon Charlotte had gone missing. Naturally, she hadn't had time to replace it.

Slowly, Ally looked around the room but couldn't see Sera or Maddie. The other teachers were all engrossed in their interviews, and those parents who loitered across the auditorium were simply too far away to flag down.

She tried to stand then gave up. Closing her laptop screen, she could barely focus on the printout of names she had in front of her. She had known from memory she had one difficult parent coming to see her around 7.15 p.m. If she could hold out until then, she'd be fine.

Breathing in, she focused on the pain, trying to channel it through her fingers, to visualise it. That's what her doctor had recommended when she was in a bind. Bile rose at the back of her throat. She couldn't be sick. Not here. Not now.

Sitting up straight, she lowered her shoulders, but didn't dare move her head. The pain spiked, hammering at her eye lids.

Her body relaxed when she heard Owen and Charlotte. She opened her eyes, then cried out, cradling her head when the fluorescent lights lanced through her, drilling holes in her resilience.

"Ally. Are you okay?" Owen's hand was a comforting weight at her shoulder.

"I'm fine." She squinted at them both. "Just a slight headache. Hello, Charlotte."

"It sure as hell doesn't look like a slight headache. You're as pale as a sheet and you're shaking." He crouched down beside her chair. "You need to go home."

"No. I can't," she gasped. "Interviews."

"To hell with interviews, you can barely look at me, let alone open your eyes."

She breathed in sharply, opening them wide.

The room spun.

Owen held her in place. "It's okay. We'll get you home."

"I think I'm going to be sick," she mumbled, gripping the arm of the chair.

"Charlie, get me that bin over there."

"No. No. I need…I need air."

"Okay. That's fine. Let me get you out of here."

"My stuff."

"We'll get it later."

"No."

She could hear him packing up, the sounds only magnifying her pain. All the voices in the auditorium set her teeth on edge.

"Charlie, carry Ms. McVeigh's handbag will you, kiddo? Great." Owen guided her to standing. She sagged against him, body shaking.

He lifted her off her feet, carrying her close.

"Put me down," she whispered.

"Just relax. We're taking you home." His arms were firm around her; she had no choice but to rest her heavy head against his chest. Despite the pain, she drew comfort from the steady rhythm of his heart.

Ally heard a familiar voice, then opened her eyes a fraction when she was lowered into the back seat of a car. She blindly followed his instructions, taking the small pill he placed on her tongue, gulping down the proffered water. The last thing she heard was Charlotte's voice carry from the front seat.

She woke up next in a large bed, pain clawing at her head. She writhed and kicked, crying out in agony, only to be soothed by a familiar hand at the base of her neck. It was like this every time she came around. The cool compress at her forehead and the rhythmic pressure of Owen's fingers offered her something other than the blinding white pain to focus on.

But it was the low, even voice murmuring words of encouragement that kept her calm throughout the night.

Finally, at the break of day, with the pain receding enough to allow her to fall into a deep and oblivious rest, she slept.

Ally needed to pee. It was her first thought when she woke. That, and she was starving. Which was a good sign, she supposed. She groped at her side table for her mobile and rapped her knuckles against solid wood; it was a good two inches higher and devoid of all her possessions.

She opened her eyes and blinked slowly; this wasn't her room.

Where the hell was she?

Pulling back the covers, she shivered. A mild ache still lingered at the base of her skull, but it was nothing she couldn't handle. Her singlet clung to her—perspiration had dampened it—and the air, by the smell of things. Her pencil skirt, tights and blouse lay at the foot of the bed on a low wooden chest. She had nothing on but her underwear and singlet.

She shuffled to the side table and examined the picture in the frame. It was a photo of Charlotte and the woman she presumed was Rebecca.

She was in Owen's house. In his bed.

Swift as a bird, fragments of the night before swooped down on her memory. The interview. The car.

She recalled being carried. Ally pressed her head gently into her hands. What would everyone say? What would those parents think? Not a good look.

Despite her embarrassment, she couldn't wipe the smile off her face. She had never been carried like that by any man. He had literally swept her up and off her feet, tending to her as if she were a priceless jewel.

She glanced back at her clothes. Unless Charlotte's twelve-year-old outfits were super stretchy, she'd have to settle for her perspiration-soaked clothes from the day before. She hoped nobody in her office would notice.

A bathrobe lay beside her skirt, with a post-it note adhered to the breast pocket.

Wear me, it said.

She crossed to the bathroom and stared at the second post-it note stuck on the shower door.

Use me. I'm warm. Take a shower before you flee. You'll feel better for it - Owen.

Ally washed her hands, fighting back a smile. Was she that predictable? Waking up in his bed, whilst comforting, wasn't exactly the slow start to their relationship she had in mind. Not that it was bothering her as much as she expected. She trusted him. Trusted that wherever this was heading, she was in safe hands.

A toothbrush still in its plastic case sat beside toothpaste and a towel on the bathroom counter. *Ms McVeigh's stuff* was written in Charlotte's distinctive scrawl. She smiled then stepped under the spray of the double headed shower jets. The warmth of the water on her clammy body rejuvenated her. A hot meal and a good night's sleep this evening would get her back to normal.

The events of the last night played in her mind as she washed her hair. Owen had been so comforting, so gentle with her that she couldn't help but be touched by his kindness. And a little thrilled at his chivalry.

She reached for the conditioner and found none. In fact, the bathroom, like the bedroom seemed devoid of any clutter. So very different from her messy little apartment. She still had folios scattered across her dining table, and her folders were bulging with documents that had yet to be filed.

Ally's eyes flew open. She was going to be late for work. She had scheduled a before-school briefing with her team, which meant no time to linger under the warm spray.

She rinsed off and was dry in a matter of seconds. Frantically, she brushed her teeth, wrapping the towel around her. It dawned on her that she had no clue what time it was...

Racing out of the bathroom, she slammed into Owen's chest with enough force to have her tottering backwards. His hands shot out, steadying her.

It was as if all the oxygen had been sucked out of the room. She clutched at the towel, awareness rippling along her naked body. Sinful images of his hands on her breasts, his fingers stroking her until she climaxed shot through her mind.

"Ally." His eyes swept across her face, then down to her chest. He stepped back. "Sorry. I heard the shower running, so I came in to tell you about food. But then you opened...food. I made it. I wanted to see if you were hungry."

It took a few seconds for her to register his words. "Food?"

"Yeah."

"Could you hand me that robe?" She suppressed the urge to giggle.

He did so, then faced the opposite direction.

"I'm decent." She swallowed. The way his eyes raked over her body, she may as well have been naked. She tugged the sash a little tighter.

Owen reached out, touching the ends of her hair. His fingers twirled an errant strand, the back of his hand brushed against the underside of her breast. Even through the robe, her nipples strained.

His touch was filled with as much longing as tenderness— one that was reflected across his face. Her heart slammed against her ribs.

"Food."

"Hmm?" He lowered his hand, letting go of her hair.

"Food. You mentioned you made breakfast. I don't think I have time for a full meal, but I can grab some toast. I've a 7.30 meeting with my team so I need to get a wriggle on."

"I don't think so." He pulled out his mobile from his pocket. The clock read 2.30 p.m.

"No!"

"You slept like a zombie."

"No. No, no, no, no!" she paced. "I had meetings, seniors to see…a prac class! This is not happening…I forgot to call the daily organiser. Shit."

"It's all taken care of."

She stopped mid-stride. "What do you mean?"

"I bumped into Sera on our way out yesterday. She said she'd call you in sick as you looked in pretty bad shape and needed the rest. She said she'd handle all the details."

Ally rubbed her forehead.

"Is the pain back?"

"No, no. Well yes, but it's manageable. It's just all the stuff I'll have to do to catch up on Monday, that's all. Teaching isn't a gig where you can take days off easily."

"You okay?" Owen stepped closer.

"Yeah. Just frustrated." She looked up at his face. "Thanks for helping me out last night. You didn't need to do what you did, but I really appreciate it. You seem to be getting me out of a lot of binds these days."

"No problem," he replied, moving a strand of wet hair away from her face.

She shivered.

"Cold?"

"A little," she lied. His hand cupped her cheek then ran down her arm. How did you tell a man you wanted him more with every passing moment? That he made you believe you could give more than you thought possible?

She pressed her lips together. *You didn't, you idiot.* Take it slow. That's what she needed—wanted to do.

A buzzer pealed downstairs.

"That'd be the oven."

"You're baking?"

He laughed. "Don't look so alarmed. You've seen me in the kitchen. I sometimes put it on when I work over lunch to remind myself to take breaks. And that it's nearly time to stop and pick up Charlie."

"Ahh."

"I have food downstairs ready and waiting."

He leaned forward, planting a soft, fleeting kiss on her lips. The man was irresistible.

"I'll see you downstairs."

Five minutes later, with her hair beginning to dry, Ally walked into the kitchen to the heavenly smell of cooked fat and eggs. Even though it was past lunch, her stomach was craving a full fry.

Usually she couldn't eat much after a migraine, but today she was ravenous.

"Good to see you're getting some colour back." Owen was at the stove. He loaded up her plate with bacon, eggs and toast. "I assume you eat bacon?"

"I do...but the eggs and toast will probably be heavy enough for the moment. I usually don't have much of an appetite after a bad spell."

"More for me then." He winked. "Drink?"

"Peppermint tea if you have it." She settled at the breakfast bar and spread butter on her toast. She took a bite of the eggs and groaned. His head jerked up. Ally swallowed, realising her mistake. "Really yummy."

"I can see that." He placed the hot tea in front of her plate. "I might have to cook for you more often if you make sounds like that."

She sipped at the steaming tea, grateful for the quick burn

down her throat. "What do you put in them?"

"A little mint, onions, this and that."

"Chef's secret, huh? I can respect that. Though I'm surprised at your inability to bake but your acumen in the kitchen, Mr. Davies," she teased, enjoying having him close.

"I have many, many other talents outside the kitchen, Ms. McVeigh."

Ally grinned. Winced.

"Still sore?"

"A little. Do you have any Panadol Forte by any chance?"

"I'll check upstairs."

He returned with a packet, and a bottle of water.

"Thanks. Speaking of upstairs, how is it that your room is so clean? It looks like you live in a display home." Ally broke open the seal and placed two pills in her hand.

"That's not my room. It's a guest room."

She drank from the bottle wondering what his room looked like. "I don't feel like such a grub then."

"It's one of the spaces Charlie sometimes plays in. She actually insisted that you have that room to feel better."

She swallowed the second pill. "That's sweet of her."

"You may have noticed the pictures of her mother on the side table. She said you should sleep there so you have someone to watch over you."

Her heart ached. "She misses her."

"Some days more than others. Having her own area that she can dedicate to her mother's memory was something it seemed she needed when we moved. Whilst we have pictures of Rebecca in her room and in the house, she gravitated towards that space. The psych said her attachment will lessen over time, the more resilient she becomes."

"I'm sure Rebecca would be touched by it. And by the girl you've raised."

Ally rubbed at the back of her neck. The pressure on her shoulders was still persistent.

"They hit you pretty bad, huh? The migraines."

She bit into her buttered toast. "This one caught me by surprise. I had them frequently when I was younger. My parents didn't think they were bad and made me go to school. It wasn't until I was in class one day and passed out that they took me to a doctor. They realised it was more than just an attention headache."

Owen's eyes searched hers. "That sounds..."

"Cold?" She shrugged. "They had their own views on raising kids."

"Very different to your own."

"Massively so. But I'm sure that's with most people."

"Just because they raised you, doesn't mean you're a reflection of their views."

It was instinctive. The need to clam up. Change the subject. Because of it, she placed her toast on the plate and considered her words. There was no point in starting a relationship with the man if she wasn't going to be honest about her life.

"We have our differences. Namely, they think I'm wasting my time teaching, especially in a public school. They're overly controlling and don't really understand me. I struggle with finding ways to be affectionate with them the older I get. We're not exactly the warm and fuzzy kind of family."

Owen's hand covered hers briefly before moving away. "Sounds like it was tough as a kid, living in that environment."

"It was confusing as a child. As a teenager, I channelled all the hurt into being as obnoxious as I could." She picked up her tea. "I'm trying to find some middle ground with them as an adult. But I find it hard to talk about what's important."

"You're doing a fine job from where I'm standing."

"What I'm saying, or trying to, is that I want to make this work."

"Well that makes two of us, then."

Ally felt the promise; the look in his eyes warmed her bruised heart.

"Thanks for staying with me last night. I should have been more in-tune to the warning signs. I felt a bit sick coming back from Sydney—" she clamped her mouth shut, clearly incapable of finding a safe topic to discuss. She shovelled the eggs in her mouth, grateful for something to chew. "I felt it coming on during the week and it builds up if you're not careful."

"What do you do to ensure it doesn't get this bad?"

She was grateful that he brushed off her comment. She was too naked and way too comfortable with the idea of seeing him naked again to start flirting. The need to be filled had been a constant ache the past week. If Sydney was anything to go by, having sex with Owen would far surpass her expectations. But she wasn't in control of her emotions. She had to sort them out before she embarrassed herself by crying in his arms again.

"Ally?"

"Hmm?" She glanced at him and shifted. *Focus, Ally. Get a grip.* "Right. Sorry. Uhh. Migraine...my doctor has recommended anti-seizure drugs or even anti-depressants but I'm not a big fan of putting that stuff in my body." She finished off her toast next. "I usually use a cold compress or a heat pack. I turn off the lights at home, that sort of thing.

"If I take strong pain relief early on it can help. I normally get my neck adjusted at the physio or even a remedial massage, but things have been hectic of late. Report writing never fails to give me a bad back so I probably should book a massage soon."

"Really?"

She lowered her tea, swallowed.

"Owen."

"Consider this a free consult, without fees."

"That's what free means—hey, I don't want to consider any—"

He kneaded her shoulders and the protests died on her lips. He worked his way up to her neck, then to the base of her skull.

"You were saying?" His voice was low, hypnotic.

Ally closed her eyes, letting herself fantasise about those hands on her breasts. On her legs. Inside her.

She'd ask him to stop. She would. Any minute now.

The man had such glorious, skilled hands. He kneaded muscles that were tighter than she had expected.

"Is it working?"

"Mmm."

How was it that he both calmed and aroused her?

When he tugged the bathrobe down her shoulders, she froze.

"Owen. What are you doing?"

"I can't get at you with this thick robe. Relax. Have I taken advantage of you to date?"

Her cheeks burned. They both knew who had made the first move in Sydney. If only he knew what she was thinking.

She clutched the robe tighter. When it came to his touch, she was ravenous; always wanting more. Those hands on her exposed skin sent pulses of electricity across her breasts and down her stomach. She couldn't help but moan when he squeezed the nape of her neck. He threaded his fingers through her hair and massaged her scalp.

The tension she had woken up with had begun to fade. Instead, a new sensation burned inside her. A red, hot ball of lust shot through her body. Her breasts were heavy. Nipples hard.

"You keep making sounds like that and you're going to have more than just my hands on you."

Her eyes popped open. Owen stood in between her open legs. His jeans grazed against her naked thighs. All she wanted was to kiss him. Taste him. Finish what they started in Sydney.

"I'm like a teenager around you, Ally." He stroked her cheek.

"Owen."

"All I want to do is untie that robe and bury myself inside you. By the look in your eyes, I'd say you want that too."

"What look?"

She gripped his sweater, pulling him down. She had such a thirst for him.

Ally pressed herself closer, her tongue stroked his, matching need for need. His touch shook her resolve and broke down her reservations. With him, she could let go.

The peal of her ringtone startled them both. Her heart jack-hammered like a rabbit. She took her phone out of the pocket of her robe with unsteady hands.

"I have to take this." She could hear the resignation in her own voice.

He stepped back.

"Hey. I'm fine. Yes, I'm at Owen's place. He's been really, uhh...helpful." She ignored his grin. "Thanks for sorting it out, Sera, I owe you one. No, I can't...I don't have a car."

"I'll drop you."

"Hold on."

"I can drop you home if you need to go." He checked his watch. "It's nearly time for me to pick up Charlie from school so it's no problem. Unless I can convince you to stay?"

She bit her lip. "Okay. He'll drop me home. Thanks. I'll see you soon." Ally hung up. "The girls are coming over to stay this evening. But I'd be lying if I said I wasn't tempted by the offer."

"You probably need an early night, so we can take a rain check. Here, I'll clear up. You go and change." He took the plate from her then stopped her before she could leave. "Ally, I know that Sydney was just a taste of what's to come between us. It's all I can think about since we got home. But I told you I won't rush it."

"I know."

"What I'm trying to say is, you can always say no, and I won't take offence. We're in a relationship and I want to get to know you. I like you; I like what I've seen and heard and I want more of it. More of you. Whenever you're willing, however much you're willing to give. I'll take it all."

"I—"

He waited.

She shook her head. What could she say when the man left her heart full?

"I've never met a man like you before. But I want the same. Just in case you didn't know. I want it all, too."

She welcomed his tender kiss even as a whisper of fear crept inside her heart.

CHAPTER TWENTY-FIVE

*S*he had waited a day. A whole twenty-four hours, and then some before knocking on Owen's front door.

Sera and Maddie had distracted and pampered her all Friday afternoon and Saturday too. It was exactly what she needed to feel like her normal, healthy self again. But when she realised she had left her chronicle in Owen's car, she decided it was easier to just drive over and pick it up. It would be nothing more than a quick hello, pick up and goodbye. No big deal.

Plus, she wanted to see him again.

The phone call yesterday morning just wasn't enough.

She shifted the pot of herbs from hand to hand. So what if she brought a little thank you gift? That's what you did for your —what, boyfriend? She cringed at the word. Lover? It was more than just that…

Ally wiped her sweaty palms against her jacket and reminded herself not to overthink it. They hadn't really discussed labels or titles. Which was good. She wanted to take things slowly.

Then why was she shaking like a leaf?

As the seconds ticked by, she began to lose her nerve. She

presumed it was okay to just drop in, but what if Owen wanted a bit of space? Maybe that migraine spell left her with brain damage. Maybe she concussed her head and lost a couple of million brain cells resulting in dud tissue. That must be it.

She could just call and ask him to drop it off at the school in the morning.

Yes! Well done, dud cells. Great idea.

The door swung open before she could pivot. Owen's hair was damp, his sweater snug and his jeans, well, she shouldn't be looking down there anyway.

"Ally, hey." His smile was welcoming even if a little surprised. "Come on in. That for me?"

Her pulse scrambled. She thrust the plant at his chest and stepped into the warmth of the foyer.

"I forgot my chronicle."

"And you decided to exchange it for a plant?"

Her mouth twitched. "This is a thank you plant for the other day. I must have left the chronicle in your car. I didn't want to disturb your Sunday, but I need it for tomorrow."

It sounded like a lame excuse even to her ears.

"I've got it on the kitchen table. Eagle-eyed Charlie spotted it last night." He guided her inside. "We were contemplating dropping it over later this arvo."

Ally's shoulders lowered. "Is that so?"

"I wasn't sure if you were receptive to gentleman callers on a Sunday." He winked. "I was waiting for your move. Truth be told, I'm glad you couldn't resist. I'm told my appeal is very potent and far-reaching."

He bent his head to kiss her.

"Potent is it?" She stepped into him, accepting another kiss.

"Very."

"Then I'm glad I didn't call."

"I told you, I'm that magnetic you just couldn't keep away."

He tugged on her hand, leading her to the kitchen. "Feeling better?"

"Much. Thanks."

"Ms. McVeigh!" Charlotte's grin was quick. She bound around the counter in a blinged-out cooking apron. She saw the girl's eyes round slightly, noticing the way Owen's arm had slipped around her waist. Before she could move away, she felt a slight pressure, anchoring her to his side. The little girl's eyes sparkled.

"I just dropped by to grab my chronicle and say thanks for Friday." She spotted her planner on the table. "I'll just pick it up and get going."

"Are you feeling better, miss?" Charlotte played with the apron string. It had a massive unicorn on the front of it with her name alongside the rainbow above.

"Yes. Thank you for asking. You and your dad were very generous letting me stay."

"Headaches are the pits."

"They are. Okay, well, I'll let you get back to your weekend."

"Wait!" They said simultaneously.

Charlotte looked up at her dad, then back at her. "We were just about to make cookies, miss. My choc-apricot ones. Can you stay and help? You said you'd like to try them, remember?"

She hadn't expected the invitation—not from Charlotte at any rate.

"I should probably—"

"Pleeeaaase. It'll be so much fun!"

She glanced at Owen. "Your dad no doubt has work to do and I don't want to interrupt your baking time, but—"

"No interruption at all. In fact, I've got the whole day free." His smug smile proved that he was all too aware that he threw her in the deep end and was now watching her frantically tread water.

"I guess I could hang out for an hour or so."

Gutless. She was a gutless wonder. But she wanted to stay, so why fight it?

"Yes!" Charlotte clapped her hands and pulled her around the counter. "We have a spare apron, so you don't get your pretty top dirty. These are the best cookies ever, Ms. McVeigh, I promise!"

Ally glanced at Owen, who sat at the counter.

"After the last fiasco, I'm now not even allowed past the breakfast bar when the chef is baking. Apparently, I make a mess."

Her lips curved. "I remember."

She would take an hour out of her Sunday to bake cookies, and then she'd go home. It was only an hour. It couldn't hurt, right?

CHAPTER TWENTY-SIX

*I*t took only five minutes for Ally to shrug off her reserve and help Charlotte measure out her ingredients. The young girl's lively chatter chased away any of the trepidation she had felt at being in their home.

Even though her nerves had settled, she was still getting accustomed to the little touches that Owen would bestow upon her in front of his daughter. A squeeze of the waist. A brush of her hair. She didn't want to make Charlotte feel uncomfortable, but the girl barely batted an eyelid.

She was so hyped that after mixing a batch of her mother's cookies, she decided to experiment with one of her own. Ally was impressed by her knowledge of the chemistry behind baking. Their practical cooking class at school didn't give the students much of a chance to deviate from the set recipes, and she found the little baker was adventurous in her pairing of flavours; it wouldn't be long before she was teaching her a thing or two.

When the doorbell rang—to an odd rhythm—Charlotte and Owen turned to each other.

"Uncle Jack!" Charlotte squealed, running to the front door.

Owen called for her to follow. She reluctantly took off the apron. The door was flung wide open and Charlotte was clinging to her uncle like a baby koala bear.

"Hey, Big C!"

He put her down. "Gimme a twirl, little lady." Jack motioned with his hand. "You sure have grown. Gonna beat your old man soon enough."

The little lady in question exploded in chatter, stopping only when the timer beeped in the kitchen.

"Oven's ready! I'll pour them in the tins!" she called out, racing to the kitchen.

"Oven mitts, kiddo!" Owen called after her.

"I'll go," she offered.

"My kid. I'll go. Saying hello to this pretty boy can wait." Owen smirked, punching his brother lightly on the arm before leaving her alone with the Hollywood hunk.

His tanned movie-star face turned to her. His eyes—a lighter blue than Owen's—sized her up in the way only a confident man could. She wasn't sure whether she was flattered or offended.

"Please don't tell me you're hooked up to that ugly mug of a brother of mine? It'd break my heart."

Her mouth twitched. So maybe a little flattered.

"We..."

"Son of a bitch." Owen caught his brother in a bear hug. They slapped one another on the back, made male grunting noises and talked over each other.

"I was just wondering what a stunning woman like this lady is doing messing around with a dog like you."

Owen punched his shoulder. "Ignore my vain brother. The sunshine in Hollywood has given him delusions of grandeur."

"Call it as I see it." He stepped forward to shake her hand. "I'm Jack. But you can call me whatever you want."

"Ignore him."

"Ally."

She took his hand and tried not to stare. The similarities between them were clear. Both had the height thing going on and a smile that could melt butter. But where Owen was naturally broader in his shoulders, his hair a darker blonde; Jack was leaner and…dazzling was the word that came to mind. Perfect tan, sun-kissed blond hair and an all-star attitude to match.

His tailored "casual clothes" look of tan slacks and a V-neck cashmere sweater spoke of style and money. Yet his manner was easy and unpretentious. It was a potent combination.

"Easy tiger." Owen snaked an arm around her waist. "That's my partner you're hitting on. Ally and I met at Charlie's school. She's her coordinator."

Jack's grin widened. "School's certainly changed since we were kids. I'd have enjoyed the pleasure of your company at twelve, miss."

Owen reached out to cuff him on the back of the head. "Excuse my moronic brother. My parents ran out of the smart gene after I was born."

"Old man here is just sore 'coz he's as ugly as a witch's mole." Jack flicked his brother's nose. "Busted it once, can still bust it again."

Owen lunged and caught him in a headlock.

It was time to check on the little baker.

"Nice to meet ya, Ally." Jack called out, then grunted at Owen's well-placed blow to the stomach.

She stepped into the kitchen, greeted by the aroma of cinnamon and vanilla.

Partners. Well, that settled things then. It was a much better term than boyfriend that was for sure.

Charlotte skipped past her only to return a few seconds later; concern lined her small, angelic face.

"Ms. McVeigh? Why are Dad and Uncle Jack fighting?"

"They're brothers. It's what they do. In this case, it's a form of affection."

Her frown deepened.

"It's like how women complement each other or hug one another when they miss that person."

"Grabbing someone in a headlock is the boy version of a girl hug?"

Hmm.

"Sometimes. For some men. In this case, yes." She didn't think she'd have to explain male behaviour to a twelve-year-old. She crouched beside her. "Did either of them seem angry? Or in pain?"

Charlotte's eyes rolled upwards. A little line formed between her eyebrows. It was a replica of Owen's frown. And cute as hell. "No. Uncle Jack was laughing. Same as Dad."

"Well there you have it. If they were really fighting, I would have stepped in and made sure that they stopped, but they're messing around."

"Laura said her little brother jumps on her and tries to bite her. Like that?"

"Sort of. It's what happens when boys think wrestling is an acceptable form of showing affection, instead of using their words. It just adds to the male identity culture crisis we have in society—" Charlotte's eyes were wide. "Never mind."

Ally could sympathise as a fellow only child. If she hadn't witnessed Sera's brothers engage in this very ritual half a dozen times, she would have been shocked, and mildly concerned. She knew better than most to keep her distance until whatever grunting gene that embedded itself in every XY chromosome ran its course.

"They'll settle soon enough. Let's sort out this second batch of cookies while we're waiting. It smells divine."

Ten minutes later, both men entered the kitchen, twin grins

firmly in place, hair mussed. Their blue eyes shined with mischief.

Charlotte had barely put down the remaining batter before both men charged. Owen picked up his daughter, tickling her, whilst Jack stole the wooden spoon. Voice impersonations of the Cookie Monster bounced around the kitchen as each brother took turns at licking the batter. They carried her to the carpet, tickling her in turns.

Charlotte's breathless laughter echoed through the kitchen.

Ally's heart quivered. The fluttering sensation in her chest spread down to her fingertips. Heat raced along her spine, sending signals to her brain that had no right to be there.

She *couldn't*. She didn't. It wasn't possible.

Owen raised his head. Humorous blue eyes caught her in place.

Her heart sky-rocketed up and landed—heavy—in her chest. Owen barely had time to frown before he was tackled back to the ground by Charlotte and Jack.

His laughter rang out at the very moment she realised the truth; she was falling in love.

CHAPTER TWENTY-SEVEN

"*Y*ou can't just call up a man and ask for sex!"

"Why the hell not?" Maddie flicked her auburn hair back. "That's what I would do."

Sera rolled her eyes. "Not everyone is as easy as you."

Ally looked around the park, in case little kids were eavesdropping. She tugged Maddie closer and focused on keeping warm. She had barely taken off her jacket, when her friends had stopped by her apartment after work, eager to know what happened on Sunday.

She had slapped on a pair of trainers over her stockinged feet and bundled into her coat for a pre-dinner walk by the oval.

"I think the word you were looking for was "fierce." And it's not a booty call. She's in love with the man, for heaven's sake! And I think she needs to bang him to see whether those feelings are legit."

Sera tugged at her friend's braid. "Sure."

Ally intervened. "I told him I wanted to take it slow. Falling in love isn't exactly going slow. I've known him for what...nearly three months? Surely it's not love."

"When you know, you know. My parents knew within a few weeks and they've been married over thirty years," Sera added.

"I think they're an exception." Ally rubbed her hands together. Winter was proving to be particularly cold this year. "I prefer to just let things happen, naturally."

"Go the extra mile. What's sex when you've already got one another off? You know he's good in that department, so why aren't you riding him like a cowgirl and lassoing the big O?"

"Maddie!" Both Sera and Ally laughed.

"I wanted to take things slow."

"Slow, shmo. Things change. Sydney opened those floodgates, girl."

"But it was different then. I didn't feel this way two weeks ago. Falling for him changes everything. It wouldn't be just sex…"

"Then you're doing it right," Sera soothed. "Sometimes what we think we want and what we actually want are two different things. It's okay to move things along."

"It's scary, though." She pressed a hand against her chest. How was it she could feel utterly alive and petrified at the same time? "I'm sure it was written all over my face. I could tell Jack was analysing me like his next script that whole afternoon."

"Wait…*script*? Jack…Hollywood hunk, Jack Davies is Owen's *brother*?" Maddie slapped her hand on her head. "Why didn't I see it? They have that similar look about them."

"I thought you knew. I guess he doesn't make it public knowledge very often. You've seen his films?"

"Seen his films? We were in a stage production of *Hamlet* together—ages ago—before he went to America. It was when you were in Spain for the summer break, which is why you didn't meet him. Amazing stage actor."

She digested this new bit of information. It struck her sometimes, why certain people showed up at certain times in your life. If she hadn't visited on Sunday, she wouldn't have met Jack. Wouldn't have realised she was in love with Owen. Wouldn't be stressing about sex.

"How is he?"

"Who? Jack? What, you starred in the production of *Hamlet* too?"

"We met at the final wrap party after the play."

Ally studied Sera's face, cheeks glowing in the dusky cold. "Aaaand?"

"And nothing."

Maddie sniffed the air. "I smell a rat. Spill it, De Lotto."

"It was nothing…" She rolled her eyes. "Okay so we hooked up. No biggie. We were young. We spent a bit of time together over the break, then he left for America."

"You dated Jack Davies. How come I didn't know this?" Maddie prompted.

"You flew to Canada the week later. The two of you were off globe-trotting, and both Jack and I had time to spend together. It wasn't like he was famous back then. He was just…Jack." She shrugged.

"Aren't you the sly fox."

"Is he in town for long?"

"Not sure. He didn't really say. Though he's charming as all hell. It's no wonder you jumped him. He was pretty dazzling."

"I wouldn't know."

Maddie prodded her. "Wait—you haven't watched his films? His face is all over the internet."

"Nope."

"You really should. He was pretty hot back then, he's downright sex on legs now."

Ally shook her head. "Wow, you and Jack. Nice one, Sera. What else did I miss that summer?"

"Ancient history more like it. Can we get back to you and Owen?"

Maddie's mismatched eyes twinkled. They all knew she was in for a grilling later. "Sera's right. Back to the pressing matter of your sex life. Or lack of. You can all but brush the cobwebs from your lady garden, it's been that long."

"How the hell would you know?"

"Oh, sweetheart. I know. You want to bonk his brains out. You certainly know *he* wants to bonk yours. If I'm not mistaken, that's more than enough reason to do the deed."

"I don't want to stuff it up between us."

Sera stroked her hair back. "Don't get yourself worked up over it. Sex shouldn't be a stress. Freaking out about it is only going to make you more nervous."

"Take a leaf out of sneaking Sera's book."

"The *old* Sera. I'm a little more discerning these days, but yes, take a leaf. Take all the leaves."

"Are you going to go over there?" Maddie prodded.

"It's been two days since his brother arrived, Madds. I'm not just going to barge in and bonk his brains out. But when the timing is right, I'll be ready."

The girls cried out in glee and already began planning her seduction outfit.

Ally hugged the sensation close to her. Things were moving so much quicker than she had anticipated, but it was something she wanted.

She had spent most of her adult life denying her emotions, cutting herself off from loving relationships. Bloody hell, she had spent months convincing herself that a relationship with Owen wouldn't work, and now that they had begun dating, she was feeling more for him than she had thought possible. Despite the queasy sensation in the pit of her stomach, her heart knew that she was making the right decision.

She had relied so long on measuring things according to reason, to consequences, that now that she let herself go a little, she found it was difficult to rein it all in.

Owen had unlocked a part of her she thought didn't exist. She had the capacity to love. The question was, what, if anything, was she going to do about it.

CHAPTER TWENTY-EIGHT

"*S*o..."

Owen shook his head and sipped the cold beer. His brother's smile was a mile wide.

When Rebecca was still alive, they would sit on the roof of their old home, whilst the girls were asleep and chew the fat. Ever since Jack moved to America, they kept up the ritual whenever he was in town. Whilst the house had changed and so had their lives, they always managed to slip back into the habit as if it were yesterday.

Even though Jack had only been with them a week, the paparazzi hounds had sniffed him out. They sat on the back porch, away from the flashing lights and distractions. He couldn't fathom how his brother was used to all that attention. All that noise. Give him his anonymity and peace any day of the week.

Owen drew the blanket around his shoulders and leaned back, comfortably full. Ally had come over that afternoon for a Sunday roast. Followed by a ridiculously good apple pie. He hadn't been this relaxed in a long time. After spending the afternoon listening to Jack's escapades in Hollywood, his brother had taken Charlie out in the backyard to shoot some hoops whilst he spent a little time with Ally.

Now that the longest term known to man was over and the two week school break was upon them, Owen was excited to progress their relationship. To spend time together as a proper couple.

They had developed a nice rhythm, but still he wanted more.

Even though she would be busy working for most of the break, they made plans to hang out when she wasn't marking or catching up with admin. He was greedy for her company. Not that she'd have much time available if Charlie had her way. The kid was already planning a list of recipes they would bake together. No dads allowed.

He thought about how easily Ally fit in their family. How happy Charlie was having her in their lives. And with every phone call, every shared meal, he sensed her fears fading.

Owen sipped at his beer. The pieces of his life were finally coming together. All except one.

He glanced at Jack, who seemed eager to hound him about his relationship whenever he had the chance. Tonight would be no different. Not that he had revealed much. Work was busier than ever now that the Sydney deal had gone through. It hadn't left him much down time. Not that he was complaining.

"Go on, little brother, out with it."

"Sunday roast with the school-teacher. Serious vibes there. Can't blame you, when she looks like that and is smart to boot." Jack raised his bottle in a toast. "No doubt a killer in the sack, too."

"That's none of your business."

Jack paused mid-swig. "Wait a minute. You *have* done the dirty together, right?"

"Not exactly."

"Ahh. Now *that* sounds more like my brother. What's wrong, can't get it up, old man?"

"Smart-arse. Still got that mouth on you."

"Ladies love it."

"It's gonna get you in trouble one day."

"You always were a smarmy know-it-all...so are you going to tell me why you haven't had sex yet? Jesus, do I have to beat it out of you?"

Owen hunched his shoulders and ignored him. "I like her, Jack. I mean, *really* like this woman."

"But?"

"But she's...cautious. She keeps this protective layer around herself and finds it hard to open up."

"That sounds like a man deprived of sex."

"I don't mean sex, dickhead."

"That's the spirit." Jack's eyes crinkled at the corners. "She likes you just as much, you know."

"Christ, that sounds so high school."

"I know when a woman is hot for me. And that school teacher of yours only has eyes for you, brother. A woman who looks like that, who is that comfortable around Big C...well, you'd be mad to let her get away."

Owen stared at his brother. "Now who's been abducted? All that peroxide get to your brain, pretty boy?"

"I'm a natural blond, thank you. A rarity in Hollywood. Hey, you know me, I call it as it is. You've never been the bed and break-for-it type anyway."

"There's gotta be more than just skin on skin."

Jack's sigh was gusty. "I know. Much to my disappointment and the ladies I tried to set you up with...more for me."

He cringed. "God, I remember that. Stacey? Stephanie?"

Jack choked on his beer. "Fuck. Stephanie Rollard. She was convinced you were gay."

"I appreciated the effort."

"I know it. Great body doesn't guarantee great sex."

He grimaced. "Mate, that's crass even for your standards."

"That's Hollywood. Just because you own a fancy car—"

"Doesn't mean you can drive it. Yeah, yeah. It isn't that I don't want sex with Ally. It's more than that. It's…I want to know *her*—hopes, fears, dreams—everything."

"You can woo her and get to know her all you want. What I want to know is when you're gonna get horizontal."

"It's complicated."

"I invented "it's complicated." I'm gonna get us a couple more beers and you can educate me."

With the beers flowing and his tongue loose, Owen moved from the events in Sydney with Ally to the mediation trouble on his hands. His feet were cold, but the beer and his underlying anger at the Langdons had warmed him right up.

"Shit, you wait 'til now to tell me this? I've been here a week…this has been going on for months!"

"Don't get your briefs in a twist. I'm telling you now, aren't I?"

"Jesus, those bastards are really low."

"From day dot."

"I've got this lawyer—"

"Marcus is handling it."

Jack ran his tongue over his teeth. Anger turned his voice to steel. "They mess with Charlotte, they mess with me."

Owen put down his beer, his stomach turning over at the thought of what he could possibly lose. Then anger, quick as fire on gunpowder took its place. "Easy, tiger. They'll have to go through me first. We're going to mediation as they want custody, which Marcus tells me shouldn't happen as I'm her father." He explained the document he had signed before Rebecca's death.

"Fucking hell."

"I'm telling you, because I'd appreciate it if you'd hang out with Charlie that day. I'm trying to keep all this shit away from her, but the girl has ears and a good, solid brain."

"She's sharp as an arrow. Got that from her uncle." Jack smacked his brother up the side of the head. "You can bet she already knows the gist of it, idiot."

"No." His jaw was firm. Mouth hard. "I made sure to keep it all on the down-low."

"She may not know the particulars, but you can bet that girl knows something is fishy. Especially after the stunt they pulled with the ice cream. Fuckers are testing you."

"I'll let her know if something comes up and it's unavoidable. For now, I think we can assume she's none the wiser."

"I think that's a mistake, but it's your call. Is there anything you want me to do? Other than take care of Big C?"

"No, I've got this under wraps. Marcus tells me that they're demanding full custody and will likely stop at nothing to prove I'm an unfit parent—"

"What the fuck?" Jack leapt up and paced.

"They're apparently building a case."

"This is beyond ridiculous, Owen. What a waste of fucking time and energy."

He rubbed his fingers together. "Money. They have it and are sure as hell going to spend it if it means they can get their way."

He watched Jack pace back and forth.

"I have money. Loads of the stuff. You can take it. Take all of it. I'll make more. Christ almighty, I wish I didn't give up smoking right now."

He saw the moment that danger leapt into his eyes, turning all that charm to ice. It was no wonder he was in such hot demand in the film industry.

"Easy, brother. Once Marcus finalises this big case he's working on, things will move fast. All I need to know is you'll help out with Charlie."

"I've given you my word. But how can you be so matter of fact about it? So calm?"

"Trust me, I was worse when I first found out. Nearly chewed Marcus a new one. But I've had time to process it. And if it's a fight they want, you can bet all that American money of yours, that they'll be getting it."

"Wait—Marcus. Marcus Kinsey? Christ, Owen you need a proper lawyer. A shark. He'll get pissed on. Let me hook you up with my guy."

"What's an international lawyer going to do to help a custody case, Jack?"

"Not him. His brother. Family law expert extraordinaire."

"In America."

"In the world. Trust me. I'll give you Edward's number and he'll get John Shellman in your corner. It doesn't hurt to have friends in high places. We sure as hell weren't raised to rely on favours to get success, but these people, this system, it's all about who you know and how good they are, that counts. You might not like it, but you know it's true."

He didn't. But he also wasn't naïve. He knew Jack was right. Better to have an ace up his sleeve in case the hand was crummy.

"Sure. Send me his details."

Jack clapped him on the back and reached for his phone. "He owes me one anyway."

Whilst he didn't have access to a great deal of money, he'd been building enough capital, working enough over-time in his business to take this fight as far as he could. Hell, he'd sell the damn house, the business—everything—to make sure their spite didn't tear his family apart.

If they wanted Charlie, they'd have to go through him first to get her.

Ally hadn't thought twice about buying Charlotte the present. When she had been dragged by Maddie and Sera to the city for an impromptu shopping trip in the second week of the holidays, she couldn't resist. She spotted the delicate silver locket in a small jewellery store in the heart of the CBD. Naturally she bought the thing silver chain to match. A girl couldn't have enough pretty things at that age.

Not that she was any better. The girls had convinced her to buy a cute date-night dress, a new pair of jeans and half a dozen blouses that she would normally talk herself out of purchasing had she been alone. Which was rare these days. When she wasn't working, she was spending her free time with Owen and Charlotte. She couldn't be happier.

They had used her new relationship status to drill her for any nitty gritty details throughout the day; namely whether they had sealed the deal yet.

Much to Maddie's dismay, the closest thing she had come to an increased heart rate of late, was their six-hour hike over the weekend. Owen had packed a picnic, Charlotte had baked the cookies and they all devoured every bit of food as they sat along the river upon their return. Hardly a raunchy romp in the sack.

Not that she minded. She loved spending time as a unit: going to the movies, baking with Charlotte, the odd dinner out with Owen. Having Jack stay with his brother meant that they could spend a bit of time as a couple.

The few times that Jack went out with them, Ally found herself followed by paparazzi. She didn't know how he lived his life in such public scrutiny. She found it intolerable. As did Owen. Charlotte on the other hand, hadn't minded one bit. Her new friends had thought it was the coolest thing in the world that her Hollywood uncle was staying with them.

Ally parked her car outside their driveway on her trip back

from the city, relieved that any lurking photographers had fled. She hefted her haul into the house.

If Owen had been surprised by the number of items she had purchased, he didn't say a word. But she hadn't missed the way his blue eyes bulged out of his head.

She dumped her stuff on the sofa and leaned back, groaning as she slipped off her shoes.

"My feet are still killing me from that death walk on the weekend."

"Mine too." Charlotte looked up from the book she was reading. "I convinced Dad that we order a pizza to make up for it."

Ally high-fived her before settling back against the cushions.

"A successful shopping trip, I see." Owen sat on the opposite sofa, propping his feet on the coffee table. "Anything in those bags for the man of your dreams?"

"Jack? No, he'd be too difficult to shop for." She winked at Charlotte, laughing when the pillow sailed across the room, catching her square in the face.

His pout was almost worth it.

"Boys."

"Tell me about it. For your information, boy-o, I did buy you something, but you'll just have to wait." She turned to Charlotte. "I saw this in the jewellery store, and I thought you might like it."

She watched her rip open the packaging, uncertain if she had made the right choice. Her squeal of delight was a welcome sound.

"Oh! Miss McVeigh, I love it!" She launched herself into her arms, crushing the bags between them on the sofa.

"Really? You're not just saying it?"

"No, it's gorgeous!"

"I thought you might want to put a picture of your mum in the locket, to have her close to you wherever you are."

Charlotte's eyes shimmered, but she sniffed back the tears. "I think it's perfect, miss."

"I'm so happy you like it. But how do you feel about calling me Ally? Or whatever you like when we're outside of school. What do you think?"

She beamed. "Sounds good. Hey, mind if I go find a picture?"

"Sure thing, though we can re-size any image you like to fit it specifically. That way you won't need to cut up your photos."

"Cool! I'm going to go try it on, and then can we watch the *Baking Championships*?"

"We can...though we might want to watch it after this..." Ally reached into another bag and pulled out a series on baking in the 1900s. They had both been dying to watch it.

The young girl squealed again. "You found it?"

"You bet."

"You're the best, Ally! Don't move, I'll be back in a minute!"

She leaned back, pleased with her efforts.

It was odd how she seemed to fit in their lives with such ease. They had both made room for her in their own way.

They were forming a new dynamic; one wholly alien to her, but also vital. Despite her reservations, Owen never pressured her to change pace. She was struck by how very different her life had become over the past three months.

The sofa sagged beside her. Owen sat down, shifting her thoughts and a few bags between them. He raised an eyebrow.

"What? What is it?"

He drew her close. "You were away with the fairies for a second. Don't look so alarmed, nothing's wrong. You smashed it out of the park with the locket. Charlie loves it. Trust me, I've spent years getting it wrong to know when she's trying to be polite and I can tell she's touched by your gift. I'm sure she's upstairs pulling apart all her albums and texting her friends."

"I'm glad. When you told me about the photos of Rebecca, I

thought it would be nice for her to feel connected to her mum all the time. Wherever she is."

"Like I said. Really thoughtful."

"Thanks."

He frowned. "But I do have a problem."

"Oh? And what's that then?"

"I think it's time that I got my present, don't you? I'm feeling a little left out."

He dragged her onto his lap, just as she reached for two bags.

"You'll be pleased to know that you get two gifts."

"Aren't I a lucky boy."

He very well would be if she had her way. She handed him the first bag.

His eyes lit up. "The new Edwardson novel? I didn't think it was out yet."

"It's hot off the press apparently."

She welcomed his kiss, then pulled back. She'd prefer if Charlotte didn't get a glimpse of the next present.

"Gift number two. Let's just say it's more of a present for us."

Owen opened the bag and unwrapped the tissue paper. When the scrap of red lace emerged, Ally bit her lip. The look on his face was priceless.

She leaned closer. "I thought maybe we could gift ourselves this little number in the near future. But only if you're a good boy."

Owen's eyes darkened. "Yes. Hell yes. You just say when, miss." He gripped her waist and nibbled at her lips. When his hands reached up to brush against her breasts, she wound herself around him, teasing with her tongue until she felt him stirring beneath her.

"Now?" He ground out.

She laughed, moving out of his arms and back on her side of the sofa. "Easy, tiger."

"When?"

"Soon. Real soon."

Owen kissed her again. It was a caress, a sweet promise. They both drew back when they heard the retching sounds from behind them.

"Honestly, Dad." Charlotte said, throwing herself down on the sofa. "Stop distracting Ally. We have a baking championship to watch."

CHAPTER TWENTY-NINE

*A*lly glared at her computer screen and the thirty emails all marked important. She had barely begun to address two. She smoothed back the strands of hair that had snuck out of place and wished she could rewind time.

Another Wednesday. Another manic day. Added to the pressure was the prep she'd need to do for her approved leave. Her father's surgery was in a little over a week. Even though she'd booked in the best nurse to care for him at home, she would take a few days of leave to help him adjust in his transition home from the hospital. Which meant even more work when she returned.

Whilst the new semester had started well, it had taken only a few mishaps for her to feel like she was back at square one. Not to mention behind in every task she had set. Before she had time to catch her breath, they were halfway through the term with no signs of slowing down.

She'd need to start pulling some late nights if she had any hope in finishing before the next century. Which meant a little less fun time on the weekends. That wouldn't have been a problem four months ago. But now all she wanted to do was spend time with Owen. She pressed a hand against her chest. If she thought about her feelings for him for too long, she'd freak out.

She hadn't expected to fall so hard, so fast.

She checked her phone again, knowing he would be back this time tomorrow. He had spent the past few weeks travelling back and forth between Melbourne and Sydney to secure a deal with another established company. His business was growing, and she knew how important it was for him to be able to support his family.

It was yet another thing she had learned in their time together. That, and he stubbornly refused to talk about the custody case. No matter how many times she broached the subject, he shut down. He wanted to handle it, and that included when he told his daughter. She had hoped that this new American lawyer would make him see sense. But he wouldn't budge. He would only tell Charlotte when he was ready.

It wasn't her call. She understood that. She'd never want to pressure him when he was so patient with her. Especially when the thought of losing his daughter caused him so much pain. It didn't bear thinking about.

Even though she missed him when he was away, his absence had given her a chance to spend a lot more time with Charlotte. Their relationship had developed beyond just their shared interests; she was beginning to seek her advice, to talk about what worried her. It was a good sign. Even if it did make her second-guess her ability as a parent, she was happy they were making progress.

Ally focused on the next email. Now was not the time to give in to her doubts; she had too much work to do. Applications for next year's leadership positions would open soon. If she wanted to be reappointed in this role, she needed to ensure she hit her targets. She had managed to make some changes, but it wasn't enough.

She was lost in thought when Charlotte ran into her office, tears streaming down her face.

"What's happened? Are you okay?"

"It was my fault," she sobbed.

Ally stood. "Come into the spare room, and we can chat." She guided her past the small group of students that had begun to trickle in to pick up confiscated items or sit their detention. The ten or fifteen minutes of the after-school rush was always busy, but she was becoming accustomed to blocking out the noise and chatter. She'd never get a thing done if she kept getting drawn into the conversations.

Charlotte's outburst wasn't surprising. They'd had a fundraiser for the Cancer Council this afternoon, and whilst she had checked in, Ally knew it was only time before those emotions surfaced. Sitting down in the chair opposite, she waited for the little girl to settle.

"What's your fault?"

"It's my fault that Mamma died. I wished for them to stop arguing. I prayed to God for them to stop and to take it all away, and he did. He took Mum away and punished me and Dad because I was bad. Grandma and Grandpa say it's his fault she died but it isn't. They don't know I'm to blame."

She wept with all the heartache of a child who had the weight of the world on her shoulders.

"Today has been a big day for you. Lots of emotions, which is perfectly normal. But it isn't true."

"It *is* true," she wailed.

Ally held her, rubbing her back in big soothing sweeps. She knew she wouldn't get much of an explanation if she didn't let the tears run their course. Her heart bled.

This little girl deserved to have a mother who made her feel safe and supported. The bond she had developed with Charlotte was growing stronger, as was her fondness for her. But that didn't necessarily qualify her to be a mother. She had no idea what it meant to be a good parent. What could she offer a small child? She hadn't even sorted out issues she had with her own parents.

"I know without a doubt that you are not responsible for your mother's death. She had cancer; from what you dad told me, she had it when she was a little girl, but fought it. She thought she'd be cancer-free, but it came back again, and it was nastier than before. Your parents didn't want to worry you with all the details, especially as you were very young when the cancer came back."

"But I—"

"No. No amount of wishing that your parents would stop fighting could change that. Parents fight. It happens."

"But they were—they were going to get a d-d-divorce," she sobbed.

"Maybe they were, but that doesn't mean that it's your fault or that it happened because you wished they stopped arguing. I know what that's like."

She had wished she had someone to go to for advice as a child, especially when she felt so alone, and somehow at fault for her parents' acrimonious marriage.

"My parents used to fight a lot when I was your age. It really got me down. I used to think that if I was a little bit smarter, a little bit braver, or prettier or better that they would stop arguing and be happy. It took me a long time to realise that their unhappiness wasn't my fault. Just like your mum's cancer or your parents' arguments weren't your fault."

No matter how many times she had told herself this over the years, something deep down had rejected it. Somehow telling Charlotte brought it all into sharp focus.

She was never responsible for her parents' misery. She had carried theirs around deep inside of her for so long that she hadn't realised, really realised that she wasn't to blame. She couldn't change it. For so long she tried not to wallow, but maybe she needed to—instead of shoving aside the misery and burying it deep, perhaps she needed to remember. To give it a voice. To let it go.

She hugged Charlotte tighter, hands trembling.

"How do you know?"

"No one caused her cancer—not your mum, not your dad, and certainly not yourself. It just happens sometimes—it's awful and heartbreaking, but what I know without a doubt is that she wouldn't want you to blame yourself."

"But that's what Grandma and Grandpa think. They think my dad killed her."

"I'm sure they don't."

"They do. They told me," she whispered.

Curses hovered on her tongue. She swallowed them with difficulty. What gave them the right to twist a child's innocence that way? To poison her mind with lies?

"Sometimes grief can make people say things that aren't very nice. I don't think they meant it literally. Your dad didn't kill your mum. It was an unfortunate circumstance, and a tragedy that you had to lose her so young. But it was nobody's fault.

"That's why fundraisers like today's one is so important. We've raised so much money that will help so many people. That's a good, solid thing. It's hard sometimes to remember those we've lost, but your mum will always be beside you. You just have to think about her and she's there. She'll be watching over you, always."

"Ally? I mean, Ms. McVeigh? You're the best teacher ever. And…well, you'd make a really good mum. I just wanted to say that. But…can you promise not to tell my dad?"

She swallowed against the lump in her throat. She was sure the little girl could hear her heart thumping. "Thanks, kiddo.

That's sweet of you to say. But I have to let your dad know. Just like I need to tell Mr. Taylor for your next session. This is big stuff that's been weighing you down. We can't keep it between ourselves."

"Well can you wait, then? Please? I want to tell Dad on my own. I don't want him to yell at Grandma and Grandpa. Please." Tears welled in her eyes; her voice shook.

"I'm sorry, sweetheart, but I have to say something."

"Did you tell your parents? About them fighting?"

The vibration of guilt resounded low in her belly. She was giving advice to a little girl that she hadn't taken herself. "It's complicated."

"You totally understand then. I know he'll be upset at me for not telling him ages ago. Please, Ally. He comes home tomorrow night. Let me tell him first."

"How about this? I'll chat to my parents if you chat to your dad ASAP. I'll give you the next few days, but after that, I have to let him know. In the meantime, I'll talk to Mr. Taylor and maybe he can help us speak to your dad. He won't be mad, Charlotte. He'll be concerned, but not angry. Those are two different emotions. Deal?"

"Deal."

She didn't analyse her guilt too closely. She would talk to Owen about this. It was her duty of care to do so—and a personal priority. Charlotte's wellbeing was paramount.

What harm would there be in waiting a few more days?

CHAPTER THIRTY

*O*wen waited in the small, windowless room of the courthouse. It had been less than twenty-four hours since he returned from his business trip, tired from travel and wanting nothing more than a break, when reality had kicked in.

He had tried to put the upcoming mediation out of his head, to not to think about it; but as he waited for his lawyer to come back in the room, he wished he had mentally prepared. He couldn't believe he was in this position. That this day had come.

He tapped the pencil against the edge of the square table. He knew they'd throw their weight and money at him. That was always the way with Henry and Anita. But Christ, he wished it didn't have to be this way.

His in-laws loved Charlie—he knew that—and because of it, he endured the disapproval from them; their belief that he was a failure as a father, a provider and a husband.

It would be a cold day in hell before he gave in to their bullshit.

He sat up when John re-entered.

"Owen, let me go through this one more time." John Shellman's American accent was tinged with flavours of the world.

The man was in his late fifties and looked at least ten years younger despite his profession. He had been so confident and had shown a depth of knowledge about custody cases, that Owen knew in his gut he had made the right decision. John outlined the Langdons' position, all the while exuding an air of calm assurance. "You know they're still threatening full custody."

"Yes. I've told you where I stand on this."

"I do. And you know they're using this guardianship claim to taint your case?"

"Which never saw the light of day!" Owen lost his temper. "This is a waste of time."

"It is. We know this. And I'm sorry to say they're playing dirty. You're the surviving parent. You've provided a stable and loving home for your child. Short of great abuse or even negligence, it will be difficult for them to make this claim stick. I will make damn well sure that this mediation gets settled with as little pain to you as possible, so we don't go before the judge."

Owen shook his head. "This is ridiculous. I'm not agreeing to full custody."

"For argument's sake, what about 50/50?"

"No way. I'm Charlotte's father. I've given them access to her and haven't kept her from seeing them. What I don't appreciate is their entitled assumption that they have a right to her."

"Good. Stay firm to this. Mediation can get messy and being cooped up in this coffin of a room can break even the most well-intentioned men. I'll be moving back and forth with their council, coming to you with their offers. I've already pre-empted all their claims. I've seen this a thousand times over. But to you, this is all new. Know this, Owen. I'm on your side. I'm your council. I might come back with offers that are repulsive to you, but it's all about wearing them down."

"They're out for blood. They're not going to be accepting a half bargain."

"Let me handle them. You sit tight. Your brother will be here soon."

He sat back and clenched his fist. No doubt they were sitting in a similar boxed up room with their big-shot lawyer, gloating. *Focus, Owen.* He ran an unsteady hand across his jaw. What would he agree to? They already had access every second weekend. Part of the holidays. Maybe he could increase that...and then what?

Everything was always on their terms. Nothing had changed over the years. He assumed Charlie wouldn't mind seeing them, but he needed to have that conversation with her. He rubbed his hands over his face. Ally had been right. It was stupid of him to have kept this all a secret from her. His little girl was growing up, establishing her own friendship groups, pursuing her own interests. She had as much a say in this as her grandparents.

He would mention that to John. If he could get some time to talk to her, break it to her gently, maybe it would work out.

He laid out his terms on the sheet of paper in front of him, biting his tongue. He was certain, no matter how sad Rebecca was about their marriage failing, that she wouldn't have wanted this.

John came back in the room thirty minutes later. "They won't budge on 50/50."

Owen passed him the sheet of paper. "These are my terms. Take it or leave it."

And so it went, for hours. His lawyer cajoled, calmed and implored him to be patient.

In the end, they wouldn't agree to his terms, intent on proving that he was an unfit parent. Intent on taking this before the judge.

After hours of sitting in that cramped room, Owen's muscles were tight, his head pounding. He had sent Jack to pick up

Charlie, who had spent the Curriculum Day off school with Holly.

His brother had insisted that he take her up to the mountains for the weekend, sensing he'd need some space after being in court all day. He wasn't wrong. Owen made up his mind to tell Charlie the truth when she returned. He just needed to figure out how to do it.

Henry and Anita wanted custody and it wasn't something he would ever accept. What angered him was their disregard for Charlie's wellbeing. They had no understanding of how this would crush her. He supposed they hadn't understood Rebecca all those years ago either.

Owen walked out feeling frustrated. A tiny part of him had hoped they would be able to come to an agreement and move on. But the day's failed proceedings meant they needed to take it to the next level.

John reassured him that going before the judge might work in his favour. Their claims of negligent parenting were spurious. It was now just a waiting game until they could be seen in family court.

Despite John's confidence, Owen was certain going to court was a mistake. If they couldn't agree that he was the sole caregiver now, what would standing before a judge prove? Other than cause emotional turmoil for his family—not to mention leave a big hole in his earnings. Not that that mattered to the Langdons. They wouldn't spare any expense to get what they wanted.

A shiver ran through him, turning his blood cold. He punched in Jack's number and headed to his car. He needed to speak to his daughter before they went camping; he wanted to hear she was okay.

It was more for his bruised heart than anything else.

Ally didn't know what had possessed her to stop by. Or why she needed to bake cookies. That wasn't true. Something was off. She had sensed it when she spoke to Owen on the phone yesterday evening. He had sounded weary and...she couldn't put her finger on it. She just knew she had to see him. It didn't help that the gnawing guilt in her gut hadn't abated.

Charlotte's admission a few days before had plagued her. She hoped that the day off school today had given her a chance to tell her dad. If anything, it might help his custody case to know exactly what his in-laws had been saying. It was a relief that there had been no other incidents with the Langdons, but that didn't mean they could be trusted.

She wasn't familiar with the mediation process, but she could only imagine it would be difficult to handle. She could only hope to offer him comfort when the time came. To support him through the process, regardless of the outcome.

She rang the bell and waited.

Leaving the Tupperware container on the porch, she patted her pockets for her phone, about to send a quick text, when Owen's car pulled into the driveway.

He slammed the door, stalking up the path in long strides. Tension vibrated around him in palpable waves. Ally noted the set of his mouth and the scowl marring his usually carefree face. He climbed the stairs and stopped.

Charlotte wasn't with him. Neither was Jack.

"Are you okay?" She took a tentative step forward.

"Crappy day."

"Looks it." His eyes didn't leave her face, not for a moment. The scowl was replaced with a look that left her mouth dry, and her body tingling. A look that spoke of promises and desires that she craved but feared. She focused on the rain.

"You should probably get inside. You're getting the brunt of that." She gestured behind him. "I baked brownies. We had a Curriculum Day. You know that. Anyway, I wanted to talk to

Charlotte. And you. There's a few things we need to discuss about—"

The kiss was greedy, almost unrestrained with need. It was like being struck by lightning, she thought briefly, before succumbing to the downpour of sensations.

Owen tugged her against him and propelled them both up against the front door. He stroked, teased and raced over her in a glorious promise of what was to come.

She gasped when his mouth found the sensitive spot beneath her ear.

"Ally...I want you."

Her voice was unsteady. "Owen..." In it she heard her own desperation. She fisted her hands through his hair. His mouth curved against her neck, teeth scraping her earlobe. "Wait...wait."

His eyes were stormy, his hands firm against her hips. "What's wrong?"

"What about Charlotte?"

"Jack's taken her camping for the weekend."

"But—"

"Do you want this? Forget about everything else for a damn minute and tell me. Do you want me? If you come inside, I'm going to finish what we started in Sydney."

She swallowed. "I—"

"Do you?"

Her body tingled. "Yes. Owen, yes I want you."

"That's settled then."

She suppressed her protests when he swept her off her feet and carried her inside. She couldn't resist him, even if she tried. At that moment, she didn't want to try at all.

CHAPTER THIRTY-ONE

*W*ith each step upstairs she could sense Owen's anger fading. His eyes clouded over—a storm across the bright blue sky. Whatever it was that troubled him seemed to disappear. Or at least was channelled into his need. For her.

He placed her gently on his bed. The room smelled of him. She was surrounded and enticed by it, wanting more.

With slow but careful movements, he undressed her, replacing her clothes with his mouth. All thought flew from her brain. It was like he was feasting on her body, savouring every morsel.

He touched her like she was the most sacred thing in the world. He touched her in a way that marked her heart and body, wrapping those ribbons of lust with love, so entirely, that she was bound to him on every level. Her eyes stung. Who knew that her love for him was so encompassing?

He nibbled up the column of her throat, stroking her breasts. His groan sent a quiver of need straight through her. The sound was so elemental, so appreciative that Ally stifled a smile. She reached for him when the fever reached its pitch. His mouth crushed hers, then lowered further, latching on to her breast. She cried out, vision blurring.

With teeth and tongue, he drove her to the edge of pleasure, building the layers of lust with deft, gentle hands.

"Owen—please, I can't stand it."

He arched over her, a satisfied smile on his face then shifted lower.

He travelled over her naked thighs and found her wet and willing. Shivers of expectation coursed through her. When his tongue moved over her clit, her body tensed, then went limp. Sensation after sensation flowed through her. She couldn't quite catch her breath.

Gripping his hair, she bucked beneath him, but still he held her in place, punishing her until she shattered. Before she could cry out, she had peaked, the orgasm rushing through her.

Owen's lips curved against her hip.

"That, Ms. McVeigh, was handled very well."

Her laugh was breathless. But she craved his naked body against her own. Chest to chest. Joined completely. He ripped off his sweater and pants. She wasted no time in exploring the smooth bands of muscle at his shoulders. She raked her fingers down his abdomen, until she found him, hard and proud. She stroked slowly, revelling in the satisfied growls that he couldn't seem to contain.

His hips jerked, but his hand caught her wrist. "Not yet."

"I want you inside me." She touched him again, delighting in his length.

His laboured breathing urged her on. He reared back. "Ally. You're driving me insane."

His eyes spoke of more than lust. It was a storm of emotions, a terrifying force, meant for her.

"Now," she urged, rubbing against him.

Ripping open the packet, Owen covered himself. Tilting her

hips, he entered her slowly, rocking by gentle degrees until she had taken him all in. Ally shivered at the intrusion.

His body was hard as marble and beginning to pulse with apparent restraint.

"Are you okay?"

She'd never be the same because of this man. She was greedy for everything he could give her, greedier still for the dreams she had long denied herself. Dreams that seemed possible now with him.

"Yes," she whispered, wrapping her legs around his waist.

His mouth found hers, and he set a slow, torturous pace. When they both were slick and shaking, he took them higher.

"Ally."

The sensation of her breasts brushing against his chest drove her to the edge, she clawed at his back, desperate for more. His control snapped; the rhythm matched the frenetic pounding of her heart. With every thrust, she teetered on the edge.

The sound of his pleasure was a greater turn on than anything she'd experienced before. She was at his mercy.

"Owen..."

When he pinched her nipple, the tension that had coiled inside of her snapped. She shuddered, clenching around him as she came. His own release followed.

Sweaty and sated, he held her close. She ran her fingers in lazy, long strokes down his back, revelling in the weight of him. She couldn't wipe the grin off her face.

"Ally...that was..."

"Yep." She giggled. He looked stunned.

"We should do that a lot. I'd have no objections. In case you were wondering."

Owen pulled up the throw at the base of the bed. His quick, boy-ish grin had her floating up to the ceiling.

She relaxed under his touch; his fingers tracing her shoulder, the outline of her mouth, her nose, soothing her by degrees.

She didn't fight the sleep that blanketed her moments later. She was too sated to care.

Ally woke to a rumbling stomach, with Owen's warm, blue eyes on her. She rubbed at her face self-consciously.

"How long have you been awake for?"

"Long enough to know you look like an angel when you sleep." He trailed a hand up her thigh. "A very sexy one."

Heat flooded her cheeks. "I'm a mess."

"Nope."

"I have bed hair."

"Wrong again. You're perfect."

The monstrous rumbling from her stomach cut her retaliation short.

She cringed. "That was definitely not angelic or sexy."

"I wish my stomach could speak Klingon as well as yours. I was thinking I could cook us up some pasta. Open a bottle of wine. Sit in front of the fire."

As the rain hammered down outside, she looked at the man whom she loved, knowing she wouldn't be the same again. Which suited her just fine.

"Sounds perfect."

The look of pure happiness on his face made her throat close over.

His eyes suddenly turned mischievous. "I'm getting pretty hungry myself."

"Is that right?"

He stirred.

"Yes, miss. In fact, I'm starving all of a sudden."

She arched above him. When he was rock hard and straining against her hand, she dipped her head and took him in her mouth. Ally moved slowly down his length, breathing in his musky scent, enjoying the sounds of his pleasure.

Yearning to be filled, she sat up, licking her lips. Straddling his legs, she guided him inside her wet centre.

"Well, Mr. Davies, I think I can whip us up a meal that we'd both enjoy."

An hour later, showered and wrapped in a fluffy bathrobe, Ally followed her nose downstairs to the kitchen. The smell of Owen's carbonara sauce had her stomach rumbling again.

"Glass of wine?" He pointed to the bottle of Pinot Grigio on the counter. "There's chardonnay in the bar fridge if you prefer."

"Pinot is great. Thanks."

She poured them both a glass and motioned to the salad on the table. "You really work fast."

"Wait until you taste the food, then you can praise me."

"Anything I can do?"

"Yep. Sit back and watch me make garlic bread."

Ally did as instructed. The combination of good wine and great sex had left her body tingling. She was in a languid state of bliss.

Owen chopped garlic and parsley, checking on the pasta every now and then, regaling her with stories of his childhood. She hadn't laughed as much with a man in...forever.

She was about to bring up her conversation with Charlotte, when the phone rang. The easy expression on his face disappeared in an instant.

"I appreciate the call, but I can't talk now. Yes, I understand." His tone was icy. "Can you email that through then? Fine. No. I'll call you. Monday. Yes, whatever you have to tell me can bloody wait." He hung his head. "Right. Sorry. Yes." He rang off with a muttered oath.

She walked up to him, rubbing his shoulder. "Are you okay?"

He turned slowly. "Not really."

"Is Charlotte okay? Has something happened?"

"She's fine." His eyes turned distant. "That was my lawyer. I just...I need some time to not think about custody issues and lawyers. It's too fresh. I want to enjoy our evening together without all that hanging over my head."

A trickle of unease flittered around her stomach. Something wasn't right. She knew when someone was lying to her. And Owen was keeping secrets.

They still had so much to learn about one another. Yet she had fallen for the man already. Given herself to him in more ways than he knew.

"Sure you don't want to talk about it?"

His eyes were troubled; they searched her own, as if looking for something. "No...but thanks for the offer." He stroked her cheek. "Knowing you care enough to ask is good enough for now. I just want to enjoy this meal, with you. Maybe taste whatever sweet treat it is you brought over earlier, and then try to convince you to stay the night. You don't have work tomorrow." He kissed her lightly. "Screw that. I'm asking you to stay tonight. I need the company. Your company. And I want to look at you during dinner knowing that I get to wake up beside you."

Curse her bleeding heart.

She went from keeping a firm and necessary barrier in place, to not being able to refuse him in a heartbeat. Was this what it meant to be in love?

"I'll see how good that pasta is, and then I'll decide."

"Aye aye, Chef."

It took a little over a glass of wine and a half a course of dinner for the guarded look to vanish from Owen's eyes. It had taken her less than half that time to know she would stay.

Owen sat in front of the fire, waiting for Ally to come back in with dessert. Without her in the room, his mind began to wander.

The events of the day cascaded through his brain. Coming home after the failed mediation to find Ally on his doorstep was like a blessing.

His control had snapped when he saw her standing there, waiting for him. Sex with Ally—her company at dinner—had kept his mind away from the mediation fiasco, and firmly on the woman who he wanted more than just a tumble with—he wanted forever.

Guilt stabbed at his conscience. He should have told her what happened. But for whatever reason, he didn't want to expose her to all the heartache.

She wanted to keep her professional and personal lives separate. Having her in court would only make her job even more difficult. Especially given their relationship status. Her reputation was important to her and he respected the fact that her job —this sub-school position—was her world.

Owen gripped the stem of his wine glass. The overwhelming urge to protect her increased the more time they spent together. More than anything, he wanted their relationship to remain unmarred by the Langdons.

Hell, he'd had a gutful of their games when he had been married to Rebecca. The last thing he needed was to taint this relationship with their nasty words hanging over them.

It still scraped at his confidence that his first marriage had failed.

Re-filling his glass, and hers, Owen willed himself to let it go, to give himself a chance at happiness—an escape from reality—for one night at least. He would enjoy a greedy evening of pleasure with the woman...with the woman he loved.

The force of it punched him in the gut. It left him shaken, yet wired, like a live current of electricity shooting through his system.

It was with some relief that he truly knew he wanted to tell her everything. That there wasn't a fear of mistrust holding him back. Going through mediation made him appreciate what was good in his life. Now. Because tomorrow there were no guarantees.

Owen sipped at the wine. He would just take this night for themselves. No court battles. No lawyers. Nothing but the two of them. There'd be enough troubles in the morning.

Ally came in with the warmed brownies.

"I couldn't resist putting them back in the oven. Makes it taste so much better."

"They smell great."

He placed his glass on the coffee table and linked his fingers with hers. She had a pianist's hands—long and slim and unadorned. He couldn't help but wonder what a jewel might look like on her finger. An emerald perhaps, to match her eyes.

"Stay with me tonight?"

He caught the far-off look that stole over her expression.

"Hey—where do you go?"

"Excuse me?"

"When you drift like that. You take a step back. In here." He tapped a finger, once at her temple. "Why?"

She let go of his hand and shifted closer to him. "This easy intimacy isn't something I'm familiar with; I never grew up with any kind of casual tenderness. I really wasn't aware of what I was missing out on until I was older."

"You've mentioned your parents weren't very forthcoming with affection."

"That's an understatement."

"If this is too painful—"

"No. I want to tell you. You need to know this. You've talked about your parents with such admiration, I can tell how deeply you love them. How much you miss them. It isn't like that with my parents.

"I don't have that rapport with them because they didn't really have an easy, free-spirited manner in themselves. And that's describing them in the nicest of possible ways." She sat up, eyes intent.

She would tell him even if it caused her pain; it was no wonder he was crazy about her.

"Owen, I hated my childhood. I clashed with my parents all the time. They didn't understand how to raise a child, I can see that now. Especially not one who was so different from their ideals.

"They married for money I suppose. All they care about is maintaining their reputation. They were cold, oftentimes spiteful and bitter; so very bitter to think that I could favour one over the other. They didn't realise that love isn't about playing favourites. The sad truth is, I'm not sure they even know what it is to love. I grew up in that environment. It's all I've known."

"You're more than that, Ally." He rubbed her arms when she shivered and drew her to him, closer to the fire.

"I grew up without knowing what unconditional love is. I know that's warped the way I act in relationships. We never said, 'I love you.' I don't know if I've ever said it to them. It's not something I remember anyway.

"I suppose all of this has been playing on my mind lately. My father is finally going in for his surgery on Friday and I can't help but think about our relationship. How I would feel if something happened to him. Perhaps I'm being unfair in all this…" She gazed into the fire. Private memories flickered across her eyes. "Point is, I'm not comfortable with small inti-macies, or at least not at first."

"I've said before that I think you're doing a fine job of it. I'm certainly not complaining. And your father will come out of this stronger than ever. Don't let it plague you."

"I've been avoiding thinking about it for a while, but lately I can't keep a hold of all these emotions. You give so freely of yourself, but I don't know how to do that. I have these…"

"Force fields up."

She breathed out, a part of her seemed relieved. "Yeah. I have them—I need them—to function. It's not that I don't want to be carefree and affectionate—"

"You just don't know how to allow yourself."

"Exactly. I think sometimes I don't trust myself to—because of how I was raised. I don't trust that it's the right reaction. I check in with myself, test my own boundaries to see what I'm comfortable with—that's probably the look you see."

Owen knew that she stepped away from the things that made her feel. That she didn't want to risk a part of herself for fear of what she'd find. In doing so she doubted her own capacity for love, for emotion. He could see that. But she needed to know that she was more. That she was able to give love. More so, that she deserved it.

"So that was a long way of explaining that I'm staying the night."

"You sure?"

"Why? Have you any doubts?"

"Hell no. Just checking."

"Time for dessert then."

He shifted her onto his lap. "I had another kind in mind."

He wanted—for tonight—to show her how cherished she was—in every possible way.

When her eyes clouded over in pleasure, he knew it was the right move. It was exactly what they both needed.

It had been a long time since Owen had eaten brownies for breakfast.

An age since he had a woman in his bed.

The fact that said woman was ridiculously sexy and just as enthusiastic about his breakfast suggestion was just a bonus. He justified it by reminding Ally that they had exercised Saturday morning away in bed and deserved a slice of indulgence.

He wanted to indulge in this woman for the rest of his life. Even though he promised her to take it slow, his heart had other plans.

He turned to her, saw that her eyes were bright, hair tousled. And he wanted her all over again.

"You've got a bit of—" she gestured to his lip, reaching out to brush away a crumb.

She squealed when he nipped at her finger and tumbled them both back on the mattress.

"Owen! You'll get crumbs on the bed." She gasped, laughing when he rubbed his face along hers, nibbling down to her neck.

"I think it's best we have a shower then, don't you?"

He carried her in his arms to the adjoining bathroom, addicted to the sound of her laughter.

When they wrapped themselves in robes and slunk downstairs for coffee, he wondered how he could convince her to stay. He didn't want this weekend to end. Not yet. Not when his heart was full and his house empty.

He turned to her whilst the coffee brewed.

"Stay," he murmured, unable to resist touching her.

Her green eyes widened slightly, then glowed.

"For the whole weekend, I mean. I don't want you to leave just yet." He stepped towards her, drawing her close.

"But I've nothing to wear."

"What I have in mind doesn't require clothes." He kissed her nose. "Stay with me, Ally. I don't want you to go."

She trembled in his arms. "I don't want to go either."

He held his breath, waiting for the "but."

"I'll stay on one condition. We go back to mine to pick up some clothes and underwear."

Owen affected a disappointed sigh. "It'll just end up on the bedroom floor." His heart all but bounded in his chest.

"Oh, I think you'll appreciate a certain scrap of lingerie that I'll be picking up."

Images of her in red lace flashed through his overheated imagination. "I finally get my present?"

"You've been a very good boy. I think you deserve it."

He kissed her. "I'll drive."

Ally wasn't certain at what point she had lost her will to talk to him about Charlotte. It might have been on the romantic walk they took along the local trail, holding hands and stealing kisses; or when they brought the weekend paper home with provisions for dinner, calling out crossword puzzle clues to one another. She wanted to tell him. But she also knew that the easy, carefree weekend they were spending together was something they both needed.

By the time he led her upstairs, candles glowing and a bubble bath waiting, she had truly lost any capacity for cogent thought.

She was being wooed. And she didn't mind it one bit. A part of her recognised the shift between them, felt it within herself after telling him about her parents.

He made it easy to love. He showed her a glimpse of what sharing a life together might look like. Even though there was so much more to learn, she was happy to take her time, to trust in what they were building. She craved it even more knowing it was within reach.

It had been easy to dismiss it before—to dismiss him—at the beginning. Now that he was here, in her life, she couldn't imagine existing without him.

She glanced at the glowing candles, the champagne and turned in his arms. She was overcome by his tenderness.

"This is wonderful."

"This is just the beginning."

She stepped into the warm water and stretched out. He nudged her forward, sitting behind her, his arms twin bands of comfort and security.

"I think you've outdone my brownies."

"Not possible. Though I'll always be a willing subject if you ever want to try them out again. For evaluation purposes, that is."

"Oh, is that so?" she murmured as his hands stroked her belly.

"Definitely."

Utterly relaxed, her thoughts drifted. "What made you choose this house? It's gorgeous, but pretty big for just the two of you."

"It seems ridiculous, but I wanted us to start fresh. To have a family home. The last place we were in was small, and well, all we could afford as teenage parents. When Rebecca died it held too many memories. I thought staying there would help Charlie deal with her death, but it only reminded her of her sickness."

"Sorry, I shouldn't have asked." She laced her fingers in his.

"No, it's a good thing. I wanted what my parents had created for us boys growing up. I wanted to give that to Charlie. Some space to run around. Maybe a dog in the future."

"And more kids?" Ally bit her lip.

He placed a kiss on her ear. "And more kids. Not that I had been thinking about that, until recently."

She turned in his arms. She wasn't sure what he would see, or even what she felt, not entirely. Her natural reaction was fear, but the odd tattoo that danced in her chest was something else...

Hope.

"Really?"

Owen brushed at her hair, stroking the strands between his fingers. "You make me want things I haven't thought about in a long time. I know we said we'd take it slow, and I'll hold my word on that, but I want to be honest. I see it all with you. That includes children."

Her eyes stung. "You make me want things I didn't think possible, too."

"That's more than enough. What we have between us, what we're building is something good. I didn't think I'd have it in me to build a future again with another woman. Rebecca's death was painful. Long and painful. Our marriage wasn't perfect. And I still hold a lot of guilt over that."

"You can't blame yourself for what happened."

"I don't—not entirely. But the guilt still sits there. Applying for a divorce—starting that process—it broke something in me. I know it was hard struggling with money, especially when her parents were wealthy and reminded her of it. It took its toll when I worked so much and studied in my spare time, with a small baby.

"To see how much that pressure broke us...it was the last thing I ever thought would happen. But we had changed. We both hated arguing about every little issue. In the end, I honestly think she was relieved. The pressure from her parents was a lot for her to manage as a young mum. And then she got sick..."

"I'm so sorry. For everything you've lost, Owen. But you're raising a resilient girl; a smart, sweet, talented child who loves you, and her mother."

He kissed her hand. "You're right. It is the past. I don't know why I'm bringing it up."

"It's cathartic. And I don't mind listening."

They lapsed into a comforting silence and she settled back against his chest, enjoying the sensation of his hands stroking her thighs.

"About the mediation. Charlotte—"

"No." He tensed behind her.

"She—"

"Not tonight, Ally. Not here."

She opened her mouth, sighing when his teeth grazed her neck. "Owen…"

"Later. Let me touch you. Make love to you." His hands stroked at her nipples, teasing her into submission.

She told herself it was weak to resist. But what was another night when there would be so many more between them?

Arching against him, she guided his hands lower, to the place where she yearned for him most. Closing her eyes, she succumbed to the pleasure. And him.

CHAPTER THIRTY-TWO

*I*t was a few days later when Owen stormed into her office, his face set in an angry scowl. She hadn't seen him since Sunday afternoon, but their indulgent weekend had kept her buoyed as she worked through her mounting to-do list. Not even the prospect of her father's surgery this week had been able to dampen her spirits. She'd be away from Friday through to Monday to care for him. Four whole days and nights with her parents. Four days and nights without Owen. It didn't bear thinking about.

She glanced out the window and wasn't surprised to find that dusk was setting in; it would be dark within the next half hour. She seemed to be here most nights when the cleaning crew began their shift that she didn't really notice the late hours.

This new routine wouldn't be something that would change any time soon but gone was the tension that had accompanied her since beginning the new role. In fact, a degree of calm had entered her life since she had begun dating Owen.

He stared at her now, his face set, arms crossed. She was glad the office was empty.

"Why the hell didn't you let me know about her grand-parents?"

Dread settled low in her belly. "Pardon?"

"Sorry. Let me start again. Hi, Ally. How are you? Keeping anything from me? How about that you neglected to tell me over the 48 hours we spent together on the weekend, that Charlie's grandparents were spewing lies about me. Why the hell did you keep that a secret?"

Her stomach churned. *This*. This was why she didn't allow herself to get too close. Not only was her judgement impaired by a promise to a little girl that she shouldn't have made, she was also vulnerable to Owen's anger. The professional and the personal were getting all tangled, and she was afraid that she wasn't dealing with either in the way she had planned.

Mistakes. So many mistakes.

"I was going to tell you on Friday. Charlotte was upset about it and asked for some time to tell you herself. I didn't know she was going off camping with Jack for the weekend, so I thought it best to give her those few days. I meant to check in with her this afternoon..."

"Christ!" Owen paced the office. "To think we went to court and I had no idea. This could have changed everything."

"Court?" A spasm of fear seized her lungs. "When did you go to court?"

"Don't you have a duty of care or something? I should have been told by Charlie's coordinator—that'd be you."

His words may as well have drawn blood.

"I was doing my duty—to Charlotte."

"I'm her dad. I have a right to know."

"I was going to tell you!"

"When? When I lost custody?" He paced, frustration radiating in waves off his tense shoulders. His eyes were every shade of pissed off known to man.

"I tried to tell you on Saturday night. In the bath. I should have mentioned it earlier." Her cheeks heated with embarrassment and guilt. "Would you please explain to me what is going on?"

"Not before you tell me what Charlie told you."

Ally tried to summon all the patience in the world, even though she was itching for answers. "She said her grandparents claim that you killed her mother. I told her that was just grief talking and wasn't true. When she was little, she wished you would both get a divorce because you fought so often. Then when Rebecca died, she blamed herself."

Owen's face crumpled. "She thought the wish came true."

She nodded. "Charlotte knows that the Langdons don't like you. She was upset to think you'd hear about it from me first. That's why I came over on Friday. I thought she would have told you by then and I wanted for us to talk about it."

"When you had to choose between Charlie or me—you chose my child."

Her pulse scrambled. "No...I..."

"Yeah, you did." His smile was slow, thoughtful. "And as pissed as I am, I can appreciate that you put her first. Or I will...tomorrow. She seemed to tell everyone but me."

"Excuse me?"

"At their camping trip, she told Jack. He made sure she told me when they returned."

"Point taken."

She reminded herself that he was a parent first. She shouldn't be upset by his disappointment. Or fearful because of his anger. She straightened, compressing her hands together behind her back. "Now could you please tell me about this court business?"

"Back behind that shell of yours?"

Those barriers enabled her to face any criticism. If that made her cold, then so be it. You couldn't change who you were after all.

"The courts?" she prompted again.

"We went to mediation on Friday. Hence my stellar mood. They didn't agree to the increased hours I was willing to offer and they're intent on full custody. We're waiting to go before a judge to decide."

Ally tried to shove aside the stabbing pain. Was this what it felt like when someone didn't let you in? When there was no trust?

"Why didn't you tell me? I could have been there with you."

"For the very same reason you didn't tell me about Charlie. You're already torn between being her coordinator and being my partner. I didn't want to put you in that situation, to bring you into this mess."

"I'm already in it, Owen. I'm trying to balance my personal and professional life, but if I want to support you as your partner, that decision should be mine."

He rubbed his hand across his jaw. "I didn't say I was justified in my choice. My judgement seems to be skewed of late. I wanted to handle it on my own, so we didn't have this hanging over our heads. I didn't—"

She walked over to him. "What is it?"

"I didn't want you to think their claims were possibly true."

"That you're an unfit parent?" Ally sputtered. "You're kidding me, right?"

Owen winced, then took her hands. "Before Rebecca died, she wanted me to give her parents some guardianship rights over Charlie. I agreed, signing a document allowing them to be with her on weekends and some parts of the holidays."

She could see how much it pained him to tell her. How hurtful it must have been to hand over his rights as a parent. She squeezed his hands. "Oh, Owen. I'm so sorry."

"I know her parents would have harassed her about Charlie's well-being, gotten into her head when she was weak and vulnerable, making her see their claim as a supportive act rather than a vindictive one. Rebecca loved her parents, so I don't blame her for asking. I made that promise in those final months and I've kept it."

"But it hurts. That you feel she didn't trust you enough not to do that."

Owen's shoulders sagged. "Exactly. She was always torn between her parents and our marriage. She couldn't be both the dutiful daughter and the devoted wife. It was too much of a strain on her. She had convinced herself she'd be able to live without her parents' approval and support, but I saw how much it hurt. I was there when she cried over the way they treated me, treated us when we were together. It broke her." He cleared his throat, blinking away the shimmer of tears.

"And your marriage...I deal with unfit parents more often than I would care to in this job. I would never and have never thought that you weren't a loving and devoted father. Charlotte is proof of how much you care for her. Anyone can see that."

"I didn't want them to taint us. To taint this, or your perception of me. I should have told you, Ally. I just can't see clearly when it comes to them. To Charlie."

"Then let me be your eyes. Let me help you in this. You're not alone in facing them."

"Funny that. With you, I don't feel I am."

"Have you told her?"

"I did. This afternoon. I had been planning on telling her anyway. You were right, she needs to know. I think she should have a say in what she wants. I just wish I had told her earlier."

"She's nearly thirteen. The judge may take that into consideration."

He shrugged, then paced. "I don't know. I don't know anything anymore. The fact that we signed that document gives them some leverage, even though John doesn't think it's an issue. The Langdons are rich, entitled people. You know the type, you come from that world, understand that mentality. They'll stop at nothing to get what they want."

He hadn't meant the comment to sting. He hadn't said it that way. But she wished she didn't understand; wished she wasn't familiar with the entitled mindset that the very wealthy people —the type who mingled with her parents—had about such matters.

"Custody battles get ugly and people can act in drastic ways. They'll manipulate the situation to get what they want. Who knows what they could do again?"

"She's safe."

"For now."

"Forever, if I have anything to do with it."

"For now, Owen. I'm sure her grandparents will do anything to ensure that she stays with them."

"Not after this they won't. I refuse to grant them access to her if they're poisoning her mind with this crap. To think Charlie felt guilty for years since her mother's death. She's been punishing herself for no bloody good reason."

"I agree. It's in the best interest of the child to keep her away from them. But that might be adding fuel to the fire."

"You'd know that would you?"

She saw the fear in his eyes. The screaming terror of a father desperately trying to hold on to his child. His family. It was there, lurking beneath his annoyance. He couldn't face the unthinkable. Not yet. Not ever. She didn't blame him one bit.

But she knew that if they won, if Henry and Anita Langdon succeeded in court, that it would break him. Charlie was his world. He wouldn't ever recover from that.

"You can stay mad at me for all I care, but from a professional position, I'm making it clear that her grandparents are not to be allowed access to her at school, if that's your wish. I think we need to escalate things given the mediation stalling."

Owen continued to pace. "How could I have not seen it? She never once said she didn't like going over there."

"Children of abuse rarely do..." Ally struggled to stay in the present. She didn't want to think about her parents. Didn't want to worry over the child she had been. It was her duty to help Charlotte now. To stop the lies and manipulation. "Seeing as though she was able to tell me about their verbal abuse, I'd say she's beginning to trust others again, especially authority figures. That's a good thing. Can I offer some advice?"

Owen didn't respond.

"I think you should get a restraining order against them. They'll stop at nothing to get what they want, and I think you have a good case. I know the courts can frown upon hearing child testimonies, but they may take her opinion into consideration. You're her father. You've been nothing but supportive and stable. The Langdons are just making false accusations without evidence. No doubt a judge will see that."

She suppressed a shiver, knowing all too well how parents could manipulate. She had heard the word divorce thrown back and forth so often by the time she was eight, she no longer feared it, and had by the time she hit double digits, hoped that it would happen. She understood Charlotte's reticence to say anything and was impressed that she had said spoken to her about what was happening.

"They don't seem to care about the effect on Charlotte. Or are at least careless about it. Both are bad. They'll use her as a pawn to get the one up over you, so I'd be very careful about how you proceed."

"I know this, Ally. I've dealt with these people for a long time."

"Then you'll know what to do. I'll send out an email to my colleagues and will keep you informed about our stance once we've had our coordinators meeting."

They had hurt each other in this process. Something she

never wanted to do. She was blundering her way through this relationship, fooling herself into thinking she could handle someone else's baggage, when she could barely handle her own.

"I'll start that email now, if that's okay? I think it's a matter of urgency."

Owen stepped towards her. "All business I see?"

She threw up her hands. "I don't know what you want me to say. I apologised already for jeopardising your mediation. I let my feelings get in the way. I'm doing the best I can. That's all you can ask of me."

"Is it? Is that all I can ask of you?"

Her pulse hammered. His expression was too intense, too direct. It made all the alarms in her head go off at the same time.

"I don't know what you mean."

The secret she couldn't quite decipher danced across his blue eyes. "Never mind." He pulled out one of the chairs at the circular table. "I'll give you some time to send that email. Then we can go to dinner."

Ally's eyebrows shot up. "I beg your pardon?"

"I figure by that stage I'll have worked off the mad enough to go out for a steak. Maybe a glass of wine."

"I'm sorry, what? We've just had an argument. A pretty big one, I might add. I'm not going to dinner with you." She wanted to go home and lick her wounds. Maybe wallow over some cookie dough she had leftover in the freezer.

Owen shrugged. "So? People have arguments all the time. I've said what I had to say. You said what you had to say. I'm sorry for not telling you, you're sorry for not telling me. Nothing left to do but move forward."

"And eat steak?"

"Can't think of a better meal…unless you're talking about another kind of meal entirely."

Ally's suppressed the shiver. "I meant—"

"You expected that I'd storm off in a huff. Maybe not talk to you for a few days, give you the cold shoulder, is that it?"

She was afraid and exhilarated that he knew her so well.

"We're adults. I don't see the need to resort to soap opera worthy silences to resolve our dispute. Am I still pissed off? Yeah, a little. But I'd rather be pissed off in your company than have dinner without you.

"Before you ask, Jack's taken Charlotte out for a special, ritzy meal in the city. He rightly thought she'd want some space after the chat I had with her. So, dinner with me? I can tell you about the court case, and my conversation with Charlie. We can review our battle plan, see where we stand. Together."

Ally bit her lip. She *had* expected him to storm out. To maintain an icy distance; freeze her over until she begged for forgiveness. That's what past boyfriends had done. That's what her—

Yes. That's exactly what her parents would do. Exactly what she had come to expect and fear.

He threw her off. Just when she was beginning to understand where they stood, he flipped everything upside down, leaving her dizzy and disoriented.

"I need you, Ally. I need you to help me through this. I was an idiot to think I should be doing this alone. That you needed protecting."

Little did he know that she couldn't refuse him. Wouldn't. Not when he looked at her like that. His need for her wasn't for his own power, or for his gratification. But for his heart. She could see that in a way she had never seen before. It left her speechless.

Owen crossed the room, and with eyes beginning to lose their temper, held her. "Is that a yes?"

She nodded.

On a different day, with a different question, she wondered if she would say no.

CHAPTER THIRTY-THREE

"He's dying, Allyna! Do something!" Her mother opened the front door with a dramatic sweep, her eyes wild, her movements jerky.

It had been twenty-four hours since Ally had left her father with the live-in nurse. After spending four days and nights managing his transition from the hospital, she was looking forward to some space. She was emotionally spent. The last thing she wanted to do was end up back on their doorstep again.

She received the initial call that Tuesday evening after a long day at work. She was about to make plans for a late take-away dinner with Owen, when Sandy, her father's live-in nurse called to say she was fired and was potentially being sued by her father. Concerned for his health, she had no way of checking up on her patient now that she was barred from the house.

To make matters worse, he was refusing his medication and physiotherapy to manage the pain, without which, he might have to be re-admitted to hospital. That was when Ally knew she had to go back.

The surgery hadn't been as straightforward as they had

intended, and her father had developed an infection. He had been placed on heavy antibiotics in the hope that it would keep it under control. Without it, his body would reject the metal at his hip, the infection would spread, and they'd most likely have to amputate his legs.

Ally had reassured his nurse that she would stay with him until she could convince her father to go to hospital or re-instate his at-home care. The poor woman was only doing her job. She didn't deserve his abuse, or his intimidation. Sandy had, to her surprise, laughed, saying she had dealt with worse. It wasn't her position she was worried about, but her father's health.

She shook her head in disbelief. He was acting like an ungrateful child.

By the time she had hurriedly packed a few clean clothes in her overnight bag, she had received a dozen distressed calls from her mother and had managed to work up a considerable temper. She had planned on spending the evening relaxing on the sofa with Owen and Charlotte. Instead, she would need to work through the night, writing up lesson plans so her classes could be covered for the following day. She hoped she wouldn't need to spend more than the next twenty-four hours sorting out this mess.

With any luck she would talk her father down and get Sandy to visit him in the morning without any threat of law enforcement. She took a steady, calming breath and turned to her mother.

"What do you mean he's dying? And what are you doing here still?"

Ally walked through the entrance hall, brushing aside her bird-like mother who hovered by her side.

"This is my home as much as it is his!"

"You said you were going back to your townhouse when I left. I thought you were moving out."

"And leave all this to his floozies? Never! Eleanor called this afternoon to see how I was coping. The manipulative bastard told all our friends I was to be his new nurse!"

Now that he made it public, she couldn't be seen living elsewhere. What would their friends think if she wasn't playing the devoted wife?

"You saw the way he put on such a show on Sunday when Leanne and Walter came to call. I told him no visitors but he's greeting everyone like he's some invalid. Ringing the damn bell —having me at his beck and call. He does it just to spite me, you know? He wails and hollers all hours of the day and night. And with that nurse living here, I've had no space. No peace!"

Ally rolled her eyes even while her heart thumped. Her mother was known for histrionics. Some days her behaviour was straight out of the nineteenth-century guide for how to be a housewife. Complete with smelling salts and fainting spells.

She had spent a mere twenty-four hours dealing with her husband alone, and already her mother was a bundle of nerves.

"Mother, you do know that he fired Sandy and threatened to sue her. I doubt she'll come back the way she has been treated."

"You don't think I know what is going on in my house? The old dog did it just to spite me, I'm sure. He threatened to cut *me* out of the will if I let her back in. I told him I would not care for him and he can go back to hospital if he's in all that pain."

"Did you ring the hospital?"

"I called you!"

Ally fled through the house to the spare bedroom. Her father lay in an odd contortion across the bed. His usual ruddy colour was now a sickly shade of off-white. A musky stench hung in the air, sweat had soaked through his expensive bed sheets.

"Father. Are you okay?"

One eye opened and a grimace lined his mouth. "Allyna. You deigned to show up. Finally."

A queasy sensation tickled the back of her throat.

"I've only been gone a day. Are you okay?"

"I'm dying. Oh! I'm dying!"

"Where does it hurt?"

"My back and hips. Pain in my legs."

She checked that he wasn't bleeding anywhere. That there wasn't any nasty smells or discoloration. But it was beyond her knowledge or expertise. She swallowed back the fear. "Did you take your medicine?"

"That stupid woman is responsible!" He barely raised his right arm in accusation, pointing over her shoulder. Her mother sniffed from the doorway.

"I told you, Peter, I'm not good at caring for sick people. The nurse said you need to take your medication."

"I'm dying...I'm dying and none of you care!"

Ally tried very hard not to unleash the adrenaline fuelled temper that had lodged in the back of her throat. Her mother couldn't see past her own needs. As usual. And her father was too stubborn to accept when he needed professional help.

"It's very rare to die of a hip operation. At least not post-op. But you've got an infection. If it isn't treated with medication it can become a serious problem. Why did you stop taking the tablets?"

"Kate Featherstone's sister's husband had a friend whose legs were amputated from a hip infection."

"Not helping, Mother."

"Doctors knew within hours of surgery that it was an infection, so this can't be it."

"I *am* dying...and that inebriated skunk is keen to see me off. Wants the house."

"My nerves are shot to shreds!" Vera's reply was shrill. "So what if I had a few? I'm entitled to do so in my own home. One which you invaded!"

"If it wasn't for me, you wouldn't have—"

"Enough!" Ally was fast losing her patience. "I'm calling

Sandy back for some advice as to how to proceed. You've no right to dismiss her."

"She was killing me. The medication makes me all fuzzy. They're both in on it."

She counted back from five. "Alright, James Bond, settle down. No one is trying to kill you, but if you don't let Sandy work with you on the physio and if you don't take your medication, you *will* be going back to hospital and you *will* lose your legs. The medication is strong to help you fight off the infection. The painkillers make you drowsy. That's all normal.

"Mother, go upstairs. I'll handle this. Father, I'm getting your meds. Both of you need to stay silent and out of my way until I've spoken to Sandy." Ally stormed out, shaking her head. They were worse than her rowdy Year 8 class. And nowhere near as cute.

Ally spent the next few days in her own personal hell. She had hoped she would be there for a day, maximum. It looked like she was staying for the rest of the week. Living under the same roof as her parents was enough to bring back memories of all the arguments she'd been privy to as a child. Except this time, she was wise enough to walk away.

Not that she had time to herself, what with the rounds of cooking and nursing. She could bake up a storm with her eyes closed, but cooking was another ball game entirely. Not that she sucked. It just wasn't her passion.

She wished she had asked Sera for her lamb tagine recipe that had been in her mother's family for decades. Though knowing her parents, they would barely touch it. She seemed to be the only one in the house who ate proper meals; her father would eat only if force fed, and her mother considered a vodka martini a legitimate lunch.

Ally missed her freedom. She missed her friends. Mostly she missed Owen.

She'd never known someone to handle confrontation the way he did. Angry emotions were healthy in his mind. He encouraged her to "get it all out"—so he could understand her perspective. She was learning that having feelings weren't shameful; that expressing them was healthy. It was becoming glaringly obvious that she was no longer the defiant teenager intent on finding her own independence.

Now that she had it, she accepted how restrictive this place, and her thinking had been. Pushing Owen away wasn't going to protect her from falling into the same destructive cycle of her parents' marriage. Keeping him at arm's length would only prove that she had learned nothing as an adult.

Being with Owen, sharing her life with him meant she was freeing herself of the burden of being her parents' daughter, which meant letting go of those self-destructive habits. Of allowing herself to feel and love and exist in a healthy relationship.

Everything she had always dreamed of as a child. Everything she could have as an adult.

She was stacking the dishwasher, being mindful not to chip the glasses when her phone pealed.

"Hey," she whispered.

"Hey, yourself." Owen replied in hushed tones. "Are you in a church or something, or did you finally lose it with your parents and we have to go into witness protection? If so, I think I'd take up the name Ronald. Sounds safe enough."

Ally snorted. "And boring. No, these walls have ears. Gimme a sec," she replied, tiptoeing out of the kitchen and upstairs to her old bedroom. She felt like she was fifteen and sneaking back home after breaking curfew.

She flopped down on her single bed. Whilst the sheets had changed long ago, most of her room was as she left it after high school. Why her parents had kept it like this she had no idea. But given that it was dust-free and gleaming, she'd say they still had their cleaners tidy it after all these years. She wasn't sure why that made her sentimental.

"You still there?" Owen whispered.

She spoke at a normal volume. "Yes. Sorry. Just getting comfortable."

"We're not going on the run?"

"You sound disappointed."

"I have a thing for playing dress up where you're concerned."

Ally toyed with strands of her hair, heart suddenly light. She looked up at her glow-in-the-dark stickers she had rebelliously put on the ceiling when she was nine. It had been the beginning of her quest for independence. Her parents had flipped. But it had remained. Along with the posters that came soon after and her mismatched attempt to paint the wall in rainbow colours.

"Is that so?"

"Mhmm. Whaddya say I come rescue Rapunzel from her tower, and you can give yourself the night off?"

She closed her eyes letting the fantasy play out in her head. "Tempting...but no. This princess is voluntarily stuck in her tower."

Even though she had managed to convince Sandy it was safe to return for a few hours every day, with a single check up in the evening, Ally needed to know that her father was improving before leaving. It had spooked her a little to see him in such a diminished state. It wasn't like she could rely on her mother to take over when he was alone.

"Don't make me beg, Ms. McVeigh."

She laughed. "Trust me, I'd be the first to be climbing out my window. I've spent way too long with my parents this past week. But then that would make me no better than my teenage self and being here has made me appreciate just how far I've come."

"Sounds deep. Sure I can't come around with a pizza? Netflix and chill?"

"I wouldn't subject you to my parents' sunny disposition. As much as that sounds appealing, I'll take a rain check."

"A man's got to try."

"I appreciate the sentiment. How's Charlotte? Any news about court?"

"She's been okay. Some teary days, others not so much. Having Jack here has been great, but his time down in Oz is limited. No news as yet about a date. Though John seems to think it'll be soon. She asks about you."

"Give her a kiss from me."

"She misses you, Ally. I miss you."

She didn't care that she probably looked like her silly teenage self, mooning over a boy and building castles in the air. She held the wonderful sensation of being cared for, close to her chest.

"I miss you both. Can't wait to see you again."

When she heard her name being called ten minutes later, she reluctantly hung up the phone. She couldn't help but compare the world she was in with the life she was creating with Owen. Everything about her parents had been built on resentment and years of hostility. She was learning that not every relationship had to be that way.

That not every parent was that way.

Even though she'd made it clear that she would be leaving on Friday, her father's health permitting, her parents had already begun to make bitter remarks about her abandoning them whenever she walked into a room. Not directly to her. But to the air itself. Or at odd times, to one another.

She would make it a priority to add another nurse to her father's care, so that Sandy could work in tandem with someone else to ensure he was monitored around the clock. He was still opposed to having a live-in carer so this would have to be the compromise. Once that was sorted, she'd convince her mother to think about moving out permanently. They were the last two people on the planet that should be sharing a home.

Getting back to work and her own life was ridiculously appealing.

When she heard the bell ring, she gritted her teeth then squared her shoulders. Tomorrow couldn't come around quick enough.

Weary and emotionally spent, Ally walked upstairs late Friday afternoon to find a flurry of messages on her phone. She had been on the go all day, having supported the new nurse who would work in shifts with Sandy. She figured that round-the-clock care would be better for his recovery in the short term. The abuse she copped because of her decision would be worth it if that meant she didn't have to set foot in this house again. Not for a long while at least.

When her father's friends had decided upon an impromptu visit, she had juggled playing hostess with the snobbish pair and setting up his account for the meal delivery service. He had very little patience for anyone other than business associates and friends, but his health seemed to have moved out of the danger zone, and for that she was grateful. Now that he had care re-established, she felt comfortable leaving.

Her mother had bid her farewell and gone upstairs to calm her nerves with a glass of sherry and a bath. She had refused to listen to her about moving out, so Ally didn't persist. She was old enough to pick her battles.

She wanted nothing more than to change her clothes and sit

on the sofa with Owen and Charlotte whilst stuffing her face full of cheesy crust pizza.

She picked up her bag and phone and saw missed calls from Sera, Maddie and Owen. Adrenaline cut through her fatigue. She tensed when she heard the doorbell peal in quick succession.

Sera and Maddie were waiting on her parents' porch. The calm expression on their faces made her stomach lurch.

"What's going on? I've had a million missed calls. Is everything okay?"

Sera hugged her.

Maddie explained whilst ushering her out of the house. "We've been trying to contact you for the past few hours, but you haven't been answering your phone."

"Sorry, it's been all go here. I've not had a chance to stop." She searched their faces. "Well?"

"It's kind of complicated," Maddie began.

"Spit it out 'coz you're only making me more nervous."

"I don't think we should talk about this here."

Ally crossed her arms and planted her feet. "Spill. Now."

"It's about you and Owen."

"Nobody is hurt. But..." Maddie looked behind her and lowered her voice. "There's been some pictures."

She gestured for her to continue.

"And an anonymous email came through to all of the school council members, with pictures of you and Owen."

"What kind of pictures?"

Sera stroked her back. "Darling, there are a few pictures of Owen with you, kissing and...you know, up against his front door."

She was suddenly so very cold, as if she had been thrown into the icy waters of the Atlantic. Her body and brain were numb. "What?"

"Then there are a few others of you just kissing outside your house or holding hands in the park. Then another one of him saying goodbye to you with his shirt off on the porch."

Heat slashed at her cheeks now. She was fire and ice. She knew the exact days those photos would have been taken. There was only one day where Owen had her up against his front door.

"By the way—hot bod." Maddie nudged her.

"Why?" she whispered.

"Let's go back to my place," Maddie took her arm. "Sera can drive your car over as she came with me. We'll talk about everything there."

Ally allowed herself to be led, like a lamb to the slaughter.

The car ride to Maddie's house gave her time to process the facts. It was more than enough time for the shame to wash over her. She was violated in the most private manner. Her personal space had been invaded; paraded around for members of the school council to see—for what? If she hadn't known better, she would have blamed her parents. But they had no knowledge of her relationship with Owen. Thank goodness.

The nausea pricked at her stomach like needles.

Poor Charlotte. If the school council had been sent those photos, then it wouldn't be long before the whole school found out. She whimpered. Maybe it had been sent to all the parents in the community as well. How would she know?

It took just one person to share the gossip and it would be news by Monday.

She sat in silence until they reached the safety of Maddie's apartment. Was she being followed right now? Did they have people watching her still? She thought about her phone call with Owen and wished she could go back to feeling trapped in her parents' home. Anything was better than this.

"Owen knows?" She looked at Sera.

"He apparently went in to see the principal today. I'm so sorry, Al."

She pressed her hand against her stomach. "So am I...so all of the council knows?"

"Yes." Maddie placed a tequila sunrise on the side table. "Drink. It'll take the edge off."

"And did they send it to the students who were on the school council as well?"

Sera's nod was mournful.

Ally put her head in her hands. Bitter tears of shame pricked her eyes. Poor, poor Charlotte. Everyone would know by now.

Her greatest fears had come in one fell swoop. Not only was Charlotte going to suffer because of her actions, but she would lose any credibility in her job. Who would want her as the head of junior school after this? Who would want her as a teacher of their children?

All those parents who were just waiting for her to screw up would pounce on this as evidence that she was not fit for the role.

Evidence...

"Those bastards!"

"What bastards?"

"Charlotte's grandparents." Her eyes were damp. "This is exactly the type of game they would play. Trying to rack up evidence to prove Owen is somehow an unfit parent. Sleeping with a teacher. Painting him in a tawdry light." She knew that because it was what her parents would do.

"That's sick." Maddie's eyes were hard. "How dare they mess with people's lives and humiliate their grandchild?"

"They did it to prove a point. This was exactly what I warned him about." Ally shook her head. "I told him they'd fight dirty. They don't care about what's best for Charlotte. They just want to get back at Owen for what they think he did to their daughter."

"Bastards are flinging your name through the mud in the process." Sera's eyes were as tough as steel.

Ally rubbed at her own. "What am I going to do? This is going to be all over the school by Monday, if it isn't already."

"You'll handle it with grace like you do all things."

"And you fucking give them hell," Maddie added.

Her phone pealed. It was Principal Cavarello. She answered on the second ring, her voice tight. "Yes, Jacinta. I've heard." She looked at the girls and shook her head, pacing. "I'm aware of the custody issue, yes. I briefed Charlotte's teachers about the situation when it arose." She made a strangled noise in the back of her throat.

Surprise lined her voice. "I suppose so. Yes." She paced again. Her voice grew serious. "I understand. I do. I'll be thinking about that over the course of the weekend. We can, yes. That time sounds fine. Thank you very much, and I'm so sorry."

"Well?" Maddie and Sera stood. "What did she say?"

Her head swam. "She said it was a shock to the school and bad for the students to be embroiled in this mess. Council obviously frowns on this kind of salacious content being passed around the student body. Not to mention not a great look as head of junior school."

"I know who on the council would say that as well...uppity bastards." Maddie tossed back her hair, anger simmering.

"But then she said that the real issue was that my privacy had been violated in the most underhanded of ways. I had every right to be angry at being used in such a manner and would be supported through this by the school. She said it was bullying and I was in my rights to contact law enforcement at being harassed in such a manner.

"Woop!" Sera pumped a fist in the air. "I love Principal C!"

"She wants to have a meeting to talk about ways I can feel supported by the school—that what I do in my personal life should have no bearing on the work I've been doing at Woodbury. She'd make sure of it."

"I'd be bloody surprised if she said otherwise."

"Why do you look so forlorn?"

"Because, whilst I might have the school's support, I'm still going to be the talk of the town. How am I going to stand in front of kids in the classroom when I'll be wondering if they've seen me getting hot and heavy with a parent? It's personal. And something I should never have to feel ashamed of, but they've put me in this awful position. And now Charlotte's going to feel the brunt of it. I can't feel happy at all because of this."

"Here, have a drink." Maddie handed her the glass, watched her sip. "You shouldn't feel responsible for any of this. You've got the support of the school and it's great that Principal C is on top of it all. That's a start."

"Maybe I should step down from the role?"

"Step down?! Are you mad?"

"You love that job, Ally. No way!"

"It might be the best thing."

"Fuck the best thing!" Maddie gave her a shake. "You're not going to let these entitled fuckers throw your career off course, just because they've hired some skeezy detective to take photos."

She shivered. "It's so creepy."

"It's a violation."

"What am I going to do? How am I going to show my face at work?"

Sera squeezed her arm, her face suddenly lit up. "I've got a plan!"

When her phone pealed again, Ally stood. "It's Owen." She walked into the spare bedroom and sat on the double bed. "Hey."

"Hey, yourself. Are you okay?"

"Yeah, I just spoke to the principal. The girls told me what happened."

"I'm so sorry. This is my fault. I didn't mean for this to happen. I should have—"

"Stop. You can't blame yourself. I should have been more careful."

"It's done now. You were right about being on my guard. I guess I didn't want to think they'd come at you."

"How's Charlotte?"

"Confused. I told her this afternoon. She took it well considering. But she doesn't want to dwell on it until she goes back on Monday."

"It'll be hard for her when she goes to school…"

"I told her she can do home-schooling for a week if she needs time out, or if it gets too tough."

"What did Jack say?"

"He's pissed but said to get John on it. He's in Sydney and will be flying back to America if all goes well at his audition. I didn't think it was a good idea for him to come back with all that paparazzi following him around too. We need a bit of calm right now."

"Fair enough. How does she feel about her grandparents?"

"She doesn't want to see them. First the custody case and now this. I tried to leave out who sent the pictures, but she needed to know the truth. She shouldn't have to feel betrayed like that. They just don't see how much they're hurting her."

"Or how this would backfire for them in court. The judge will see how manipulative their actions have been. Not to mention destructive."

"Why don't we go out for a meal? Talk it through."

"I don't think that's the best idea, right now." She didn't feel comfortable being out in public knowing there might be a detective following them still.

Her mind was already racing with plans of how to tackle this. She needed to figure out how she addressed it with her students. Maybe it was time to update the bullying workshops they had on file. Take some kind of action. "I think Charlotte should see Mr. Taylor on Monday. I can block out her classes so she can have a double session with him. If she still wants to go back to school, she can start on Tuesday, but some time away would be best for her."

"Don't do this, Ally."

"Do what?"

"Compartmentalise. You're going into work mode and it won't help right now. Don't pull away from me now that the shit has hit the fan."

"I'm not pulling away, Owen. I just...I need to *do* something. I feel so useless right now. Like there is nothing I can do to make it right and I just want—I need to fix it." Her voice hitched. "I don't want you to think this has made me second-guess our relationship. It hasn't. Not one bit.

"But you have to understand, I feel like I've failed in my duty of care here. To think that Charlotte will be teased because of it, makes me so angry, and so helpless—" Her voice broke. She allowed the fear and shame to filter through. She wouldn't close herself off from it. Or him. No matter how haunting those old habits were at times, it wasn't who she wanted to be anymore.

The past week had given her that clarity. She needed to prove to Owen, to Charlotte that she was there for them. That they could trust her and rely on her to stick it out when the going got tough.

"Ally, trust me, we'll figure this out. Together."

"I know we will. I don't think it's a good idea to go out for a meal, but I can pick up some pizza on my way over if that's okay?"

She heard the smile in his voice. "That's the best news I've had all day. We'll see you soon."

They would salvage the rest of the night on their terms. Without detectives or custody battles. They'd enjoy each other and the simple pleasures of being a unit. A family.

Work could wait for a day or two.

It was clear that Monday—and the next hurdle—would come around soon enough.

CHAPTER THIRTY-FOUR

*E*ven though conflict often left her with an ulcer, Ally spent the following two weeks channelling all her simmering anger into action.

After a few Year 8 boys decided it would be funny to tease Charlotte about her dad "cooking up something with the Foods teacher"—and other not so savoury chants—she had had enough.

Sure, she had a detention lined up for those boys anyway, but she needed to do more. The principal had directed every class to spend a few lessons reviewing the school's values, in particular the detriment of bullying and invasion of privacy. Having that support had been humbling, but still she remained restless. She needed to do something cathartic that would help ease the wrongdoing against her. Against her family.

That's what they were becoming. With every passing day, with each new battle, Ally felt the connection grow. She couldn't imagine not sharing her life with them, of building a future together. Now, more so than ever.

But the fortnight since the nasty photos surfaced had been the toughest few weeks of her career. She had spoken to her team, to the school council and the principal, and received support from all areas. But she had also faced backlash from parents who felt it their duty to remind her of how someone with greater seniority might be better suited to the role. When Jacinta had addressed the gross invasion of privacy at the whole school assembly, she was reassured that they had tackled the issue from all angles.

But in private she gave way to tears of frustration. She allowed herself to feel the humiliation, the sheer exhaustion of putting on a brave face every day without knowing if she was still being followed.

Even though she faked an air of confidence, of efficiency, she wasn't sure she was actually on top of her job.

She feared losing her position, of someone with greater experience, and less scandal behind them being appointed. She would wake up in a cold sweat, fearful that someone else's vitriol might affect her chances. Her mind conjured up terrifying possibilities.

When Charlotte began showing signs of withdrawing again, Ally had seen red. Despite Owen's reassurances that he would talk to her, she needed to act. Desperate to do something, exhausted by her fears, she knocked on the door of the opulent townhouse that Friday after work with only one aim in mind.

When it finally opened, she lifted her chin and breathed through the spider web that seemed to snare her lungs.

"Mrs. Langdon?"

The woman narrowed her eyes. "What do you want?"

"I'm from Charlotte's school and I'd like a word with you and your husband."

"I know who you are. He isn't home." Her frosty reply had her temper inching up higher than the sun.

"Just you then."

"You have to leave."

Ally placed her arm against the closing door and jerked it back. The woman yelped.

"What is it?" Came a deep rumble from inside.

"Quick, Henry!"

The tall man lumbered down the hallway then stopped short.

"This will do," she said. "I'm sure you both know that I'm Charlotte's coordinator and head of junior school at Woodbury High. Or maybe the photos weren't clear enough."

"What the hell—"

She lifted a hand. "Please, sir. Shut up."

"Get the hell out of my house." He towered over her now.

Ally stood her ground and lifted her chin. "I'm not leaving until I've said my piece. And you'd better be listening. As you know, I'm sleeping with your son-in-law. Sorry, ex-son-in-law."

She watched them flinch, satisfied. She had dealt with people like this her whole life. She knew exactly how to disgust them with her words. "And whilst my sex life is intriguing to you fine, repressed folk, I'd kindly appreciate it if you didn't meddle with my life by plastering photos around my workplace."

Their smug expression only added more fuel to her raging fire.

"This is not your concern."

"Oh, but you've made it my concern. You want custody of your granddaughter and so you've gone to the lowest common denominator to make it work. I get it. Playing dirty. But in all this, you've failed to see that your actions have led to a lot of heartache for that little girl. Your daughter's child.

"Charlotte's had to deal with the shame of what you've done and the bullying that's come of it. Sure, attack me all you want, keep attacking Owen, but when it comes to the well-being of my students and the well-being of a little girl who is innocent in all of this, then I have a duty of care to step in."

Some sane, rational part of her knew that speaking to them went outside the boundaries of her care. But her feelings had become a hell of a lot more personal than professional over the past five months.

The lines had been blurred—the ones she fought so hard to keep in place. The ones she thought were so important. None of that mattered anymore.

"How dare you come to our home and speak to us that way!" Anita almost spat.

"How dare I? When you make it personal, lady, then I get to act as I please. You're not winning this game by treating your grandchild like a chess piece. You're going to lose her, mark my words. If you don't stop playing dirty, things are going to get ugly.

"This whole surveillance thing you've got going on...you think the courts are going to like hearing about the trauma it's causing Charlotte?"

"Are you threatening me, woman?" Henry boomed.

"No, Mr. Langdon. That's not a threat. A threat would be something along the lines of telling you that my father, Peter McVeigh, is a prominent figure in the business and financial circles. My father has a lot of influence over a lot of people. You know how easy it is for information of a scandalous nature to make life difficult for individuals such as yourselves." Her voice was sugary sweet and deadly as poison. "It's all about keeping up appearances after all, isn't it, Henry?"

His mouth gaped open and closed.

Anita stepped forward. "You bitch! Get out."

"That's rich coming from a woman who cares more about revenge than her flesh and blood." Ally's shoulder's sagged. She hated being manipulative. Hated playing games. It reminded her too much of her parents. But sometimes you had to fight fire with fire. "I didn't come here to threaten you, Mr. and Mrs. Langdon, but I came here to educate you.

"What you're doing to Owen is affecting Charlotte, and if you cared an ounce about her, you'd stop this ridiculous fight. I guarantee you that he isn't going to just give up that easily. You can throw your money and your influence around, hire as many detectives as you want, but the facts remain—he's a good father and Charlotte loves him."

"He ruined our daughter's life! And now she's dead."

She swallowed, refusing to be shamed. "I'm sorry for your loss. But this isn't right. What you're doing is ruining that child's life. Think about what you're doing to *her*. You're only driving her away. Shame on you both for putting Charlotte through this."

She turned to leave. Then paused. "Oh. And if you ever come at me and jeopardise my career again, I will be taking legal action. That's a promise, Mr. and Mrs. Langdon. Now do us all a favour and grow up."

She turned away, head held high. She'd scrub herself clean of the guilt as soon as she got home.

Later that evening, after a long walk and a few hours of administrative work under her belt, Ally stepped out of the shower feeling a little less guilty about what had transpired.

She dressed, wondering if she had made the wrong decision, then accepted that she couldn't turn back the clock and reverse the events. Not that she even wanted to; it needed to be said and she could only hope that once their anger subsided that her message would sink in.

The knock on her door an hour later startled her. Placing her cup of tea on the kitchen table, she found Owen on the landing.

"Hey, you." She stepped back to let him in.

"Hey, yourself."

She leaned into his kiss, shivering at the cold that lingered on his jacket.

"Come on in."

"I can't stay for long, picking up Charlotte's from Jeremy's place."

"All they're doing is baking."

His guarded look made her smile.

"Wait a few years. It'll be a cover for more…"

"Unsavoury activities?" She winked.

Owen grunted.

"Did you talk to her? Has she said anything?"

He rubbed at his jaw. "No. You're right, though. She is holding something back. I don't like her being so closed off again. When Jeremy called and asked if she could come over after school for a few hours I all but shoved her into her jacket. She needs something normal right now. Baking, her friends, it'll keep her connected."

"I'll get her seeing the Mr. Taylor for another session. She wasn't really talking much the last meeting, which isn't abnormal given the situation."

"Hmm."

"Any news from your lawyer?"

His mouth curved upwards in a slow, knowing grin. "Funny you ask. That's actually the reason I stopped by."

Ally perched on the back of the sofa. Studying his expression, she frowned. "Okay. Good news or bad?"

"Interesting." He stepped closer. "Imagine my surprise when John rings me an hour ago to tell me that a certain someone I know went to see Charlotte's grandparents this afternoon?"

Her mouth opened.

"Shall I continue?"

She barely nodded.

"Not only did you visit them. Apparently, you gave them a

savage set down. So much so, that they felt you were threatening them—and didn't want to deal with such a volatile and rude upstart ever again." Owen grinned. "You can imagine how floored I was—thinking that this woman I can't seem to get enough of was going around fighting my battles and staking her claim."

"I wasn't—"

"Oh, yes you were, sweetheart." He drew her up and into his arms. "After I got over the shock, I realised that for you to do that, to stick up for us—for Charlotte—to confront the people who've made your life at work difficult to say the least, was a massive step. One that took a lot of courage, and a shit load of loyalty."

"Owen, I—" She held onto his arms.

"I wanted to thank you. For standing up to them even though you didn't need to. For proving I was right."

"Is that so?"

"Hell yes. I knew starting a relationship with you would be life-changing. I was just waiting for you to see it too."

"I didn't want Charlotte getting caught up in their games anymore. She's just a child. She deserves a childhood."

He cupped her face. The rhythmic stroking on her cheek was enough to distract her. He inched closer. "We'll give her one. I know I promised you to move slowly, but Ally, I want so much more. And what you did today shows me you want that too." He planted little kisses on her chin, up to her ear.

"Owen." She tugged back. His eyes were piercing. "I went to visit them today because I don't seem to have any control when it comes to you and Charlotte. That distance between my work and what we have is all jumbled."

"I know, that's why I said I wouldn't pressure you to—"

"No. It's okay. It scared me at the beginning, but what I feel for you both erases all those concerns. I'd do it again in a heartbeat."

"So maybe we can turbo charge this relationship a little? I know Charlie is excited to have you as part of the family. To have a mother again."

She wanted to be Charlotte's mother, more than anything. But she also knew that rushing it, for both of them, when everything was still so unsettled couldn't be the stability that little girl needed right now.

"Stop. Whatever it is that has put the fear of God in those eyes, stop now. All I'm saying is that Charlie likes you. More than likes you. She loves the idea of us. Don't second-guess it."

She shook her head. "No. it's not that. I was thinking that she needs stability right now. With everything going on, I don't want to push the mum card too soon. But I want you to know that I want it. Wherever this takes us. I want to be a part of your family, Owen."

His hands gripped her waist. His eyes revealed the truth. He all but beamed. "Even the psycho ex-in-laws?"

Ally feigned a look of horror. "Even the psycho ex-in-laws. Remember I've not unleashed my equally deranged parents on you."

"Sounds like a fair trade to me."

"You say that now."

"I'll say it for forever."

He nibbled at her lip, then drew her into his kiss. She floated in his arms, wrapping her hopes and dreams around them both until she quivered with need.

Heart full, she gave herself up to the moment, uncertain, but excited to be taking the next step.

CHAPTER THIRTY-FIVE

*A*lly convinced herself that if she finished the work at her desk now, then she'd be able to relax all weekend at home. It was a solid plan. An hour ago, it was an achievable one. But when her stomach rumbled in protest, she decided it was better to feed the beast, than do battle with her hangry side. It was Friday night, which meant she'd normally be enjoying a post-work drink with Owen, but she was determined to get the stack of folios graded. She had one week left of this term before their two week break; one week more of slaving at her desk, working insane hours until she could breathe a little. That thought kept her going.

She opened her bottom drawer and grabbed a fun-size Snickers bar from her stash. The relief was instant. Only to be replaced by a second gnawing pang of hunger. She knew that one morsel wouldn't be enough. She was about to indulge in a second bar of bliss when the telephone pealed.

"Ally McVeigh, junior school."

"Thank Christ! I've been trying to contact you for the past half an hour!"

"Owen? Sorry, I turned my phone on silent so I wouldn't be distracted."

"Charlotte's run away." The barely restrained terror in his voice turned the chocolate treat to metal in her mouth.

"What? Are you sure?"

"Yes, I'm sure. I was prepping dinner and she was upstairs. I said I'd call her in an hour and she was going to finish off some homework."

"Then what happened?"

"I called her. Nothing. I checked the whole house and it was empty. There was a note on my bed, saying, *I'm sorry, Dad, I didn't want to cause more trouble. Don't worry, I'll be safe. Love, Charlie.*"

Ally tried to make sense of it. "Cause more trouble?" she echoed. "I don't understand. Are you sure she isn't hiding in the house?"

"I've looked. Multiple times. She's not in her tree house and she isn't at Jeremy's or Holly's or with any of her friends. She's just a kid." His voice broke. "It's getting dark out, it's cold and hammering with rain—what if someone has taken her?"

Her stomach lurched. "Don't think that way. She couldn't have gone far."

"Her bicycle is missing."

Hell. Maybe she could.

"Any luck with her phone?"

"Switched off."

"Alright. You scour the area. Check any of our usual haunts in the neighbourhood. I'll be over soon."

"Wait! Check the school. She may have come back there?"

"Right. Contact me if you hear anything."

Ally picked up her bag and raced around the school calling out Charlotte's name. She asked the cleaners if they saw anyone matching her description, then ran back to her office to pick up a school photo of her. It would be easier if they could show people a picture.

She fired off texts to Maddie and Sera asking them to begin searching.

By the time she drove to Owen's place, every light was on in the house. He was in the front yard, pacing.

"Any sign?" She ran up and hugged him.

"No. I drove by the area. Nothing. Jesus, Ally. It's dark. How is she going to be okay? What if something bad has happened?"

"You can't think that way. Owen, you'll drive yourself insane with worry. I've got Maddie and Sera on it. She'll turn up."

His mouth was grim, his hair drenched from the rain.

She gnawed at her lip. "Is it possible that she's gone to her grandparents' house? Or that they're somehow involved?"

His face grew hard. "I doubt that. She wouldn't have left the note if they were coercing her to go there. And they're the last two people she wants to see right now. Plus, I haven't told them yet. I had hoped I'd find her by now. Christ, this is bad. What kind of a parent loses their daughter under their own roof?" He paced, treading a worn path in the damp grass.

As if to smite them, there was a rumble and the heavens opened with a fresh deluge. She scrambled under the porch; Owen wearily followed.

"You need to call the Langdons. At least get them on the search."

He nodded. "I'm going back out again. I'll call them on the way. I can't sit around just waiting for something to happen."

"I'll go in my car. You in yours. It'll widen the search."

"What if she comes back?"

"Call your neighbours to stay here in case she comes home. We might want to search the house again. My friend's cousin left a runaway note and they found him four hours later in the cupboard under a pile of plush toys. He thought it would be funny to scare them all."

"Jesus." He rubbed at his chest.

"My point is, she might be closer than we think." She ushered him into the house and reminded him to bring a recent photo.

Hours of searching came and went, to no avail. The rain became a downpour, and a last wintery cold snap froze the city in deference to the past season and a blatant snub at spring.

Owen had called the police as soon as he had found the note. Ally looked at their advice page on her phone for tips.

Despite scouring the house and the surrounding suburbs, they came up with nothing. The scary truth remained that she could be anywhere, and they wouldn't be able to find her. Not if she didn't want to be found.

Owen's face had turned a whiter shade of pale after speaking to the Langdons, who had no luck in finding her either. They hadn't passed up the opportunity to berate him in the meantime, no doubt waiting for their chance to use this against him.

They brainstormed and made phone calls, going out in search parties with every new idea for where she could be. They enlisted friends to search the neighbourhood just to make sure they had all areas covered. Yet Saturday morning arrived and there was still no sight of her.

By Saturday evening, Owen was even more dishevelled. Ally tried to convince him to get some rest, but he was relentless. She had visited Charlotte's friends numerous times over the past twenty-four hours but no one had seen or heard from her.

The police were trying to do everything possible, but it took time.

She finally convinced him to take an hour to sleep and shower late that evening, despite his protests.

Feeling worse for wear herself, she drove home to change

and pack a few fresh clothes to bring back. They needed to keep up their strength if they were going to be of any use.

Every time she thought of Charlotte out in the cold, alone, she wanted to scream. She suppressed the dread that wrapped around her limbs, weighing down her mind. Her eyes stung with fatigue, but she wouldn't sleep. Not until she was found.

She had tried her best to comfort Owen, but he was caught up in his own nightmare, unable to let go of the terror that his baby girl was somehow in danger. She wouldn't let herself believe that was true.

With weary eyes and a pounding head, Ally got out of the car. Her mind still raced. Maybe there was something they missed? The ground was still slippery from the twenty-four-hour deluge and fatigue threw her balance off kilter. Before she could correct herself, she slipped down the ramp, staggering into the drenched wheelie bins at the side of her building.

Her half-consumed latte spilled out over the concrete. She cried out as the gravel scraped at her palms, now stinging and blood speckled. Ally tried to sit up. Then froze. She was certain she had heard a noise. Brushing aside the low hanging branches, she found a small figure lying in the muddy ground. Its tiny, bare legs were curled up, blonde hair dishevelled and dirty.

Her heart leapt.

Charlotte's limp body lay in the bushes. Her face, arms and legs were icy cold, faint tinges of blue marred her lips.

Relief was soon overcome by terror.

"Charlotte! Honey, wake up." A little mewl escaped her lips. "Charlotte, open your eyes. It's Ally. It's Ally, sweetheart." Her eyelids fluttered. In the light from her phone, she thought she could see her lips working.

She punched in 000, relieved when she found a faint pulse.

Next, she called Owen. "I've found her. At my place. I don't know. But I've called an ambulance. You best come quick."

CHAPTER THIRTY-SIX

The next twenty-four hours were a blur.

Ally didn't leave Owen and Charlotte's side, even when her eyes drooped, and her body heaved with nausea.

It had been sleeping in the freezing cold on Friday night, accompanied by a day of wandering around in the storm that had led to the young girl's hypothermia. Doctors were trying to treat her as best as they could, and the waiting game for her to recover was a slow, torturous event. Especially as she had suffered a head injury. Charlotte's bike was mangled; Ally hadn't noticed the bruise on her head until she had been admitted.

In the light of the hospital room she could see how her blonde hair was dirtied by blood; stained and almost blackened with it.

It was no wonder that her case was so severe.

She bit her lip and cursed for the millionth time that day. Why hadn't she gone home earlier? If she had, then Charlotte wouldn't be lying in a hospital bed. Then again if she hadn't slipped would she even noticed her in the bushes? She shuddered to think of the alternative.

"How is she?" she asked when Owen came out of the room.

"They've got her on an intravenous drip. They're trying to slowly increase her core temperature, but it doesn't help that she sustained a head injury."

"I'm so sorry."

His tired eyes turned sharp. "What are you apologising for?"

"I didn't think to check my place. I wouldn't have thought she would end up there. We never go there."

Owen's mouth was grim. "It isn't your fault. You did everything you could. I should have forced her to tell me what was troubling her, but I didn't want to push too hard. I knew the photos really bothered her, on top of the custody crap...but I never thought she'd run away."

"We'll find out in time. The doctors are happy with her progress?"

"They're cautious but are optimistic that she'll recover well. Age is on her side. Though they still want to do tests. The fact that she's slipping in and out of consciousness can't be good."

She gripped his arm. "She'll make it through. We have to believe that."

His eyes grew wary. "I hope so. Hey, you need some rest. You've been up two days straight."

"As have you. I'm staying, Owen. That's what family does."

He gripped her hand, then kissed her palm. "I appreciate it."

Owen only managed to convince her to go home when the doctors stipulated that only one parent could stay. They made up a cot for him to sleep in that Sunday evening, so Ally had no choice but to head back to her apartment.

She called in sick and slept for twelve hours straight that

night. When she woke on Monday morning, her body was still fatigued, but she had energy. That was something.

When she arrived at the hospital, it was with relief that Charlotte's colour had returned somewhat.

By Tuesday, she was awake for more than snatches at a time and strong enough to talk.

Owen held her hand. Whilst he looked relieved, the concern for his daughter's wellbeing shadowed his every action. "What happened, kiddo? We need to understand why you ran away."

Her slim little shoulders shrugged. Tears swam in her eyes.

"Your dad isn't mad at you," Ally added. "He was more worried sick. Whatever it is you're feeling, that's okay. You can tell us anything."

"I knew it was my fault," she whispered mournfully.

"What's your fault, baby doll? Help us understand." Owen let go of her hand and sat beside her on the bed. He stroked her hair back, holding her close.

"If it wasn't for me, then Grandpa and Grandma wouldn't be taking you to court."

Owen's eyes hardened.

"Let her finish."

"And—and if I wasn't here, then they wouldn't be trying to hurt you, or Ally. It's because of me that they did this. And now they're trying to attack you and get a constraining order."

Ally sat on the other side of the bed. "A *restraining* order. How do you know that?"

"I overheard Dad's lawyer on the phone. I kind of listened in when they were talking. They said after you went over to their place, they wanted to take action and bring you all down."

She could tell Owen was trying to steady his breathing, calm the storm raging—barely restrained—beneath the surface, before he spoke.

"Charlie, that was an adult conversation. One that you shouldn't have been listening to."

"So, what did you think would happen?"

She shrugged again. "I knew that they were making trouble and I didn't want to cause it anymore. I thought that if I ran away then nobody would fight."

"Oh, darling girl." Ally's eyes stung. She squeezed the child's arm, remembering exactly what it was like being a frightened child who only wanted peace. Guilt at her actions, at potentially making the situation worse, left her hollow. All she wanted to do was protect her, but she had made it worse.

It struck her then. The overwhelming urge to protect and care for her—to love the little girl like she was her own flesh and blood. Alongside that feeling came the fear: that she wasn't enough. She straightened.

"This was not your fault. I should never have confronted them. I was acting out of anger; that was my mistake and I apologise. Sweetheart, you shouldn't be worrying about any of this. It doesn't change how much we all love you."

"Nobody is taking my baby girl away from me. You hear?" Owen kissed the top of her head. "Your grandparents just want what they think is best for you. They're angry at me because your mum died too soon. Sometimes when people haven't grieved properly, they make mistakes. They're hurting but don't know how to deal with that pain. All you can do is fight for what you believe in and hope they come around eventually."

"But they're wrong! You're the best dad ever!" She flung her arms around him.

"And you're the best kid a dad could have. But that doesn't mean you take the situation in your own hands. You should have come to me or Ally with how you were feeling." He drew back and wiped the tears from her small, round face.

"But what about—"

"Nobody is going to do anything to put us at risk. Or tear us apart. They're just words that lawyers use, and Grandma and Grandpa are torn right now."

"You don't know that!" she sobbed.

Owen kissed Charlotte's small fingers. "I do. Because we're a team, kiddo." He reached out for Ally's hand. "We're family. And family sticks together and can't be torn apart. I'm trying to talk things through with them, so I'm sure they'll come around soon enough."

"And if they don't?"

She shifted closer. "I know how scary it is not to be able to control things. I felt the same when I was your age. But you know what you have? An amazing family. A father and uncle who love you, plus heaps of friends who will be happy to know you're safe."

"And you?" She looked at her tentatively.

Ally's heart bled. "And me. We all love you. You can always rely on me, sweetheart. I've got your back, okay?"

The little girl nodded.

"How did you end up at my place?"

Charlotte explained how she didn't have a plan. "I was just going to ride around for a bit. But then I got lost. The rain was so heavy. I recognised that park near your apartment, so I knew I was near, but my phone had died and I had crashed my bike over a fallen branch. I got dizzy and slept under the bench by the oval somewhere. I eventually found your place but felt sick and blacked out...I'm sorry. I didn't mean for you to worry."

"I'm just happy that you're well. Promise me that you won't do that again? If you have a problem you've got to talk about it. Running away doesn't solve anything. Deal?"

"Deal." Charlotte stifled a yawn.

"You should get some rest. I'm relieved to have you back again. I've missed you."

"Thanks. I've missed you too."

Ally hugged her, motioning for Owen to sit. She'd see herself out.

It wasn't until she reached the parking lot that her fear dissolved into tears. She was relieved that Charlotte was recovering, but she realised there was much to learn about being a mother. She had no idea where to start.

CHAPTER THIRTY-SEVEN

*A*lly had naively believed that the final term of the school year would start with good news. But after the first week back, she had more issues than ever. Exams were looming for her senior students, final rounds of reports would be due, and she needed to write up her application if she wanted to be reappointed as head of junior school in an ongoing capacity.

To top it all off, she had woken up that Saturday morning to voicemail messages from both her parents. She had somehow believed that their silence over the past month meant they were finally able to function without her.

She supposed it wasn't all bad. She had spent most of the term break with Charlotte and Owen. It was a relief to see the little girl slowly getting her energy back.

But she had been adamant to stay at her own apartment at least a few nights a week. Until the case was settled, she didn't want to force this new family dynamic onto her. Not yet. Not until they knew where they stood.

If she was honest with herself, the idea of being a mother to Charlotte was exciting yet confusing. Was she supposed to discipline her when she was sassy, or did she leave that to Owen? Would the little girl resent her for taking time away from her dad? It was all foreign territory.

It wasn't like she could ask her parents for advice. Not that she ever could.

She arrived at the family home—as per their instructions—in a foul mood.

"What's going on?"

Her mother tilted her nose up and moved aside to let her in.

"Is there a reason that I have a million voicemail messages on my phone? All of them cryptic." What pissed her off even more than the barrage of messages, was the fact that her parents never deigned to tell her what the problem was, or even why they were calling. There was no, "oh darling, just ringing to see you were alright" or "I seem to have sawed off my arm, be a dear and visit me in hospital."

Instead, she received hieroglyphic inspired messages that made her want to move state.

Whilst the two week break had been exactly what they all needed, the court case still loomed on the horizon. On top of that, she was afraid she wouldn't be reappointed as the head of junior school.

Her eyes stung; she was at the end of her tether. Not that she would ever cry in front of her parents. They wouldn't understand.

Better to remain detached. Cold. The McVeigh way. It meant you never got hurt. More so, no one knew if you did. It was destructive behaviour; a pretence she was finding harder to adopt these days. She supposed that was a good sign.

Her mother barely spared her a glance. "Your father is in the sitting room."

Ally rolled her eyes and slunk off, hoping the visit would be short.

"You look terrible, Allyna," she said at her back. "You really need to dress more appropriately. Those clothes make you look like a beggar. People in this area don't dress that way you know."

"I know, Mother. You've told me. And I still don't care."

She heard her mother delicately sniff behind her and ground her teeth. She would not be provoked to react. She would remain calm. Three, two, one...

"I thought you forgot you had parents."

She looked at her father, sitting against the antique chaise, his feet propped up, a drink in his hand.

"Hello. How's the hip?"

He sipped. "Between you and your mother, I'm feeling very taken care of actually."

"Sarcasm doesn't become you, Peter." Her mother reached for her drink off the heavy marble side table.

"Sandy, your nurse called. She's been keeping me updated on your progress and it seems like you're as good as new."

"Apparently it's too difficult for you to speak to me yourself now. Abandoning me to carers was heartless, even for you."

"You've had the best care possible, Father. I've told you that many times. The physio seems to be working wonders, which is why you've needed them to be with you so often. You know very well that I've called to check up on you. I've left dozens of voicemail messages. I don't know what else you need from me. I do have to work for a living."

"Ahh, yes. Work. Sit. That's what we wanted to speak to you about."

"Look, if this is another conversation about a career change, then I'd really rather not hear it."

Ally sat down. Her bones were like lead weights. Her mind fatigued. The sooner she left this house, the better. She never liked the memories that hovered behind its perfect façade. Being in close proximity to her parents never failed to tear open old wounds.

Lately, the thought of being a mother to Charlotte had brought up all the unresolved trauma from her childhood. She thought she had moved on. And she had—in part. But she also knew, deep inside, that she hadn't let go of all that pain. The sad thought was, perhaps she never would.

"We've heard, from a range of reliable sources, that you have gone about threatening a well-respected family in our social circle. Is this true?"

Ally's stomach dropped. Was she ever going to be able to get away from that?

"Is this true?" her mother pressed. "Answer your father, please."

"It's complicated."

Part of her was surprised it had taken them over three weeks to hear about it. Knowing her parents, it had taken them that long to decide how to broach it with her.

"Complicated?" Her mother screeched.

"Please, Vera, I'll handle this. Allyna, this family prides itself on our reputation. I'm a very influential and a well-known figure in this society. In business. How do you think it looks when my only daughter is caught *threatening* another family?"

"You don't have the full picture. Yes, I threatened them, but the welfare of a child was at stake."

"Oh, don't be so melodramatic." Her father waved his hand. "You've got to separate work from your personal life."

"And stop getting involved with that no-good widower," her mother cut in. "What do you know of that man?"

Her attempt at composure was fast unravelling. "Who I sleep with, Mother, is none of your concern."

"Don't you speak to me that way. We didn't raise you to be vulgar."

Ally stood. "No? Well vulgar would be saying that I'm fucking Owen Davies. Is that better?"

Her mother's horrified gasp gave her sick satisfaction. She

was fifteen and rebellious. She itched with self-disgust even when a small part of her relished their reaction.

"I will not have you speak that way under this roof. Your mother is simply warning you about marrying a man who isn't of your class. Knocking up that poor girl when she was a teenager." He shook his head.

"And he married her!"

"Yes, but what of his family?" Her mother recovered the use of her tongue. "What of his parents? Middle class—if that—and he's not even making a fortune for himself. He'd hardly fit in our circles."

"Your circles? No one fits in *your* circles, because they're cyclones of destruction. Owen does very well for himself as a single parent. And who the hell spoke about marriage?"

"I don't think it's an appropriate match." Her mother sniffed.

"That's none of your business. My private life has nothing to do with you."

"It does when you go around threatening decent people!" Her father's face turned red. "The Langdons, whilst not as wealthy as us, are still members of our community. They have serious reservations about that boy. The stress he put that poor girl through surely killed her. You know they were considering a divorce."

She bit her tongue. She wouldn't bring up their own dysfunctional marriage. Any time she had tried, they had feigned ignorance.

Ally's conscience pinged. Her conversation with Charlotte, months ago, echoed through her mind. How could she ask a twelve-year-old to be honest with her dad, if she couldn't be herself?

"You know, you look down on others—those without wealth, those who've been divorced, but you forget that the both of you are separated and have been for decades. You're playing a charade to everyone in the world—including yourselves."

"I don't know what you mean." Vera looked away.

"You can feign ignorance all you want, but I had to grow up playing pretend and I'm sick of it. The two of you need to learn to grow up and sort out your issues. I had to put up with it when I was a kid, but I won't do it now. You want to speak to me like an adult, then do it, but don't bring me here to lecture me like a child."

"You need to stop hanging out with these people. It's changing your attitude."

Yet again her parents were unable to acknowledge their behaviour. Or even admit to the truth.

"I don't expect you to understand, Father. I needed more than just a good education and good society growing up. I needed you both to show me how much you cared. I needed… do you even love one another? Or me?"

Her parents spared each other a glance.

"Don't be silly, child. You had the best of everything. This talk is beneath you."

Ally shrugged. "I don't even know why I bother."

"We've done everything we could to bring you up right. Instead of gratitude, you showed disrespect. It seems we'll never see eye to eye on it, but your mother and I would appreciate it if you didn't insult respectable members of society. I fear this job of yours is a bad influence. How will anyone take you seriously if you're in a relationship with a parent? It's not professional."

The fact that she was questioning whether she was right for the position in junior school hit too close to home.

"You're one to talk. At least I'm in a loving relationship, which is far more than your little bits on the side ever were." She heard her mother's gasp and felt the weight of her family expectations crushing her confidence. She needed to keep far away from them. For her own mental health. "What I do or don't do in my life is none of your concern."

"It is when you sully our name. Sleeping with a divorcé. Are you going to be looking after his child as well like some nanny? You deserve someone of the same background as you."

"Enough!" Ally yelled. "I'm sick of the two of you telling me what to do instead of asking how I am. You've never cared about my opinion, or how any of your decisions affected me as a child. It seems you still don't care.

"I'm a grown woman. Whoever I sleep with, threaten, marry or work for is none of your business. Regardless of whether you approve or not, I will live my life as I see fit. If that doesn't tie into your grand plans, then I'm truly sorry for you both."

"You can imagine what they're saying at the club. Mrs. Allsop had heard of your liaison with your student's father a long time ago. The pictures!" Her mother looked horrified.

"Your actions affect us whether you like it or not." Her father tried to shift out of the chair. "We've had to do a lot of damage control for your wild ways. We won't have it. You hear?"

"I'm done with listening to you both. All I've ever wanted is for you to be proud of me. To see *me* and not some image you had to mould in your likeness. But any time I've ever tried to talk to either of you, any time I showed any kind of feeling or affection, I was corrected for it. I barely remember a kind word, or even gentle encouragement. It was always what I had done wrong, what I could improve on."

"We didn't want you to be weak. If we didn't point out your faults, who would?"

Ally's throat burned. They would never understand her. Never truly listen; she was only picking at old wounds by confronting them.

"I just wanted you to show a bit of kindness. To see it from my point of view. I know I'm not the daughter you wanted. I understand the life I'm living is far from your ideal, but it's my life. As your child, all I've wanted is your acceptance, but I see I'm never going to get it. We live in two different worlds."

"Don't be so dramatic, child," her father admonished. "You need to realise that the life we have provided for you will bring you happiness—more than you have now."

"Like the two of you? You're both miserable, stuck in the same bullshit cycle. I refuse to be caught up in it any longer. If you want a relationship with me—not the version of me you think I should become—then give me a call. I'll see myself out."

"I'm not done talking to you!" her father bellowed.

The heartache she wanted to bottle up spilled over. Slamming the door, Ally left her childhood home, uncertain if she would ever make peace with her parents.

She was weary of them. Weary of always feeling inadequate. Her parents had displayed more emotion this afternoon that she had seen in decades. It was too damn bad it just wasn't the right kind. She knew with certainty that it never would be.

CHAPTER THIRTY-EIGHT

*A*lly didn't care that she looked worse than ever. Or that she needed to wash her hair. She just wanted to wallow in a tub of ice cream and read about celebrities with disgustingly perfect yet non-functioning lives. It somehow made her feel better about herself. In a morbid way.

After recounting the events to Owen that Saturday evening as they snuggled by the fire, she had fooled herself into believing that she was over it.

She woke on Sunday morning in a total funk. Breakfast with Charlotte had been a lovely distraction, but she had gone back to her apartment with her heart heavier than ever. When she opened her door a few hours later to find her two best friends looking fresh and lovely, she fought against the petty urge to sulk.

Sera gave her the once over. "You forgot?"

Maddie swanned past in jeans and a leather jacket, nabbing the tub from Ally's fingers.

"Forgot what?" She turned as the two settled on her couch.

Maddie gestured to her outfit. "Shopping trip? In the city? Followed by dinner at some nice little alleyway bistro?"

She slumped down next to them. "Totally forgot."

"And so not in the mood it seems. Did you skip wash day? Your hair's like a bird's nest."

Ally threw her a sideways death glare. "Thank you, fashion police. I hadn't noticed. Not that I care anyway." She crossed her arms, hearing her petulance and hating herself even more for it.

"Uh oh. I know that tone."

"Oh, Al. Again?"

She squirmed, hating how her friends knew her so well. She jerked her shoulders in defence. "I saw them yesterday morning."

"And it's hurt you." Sera acknowledged.

She stood, allowing her anger to spew forth. "I'm sick of having this conversation with you both. With them! Yesterday was proof that no matter what I do, I'll never be enough in their eyes. They just don't get me. They don't *want* to understand. They sat there and justified why they've treated me with cold disdain for most of my life." Her voice hitched, tears flowing freely. "I'm sick of caring. Of not being enough."

"They're idiots. And as painful as it is to have parents who just aren't supportive, you've got to remember that you've got family. You have me and Sera, and Owen and Charlotte. You have a successful job and a great life. Nothing your parents say or do will ever take that away.

"You've had a rough year. Filled with so much emotion. Take some time out and cut yourself some slack. But don't ever question who you are. You're loyal, and loving and brave. You have a goal and a vision, and you care so much about others that you're willing to sacrifice everything for their benefit. Don't let that fear make you second-guess yourself."

"I've made such a mess of things."

"Jesus, Al! Life isn't perfect!" Maddie pointed the spoon at her. "Your parents have brainwashed you to think that. But life is sticky. It's okay to colour outside the lines and get spaghetti in your hair!"

"What isn't okay is to not take risks because you're afraid," Sera soothed.

"I know this...I do. They get in my head and I'm finding it harder to distance myself from their bullshit. I just wish I knew how to not feel the pain."

"You wouldn't be you if you didn't feel it."

"Would it help to see someone?" Sera asked when Ally sat beside her. "Talk it all through and process it? You're dealing with a lot right now...it can't hurt?"

"I was actually thinking about it. I'm so anxious about Owen going to court—not that we've heard anything, and reapplying for this job...I don't know if I'm cut out—"

"Stop!" Maddie held up her hand. "That's your parents talking. They're worms inside your brain, making you think things that just aren't true. You have to reapply. You're exactly what junior school needs and if you don't do it, I will."

"What if I apply and don't get it? After everything that's happened, what if there's an external candidate that's better than me?"

"I highly doubt that, Al." Sera squeezed her arm. "But if that happens, then we'll deal with it. Go into another sub-school. Take on a different kind of leadership role. Whatever happens, we've got your back."

She was sick at the thought of not being reappointed. Of missing out on being able to make some positive changes in her career. Of living a meaningful life.

Her friends were right. No matter what happened, she would deal with it. She had gone through so much already, and with some professional counselling maybe she would be able to let go of all the baggage. Or at least lighten the load a little. She took a deep, cleansing breath.

"What do you think about grabbing a shower and having a girls' afternoon of indulgence?" Maddie nudged her.

"Give me half an hour."

She raced to the bathroom, grateful for her friends.

By the time she had finished drying her hair, she realised that the heavy sensation on her chest had been alleviated. She was feeling a little lighter already.

CHAPTER THIRTY-NINE

*O*wen couldn't quite believe it. He staggered out of his lawyer's office into the warm spring air, elated at the sudden turn of events. The fact that he wasn't staring down the end of a lengthy custody battle made him want to weep with relief. He knew he had Jack—well, Jack's lawyer's brother, John, to thank for that.

He couldn't wait to share the unexpected news with Ally. To take her and Charlie out for dinner to celebrate.

Seeing her parents had rattled her, and whilst he had wanted to go over there and give them a piece of his mind, she had pleaded with him to not get involved. He had called them instead.

He recalled the look on Ally's face when she realised who he was talking to; she had been horrified at first, but by the end of his call, her anxiety had given way to tears.

She'd never had someone stand up for her before. All her past relationships didn't want a bar of her family drama. He reminded her that he wanted it all. And he meant it.

He didn't care that her father berated him or called him

trash. But he made damn sure to let them know that the next time they upset her, they'd be dealing with him.

After her confrontation with them, Ally had decided she couldn't be a part of their lives. At least not until she received counselling. He didn't blame her.

He knew firsthand how debilitating grief and trauma could be. Healing took time.

He could only hope for Ally's sake her parents would figure out how to make things right. They'd risk losing out on the chance to get to know her, to love the woman she had become.

If they didn't, it wouldn't change a thing. Not for him at least.

Owen finished the rest of his coffee and made his way home. He wound down the windows, catching the breeze and the faint smell of freshly mowed grass.

He was grateful that he could finally move on. He had dodged a massive bullet today.

When John had called him in for a chat, he didn't think it was to tell him that the Langdons had dropped their claim for custody. But it had happened. Finally, he could build a life with the woman he loved, without any issues between them. Now that it was over, Owen realised how big a problem it been for them all. Like they were treading water, never really moving anywhere.

It surprised him when John revealed that the reason they had changed gears was because of Charlie. Running away and ending up in hospital had shaken them. He was cynical enough to know that the threat of his new attorney may have been an even greater incentive for the Langdons to let it go. Not to mention Ally's confrontation.

Blaming Owen had been their first response—every time— he just hoped that this was the beginning of some sort of amicable relationship. For his daughter's sake. But it would take time for her to trust them again. As much as it angered him that Charlie had to see her grandparents for who they really were, he knew that she still loved them. That she had been wounded and torn by their actions. In the same way her mother had been.

He was letting her take the lead when it came to seeing them again. He wouldn't force the relationship if she didn't want it— she was old enough to decide. His little girl was nearly a teenager. Owen rubbed at his chest.

The pang of sorrow that usually came when he thought of Charlie's future, without her mother, eased when he was with Ally.

They would be a family. They had already started down that path.

She was the woman for him. He had known for a while now. Knowing it, he wanted to take their relationship forward another step.

In order to do that, he had to tell her exactly how he felt. There was nothing stopping them now.

CHAPTER FORTY

*A*lly's hands shook when she hung up the phone that Friday evening. She had been about to get ready for dinner with Owen when her mobile rang. She had recognised the number and knew immediately what the call would be about.

Since she had re-applied for the sub-school position, she had forced herself to focus on other things. Which was easy enough to do at such a busy time of year. Her senior students' final folios and school tours for the new cohort of Year 7 students kept her mind engaged and her nerves at bay.

The counselling sessions had helped ease some of the fears she had carried with her for so long. At first, it was odd to challenge those thoughts, to challenge the negative self-talk that had become a crutch throughout her life. She soon realised that letting go of those habits, changing that cycle of behaviour would feel alien at first. But that shift within her was ultimately good. She couldn't control her parents, but she could her actions and reactions to them.

As spring settled across the neighbourhood, Ally embraced her new outlook. Especially now that the custody case had been dropped. It had been a restrictive noose around them all. And even though she still had her concerns, she was confident that she could handle them—that they would tackle them together, as a team.

The knock on her apartment door jolted her out of her musings. She all but threw herself into Owen's arms.

"Hello to you too."

She kissed him, buoyed.

"Ally, you're shaking. What's going on?"

She drew him closer. "I just got off the phone with the principal."

"The job?"

She nodded, her eyes filling with tears. "You're looking at the new, *permanent* head of junior school."

Owen whooped, spinning her around. "I didn't have any doubts. Congratulations, gorgeous. You deserve it."

"I think I'm still in shock."

"This calls for a celebration. Got any champagne?"

Her heart fluttered in her chest. "No. Not a drop."

"I'm sure we can rectify that. Pack a bag. Stay with us this weekend. Charlie will want to celebrate when she comes home from Holly's place tomorrow."

"That would be lovely."

He brushed at her cheek. "So why do you look like your souffle just sank?"

She held his hands. "I've wanted to talk to you."

"Sounds serious."

"It is and it isn't."

"Okay."

"It's just a few things that came out in counselling. And it's been plaguing me a little." Ally reminded herself that change was good. Necessary. "So, in a lot of the discussions about my parents, what I've come to accept is that I've had a block in my mind about the idea of being a mother."

He nodded. "I'm glad you're talking to me about it."

"So am I. I've been so fearful about turning into my parents that I think I've shut off the natural, instinctive part of myself around Charlotte when it comes to being a mother. Or step-parent. I know I'll never replace Rebecca. And I don't want to. But I'm so unsure of how to do this right, that I've backed away from doing it at all."

Owen shook his head, grinning. "You *have* been doing it, Al. You see yourself as Charlie's coordinator, but in all that time you've been a mother to her as well. An amazing one."

She jerked back, surprised.

"You do it when you sit and watch another show on the history of baking. Or when you take her out for one on one time when she's had a bad day at school. Or—when you give her a stern look when she's being a brat." He mimicked her raising an eyebrow. "Which I find sexy as hell, by the way."

She laughed, tears spilling over.

He cupped her face. "You're being a mum, a most incredible one without thinking about it. I could see your reticence at first and I didn't want to push it, or force parenting on you too fast. I wanted you to find your rhythm. And you have."

"But who disciplines her when she gets older and the issues get bigger? What do I tell her to call me? How do I introduce myself to others?"

"We both do. Mum or Ally. Her mum," he answered. "But these are things we can talk through. And maybe it was some-thing I should have brought up sooner, but I don't have all the answers either. I've never raised a teenager. You're surrounded by them every day, so you already have an advantage. I'll be looking to you, Ms. McVeigh for some guidance." He winked. "We're a team. A family. We make those decisions together. Charlie included. Sound fair?"

"Yeah. It does. It sounds wonderful."

"Great. What say we have a private little celebration. Just

you and me before heading to dinner?" Owen walked her backwards.

"I'd have no objections to that. Not one."

"Good. You better believe I've got plans for you, miss."

She squealed when he lifted her up on his shoulder, felt the thrill of him when he smacked her bottom.

She welcomed him in her arms and in her bed, her heart lighter than it had been in years.

When he undressed her, finding every sensitive area, teasing her to distraction, she begged for more. As they both rose up, greedily taking their fill, Ally allowed herself to fall completely. She wondered why she had been so fearful of it all in the first place.

CHAPTER FORTY-ONE

$\mathcal{A}$s the end of the year was fast approaching, Owen had one thing on his mind. It wasn't expanding his business, or even Christmas shopping, but his future with Ally. He wanted to take that next step, to give her the words they both needed to hear. Words that they both felt but had yet to say.

She had offered so much. Taken risks when she had been more than scared. And in doing so she had given them a chance, a real chance at being a family.

He had told Charlie his plans and sworn her to secrecy. Which was difficult given the fact that the two of them were as thick as thieves.

After spending the afternoon finalising their plans, Charlie had asked to see her grandparents, much to his surprise.

Owen put his coffee down on the counter. "Are you sure about this, kiddo?"

Charlie nodded, throwing him an exasperated look. After turning thirteen the week before, she had morphed from a child into a know-it-all teenager. It both amused and frightened him.

"Yes, Dad, I'm sure."

"What made you decide this?"

This time she flipped back her hair. Apparently bangs were all the range this season. And hair-dye. He caved in on the new hairstyle but had thwarted her demands for purple hair. Not until she could master quadratic equations. The kid had already started studying.

"I think it's time."

"You don't have to feel pressured to do this, you know. I get it's Christmas and all about family, but I don't want you to rush into anything you aren't ready for."

"I'm not stupid. Sheesh." She rolled her eyes. "Ally and I had a chat about it the other week. I wanted to make sure she was okay with my decision too."

"Would it have stopped you from seeing them if she wasn't okay with it?"

She scrunched up her face in concentration. "I'd probably wait a bit longer if she was *really* upset. But she said I'm not responsible for other people's feelings and I need to make choices that are right for me."

"Sounds about right."

"I wrote them a letter. About how they made me feel and the rules I have if they want me to visit. A truce. You can read it if you want."

He was impressed by not only her generous heart, but her courage. "I don't think that's necessary. It's between you and your grandparents."

"Cool...so can we go?"

"Now?"

"Duh."

A few hours later, Charlie held a plate of freshly baked cookies and waited for her grandparents to answer the door.

He threw his arm around her shoulder. "I'm a phone call away, kiddo. Relax, it'll be fine."

She cast him a fierce look. "Should I be saying that to you? You know you need to let go?"

Owen smirked. Smart-arse.

Henry stood in front of them both, his manner stiff. Despite the crisp cut of his polo shirt and crease-free slacks, the man looked a little worn since he had seen him last.

"Good afternoon there, Charlotte."

"Grandpa. I brought you cookies. And my letter outlining our truce."

He gave her a one arm hug and cast Owen a knowing look. "I see that."

"You coming in, Dad?"

"I'll let you have some grandparent time, but I'll be here to pick you up at five."

Charlotte hugged him.

"About that." Henry frowned. Hummed. Hawed. Eventually looked him in the eye, then down at his grandchild. "Would you care to stay for tea, Charlotte? We thought as we haven't had a chance to catch up recently, that you'd like to have dinner with us."

Her face crumpled. "I would, Grandpa, but I have Jeremy's movie party tonight."

"Ah. Barely a teenager and already you've a busy social life. Your mother was the same. Not to worry. Next time."

"With Dad and Ally too, perhaps?"

"We'll see what we can arrange, kiddo." Owen ruffled her hair and waved goodbye. He heard Charlie race down the hall, hollering. The pressure in his chest eased that final inch. His child was happy. That's all that mattered.

"Owen." Henry stood on the porch, gently closing the door behind him. "We may never see eye to eye on this, but I wanted to thank you for bringing Charlotte around."

"Don't thank me. She's your granddaughter. She wants to see you both and I won't stand in the way of that. I suppose I should thank you for dropping the custody case. I hope you can appreciate how much she loves you. The both of you." He paused, then added, "I am sorry that Rebecca isn't here to watch her grow up. I may not understand the pain of losing a child, but I hope that for Charlie's sake we can get through it amicably. Or at least in a civil manner."

Henry's silvery head bobbed.

Owen took it for what it was, an olive branch.

CHAPTER FORTY-TWO

*L*ike all best laid plans, Ally's went slightly pear-shaped.

It was the end of what had been a long week, and she had decided to surprise Owen and Charlotte at home with a three-course meal. There, she would finally tell him she loved him. Loved Charlotte. That it was well past time that she did. Her reservations about their relationship, motherhood, her job were fading with every passing week.

She no longer wanted to take it slow. Not when she had found her place.

Her relationship with her parents would always be strained. And for the first time in her life, she was okay with that. She was open to change, open to having them in their lives. But it would be on her terms.

She had gone through her plans with Maddie and Sera. Just to make sure she didn't miss a detail. She may be new to love, but this feeling was as old as a lifetime.

Ally knew how Owen felt about her. They hadn't said it in words, but she could tell in all the little ways he made her feel cherished.

She pressed a hand to her stomach. She was a little jittery.

Nerves. The good kind. She wanted to get it right. She frowned. No. Not right. Special.

She loved him. She loved his little girl.

There was nothing stopping her.

Except for some late-comer parent and their kid who had demanded a school tour. Ally swatted away her annoyance. She wouldn't let some "Difficult Dad" rob her of the joy she was feeling.

She checked the clock at reception again. Where were they? It was a Friday afternoon for heaven's sake. Most of her colleagues were having drinks at the local pub—not even the office staff had stayed late.

She should have been at the market picking up a juicy steak, not standing around an empty corridor. Alone.

Ally breathed in and tried to calm her nerves She wouldn't let her annoyance show—she was a professional after all. But she would make sure they knew that enrolments had reached full capacity. She couldn't take any more kids. Not unless the department demanded it.

She wandered up and down the corridor to keep herself occupied.

She'd called Owen yesterday to make sure he didn't have plans. Whilst she spent a lot of time at their place, she was still living for the most part in her apartment. She hoped that might change. She'd timed it so she could pick up groceries and surprise him when he got home from work just in time for dinner.

Or would if this blasted parent showed up. She glared at the clock. Okay, so maybe she'd bake the brownies after she told him. With Charlotte. She wouldn't have time to do it at home.

Parent No-Show was throwing out her entire schedule.

She picked up her phone when it pealed. It was Maddie.

"Hey! What's up?"

"We were just heading home when we noticed a parent is waiting at the junior school office. They asked after you."

"What? They've gone to my office?"

"Looks like it."

Ally was ready to scream in frustration. "Right. Thanks. I've been waiting at the front office!"

She heard Sera giggle. "Good luck for tonight!"

"Thanks…if I ever get there."

She raced down the corridor, then stopped short. Twenty minutes late wouldn't be a disaster to her schedule. The last thing she needed was to break an ankle trying to get there. She'd get through the tour and would be home in no time.

It wasn't until she was walking across the junior school courtyard that she noticed the scattered red rose petals.

She slowed her pace and looked around her. There was no one there. Ally stepped inside her office, mouth dry.

Standing in the middle of the deserted space were Owen and Charlotte. A dozen chocolate bouquets surrounded them.

Her heart soared. "What are you doing here? I have a meeting with a parent…"

Understanding bloomed in her mind.

"Sorry we're late. But we'd like that tour if you'd squeeze us in, Ms. McVeigh."

"You?" she whispered.

Owen grinned. "When you called me last night, I had a feeling. We had plans of our own you see…we wanted to surprise you, to finish how we started. Before you beat us to it."

Ally laughed, remembering the first private tour she had given him. The first day they met. "But how did you know—"

"What you'd say? I called back up to confirm it."

Ally shook her head, tears in her eyes. Maddie and Sera. "What did they tell you?"

She stepped towards him. The man she loved.

He feigned innocence. "Oh, just that you had something to tell me—us—that we might like to hear."

She bit her lip, body finally relaxing.

She no longer held hope, like a flickering flame, thready and ready to extinguish at the softest of breaths. Her love was a roaring fire, a burning blaze that would cover them in warmth from here on in.

She understood that now, that light in her heart. The sheer abundance of it, of those emotions that had once been a frightening, threatening force. She understood that what she had grown up with wasn't family. Not in the real sense. Not where it counted.

She wanted everything that this man and this child could give. More, she wanted to be the woman to give it all to them in return.

"Are you going to give us the grand tour, Ally?"

She shook her head, voice steady and sure. "I suppose I could show you the school grounds...but you've already seen it. You know that part of me pretty well by now." Her mouth curved. "What I can show you is a map of my heart, all the signs and signals, all the roads and rivers. I looked, Owen." Her voice thickened. "I looked, like you told me and I saw you and Charlotte.

"I saw a future with us. I saw the love I have for you and just how important it is for me to give Charlotte everything she deserves. I saw a life together, through good and bad. Filled with laughter, and baking and love. And I saw a happiness that I've not known before in my life." She pressed a hand against her chest, eyes swimming with tears. "And it was because of you. Because you showed me the way, that I was able to find it."

He framed her face in his hands. "Happy tears?"

"Always. I love you, Owen. I want to be yours, in every way possible."

His grin was a mile wide. "You're the smartest, strongest,

bravest and most beautiful woman I've known. I love you. I want you for life. Say you'll have us. Say you'll move in?" He opened his arm for Charlotte to step into the circle. To complete it.

She held a set of keys in her hand.

Ally looked at the sunny little girl, whose eyes shone with tears.

"I will. I most certainly will."

She hugged them both against her, not wanting to hold back anymore. She looped the key ring around her finger, happier beyond belief.

Ally crouched down, tears flowing freely. "Will you have me in your life, Charlie? I know I'm going to make mistakes, but I promise to do the best I can to be there for you and your dad. I've enjoyed being your step-mum and I want you to know I love you. So much."

Charlotte nodded. Little arms wrapped around her. "I love you, Ally. And you're already my mum," she whispered.

Owen drew them both up.

"Do you think your old man can finally kiss the woman he loves now, kiddo?"

Charlotte rolled her eyes, then covered them. "Jeremy said this would happen."

Ally smiled at the man standing before her. In his eyes she saw love. Commitment. Joy. Was this what it meant to feel cherished? To be loved without restrictions.

As his mouth found hers, she knew the answer.

She had a feeling she would know it for the rest of her life.

ACKNOWLEDGMENTS

As we all deal with the ramifications of this global pandemic, I want to thank everyone who has endeavoured to make our community safe. 2020 has been a really, really tough year, not only for those who have lost loved ones, but also for the essential workers who are out in society just trying to do their jobs. Thank you, a million times over!

The Teacher Chronicles is a series that I hope you will enjoy; one which is dear to my heart. Not only because I used to be a high school teacher, but because I have close friends who are still in the education system, working tirelessly and without proper remuneration to ensure that the students in their classrooms receive the best outcomes possible.

It's oftentimes a thankless job, but a crucial one. To all my friends who are persevering though the ridiculous workload and long hours, I see you. Thank you all for supporting me over the years. Your friendship and guidance have helped me through a lot in my career, and I am eternally grateful for having you in my life.

Never in a million years would I have thought that I'd be writing these acknowledgements whilst heavily pregnant with my second child. Or that I would be having a little bub during a pandemic. Whilst this year has been difficult, the arrival of a new person in our family has brought us so much joy. I only hope that this book is released before this baby enters the world! And no, Brian, the baby will not be here in two weeks...

To my darling family. Team Brida. Brian, Adria, Hugo and this little squishy baby I've yet meet, I love you all to the moon, and back! Thank you for giving me the time and space I've needed to write. Or comforting me when I couldn't. Thank you for all your patience and understanding; this has been a mad year for us all, but in many ways a wonderful one as a family.

Once again to my family, in Australia and across the wild Atlantic, your Skype calls and texts have kept me sane and grounded. Whilst we've missed out on a lot this year, I'm hopeful that 2021 will bring us together again. Thank you for all the love and support.

Thank you to my editor, Angela James. Your honesty and eagle eye has helped 'Before You Were Mine' to become a better book. Not to mention helping me become a better writer! Here's to many more books together.

To Leanne Lovegrove, for putting up with all my questions. Let's hope we can see each other again real soon. That retreat seems like a lifetime ago...

Laurelle Cousins...my wonderful friend and writer in crime; may our chats, emails and phone calls continue long into the future! Your friendship is truly treasured, so thank you for being you, mama bear. I can't wait to see your books in print!

Once again, a big thanks to my tribe – the funny, whacky, wonderfully inappropriate gang of the Romance Writers Meetup. I couldn't have asked for a more varied, encouraging, talented group of women to call my friends. I've really loved (and anticipated) our virtual chats and cannot wait until we can celebrate together in person.

To my BETA readers, once again, your time, effort and

insight make me feel super lucky to have you all in my life. Thank you for all the feedback, encouragement and support. Especially through what has been a difficult year. Y'all ROCK!

Finally, to my readers. Whoever you are, wherever you may be, I hope that this novel gives you a chance to escape from reality, even if for a chapter or two.

With you in romance,

Ida Brady

ABOUT THE AUTHOR

Ida Brady writes contemporary romance novels that promise humour, heartbreak and a happily ever after. With all the sexy bits! A lover of chocolate (milk or dark) and thunderstorms (the bigger the better), she's usually dreaming about her next cast of characters or what she's going to eat for her next meal.

When she isn't trying to tame her intractable curls, she's running after her kids, usually with a book in hand. Ida lives in Melbourne with her Irish husband and their out of control collection of books. She sometimes daydreams about having a huge library in her apartment but will settle for stacking novels in the kitchen drawers instead.

In her past life, she taught VCE Literature and English to a gaggle of teenagers. While she misses their enthusiasm, she sure as hell doesn't miss marking papers. You might find her dancing the sexy Argentine tango in her spare time, which isn't very often these days.

She loves travelling with her family, observing strangers at café's and getting lost in a good story.

Want to hear more?

Visit: www.idabrady.com to sign up to my Newsletter for giveaways and prizes!

Or follow Ida on Social Media:

facebook.com/idabrady.author

twitter.com/the_real_ida

instagram.com/idabradyauthor

CPSIA information can be obtained
at www.ICGtesting.com
Printed in the USA
BVHW030458101120
592889BV00017B/62

9 780648 815754